Smooth TALKIN' BASTARD

Smooth TALKIN' BASTARD

DONALD A. DERY

AuthorHouse™
1663 Liberty Drive
Bloomington, IN 47403
www.authorhouse.com
Phone: 1 (800) 839-8640

Published by AuthorHouse 07/03/2015

ISBN: 978-1-5049-1968-5 (sc)
ISBN: 978-1-5049-1969-2 (hc)
ISBN: 978-1-5049-1970-8 (e)

Library of Congress Control Number: 2015910239

Print information available on the last page.

This book is printed on acid-free paper.

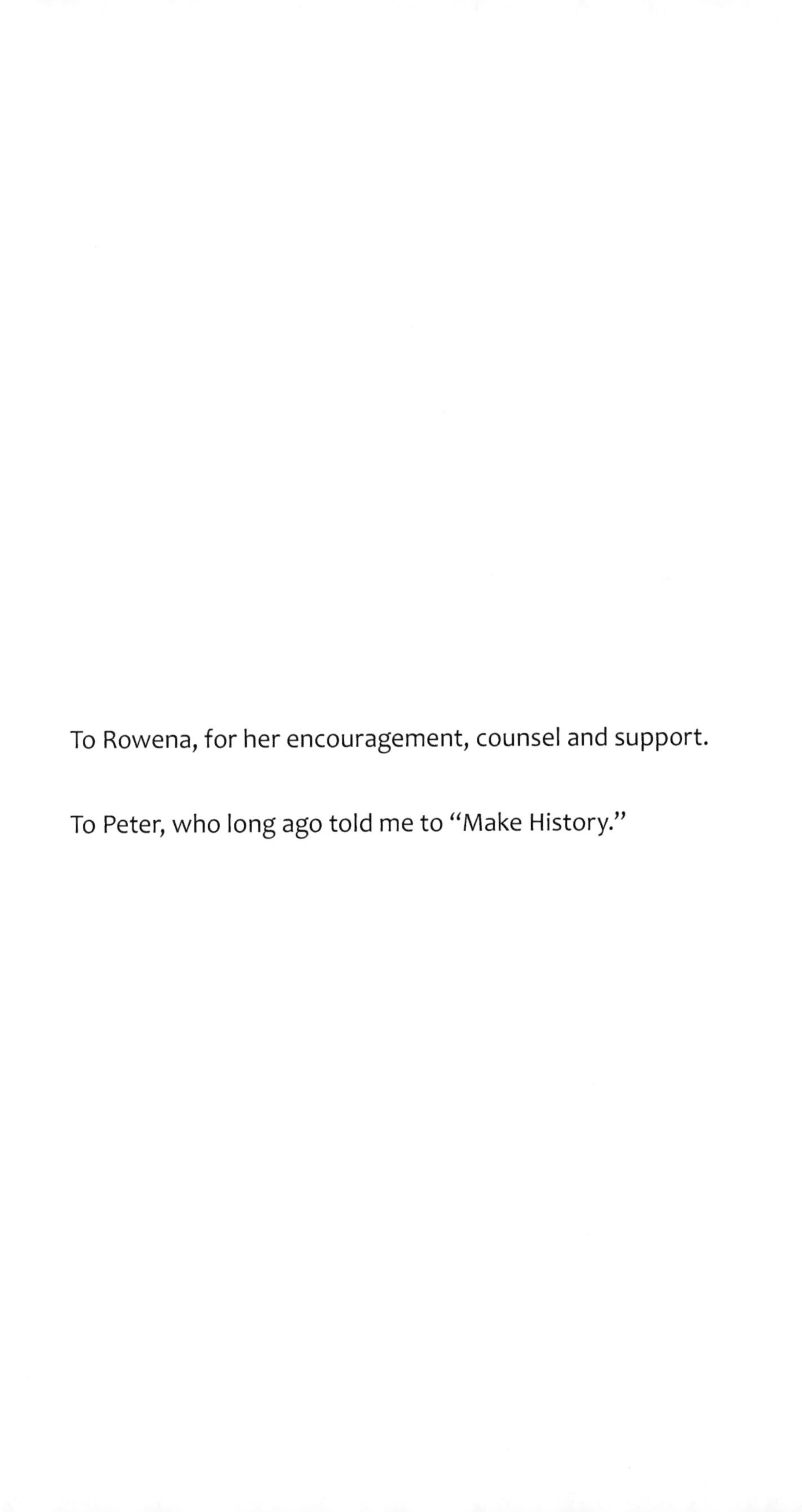

To Rowena, for her encouragement, counsel and support.

To Peter, who long ago told me to “Make History.”

1

TODAY

Pat Clauson is a highly accomplished con artist, bent on destruction. His target is a two-year-old company he's been screwing for the past five months. That's his M.O., and it's enabled him to previously rip off several start-up firms for thousands of dollars, actually hundreds of thousands. And Today! Today he's expecting to reap the biggest payoff of his so-called career.

Then he'll disappear like a bad dream, leaving the company and the State of Rhode Island in his rearview mirror.

He's dressed in his best costume: a tailored Saville Row suit, custom Hong Kong silk shirt and tie, gleaming black shoes, all contributing to his aura as an experienced, successful international businessman. To complete the image, he carries a black leather envelope-style briefcase and a copy of *The Wall Street Journal* folded so the masthead is clearly visible.

He rises quickly from his first class seat when the aircraft engines shut down and the seatbelt signs snap off. He's among the first off the jet, his long legs carrying him briskly up the jetway and into the terminal of T.F. Green Airport. He strides through the overflow throngs crowding adjacent gates, his six-four athletic frame, chiseled features, determined frown and deliberate stride screaming confidence: another serious executive hustling to an important meeting.

Not true: he's nervous as hell, scared shitless.

He maintains his rapid pace as he works his way across the broad air-conditioned terminal to the electric doors, which obediently part upon his approach. The air outside is stifling, heat and humidity make it difficult to inhale, his face and neck instantly begin to sweat, perspiration rolls down his back. He opens his suit jacket and loosens his tie as he approaches the Town Car, its uniformed driver standing alert with the rear door open, engine running, air conditioning on high.

He exchanges "Good afternoons" with the driver, new guy, chucks his jacket and briefcase onto the back seat, slides in himself relishing the cool A/C. The driver quickly closes the rear door, walks around the car, slips behind the wheel.

"Where to, Mr. Clauson?

Pat gives him an office address in Newport, settles back for the 35-minute ride. He stretches his legs, slips off his shoes, lights a cigarette. The scenery rolls by, commercial buildings with their gaudy billboards, large green direction signs alerting drivers to exits for a shopping mall, Roger Williams Park, assorted Rhode Island destinations.

His mind is elsewhere, focused on retrieving a large bundle of cash he has sashed in a locked desk drawer. No need to linger in the office, not eager to be cornered by a business associate, even for a social chat. In and out, $300,000 stuffed into his briefcase, never look back. That's his plan. He's already secured his 50,000 shares of company stock, ready to sell when the price is right. Screw restrictions; they don't apply in Canada.

It suddenly dawns on him they're headed north toward downtown Providence, the wrong direction for Newport, or at least the long way around. He has no desire to be seen in Providence.

"Where are we headed," Pat asks the new driver, younger, no mustache, full head of black hair, dark aviator sunglasses covering the upper part of the face Pat glimpses in the rearview mirror.

"Sir, I wanna avoid the heavy commuter traffic heading south on Route 95." The voice is strong, confident, self-assured. "I figure this time of day traffic will be lighter going east on 195, then south on 24, and it won't take us any longer."

"Sounds good," Pat replies. "Where's Phil, my usual driver? I was expecting him at the airport."

"He had some kinda medical appointment this afternoon, I think." The voice still strong, in control. "My name's Vince. I'm a regular driver for the company. They asked me to fill in for Phil this afternoon. Hope you're comfortable with that, Sir."

"Yea, no problem, Vince, no problem at all." Pat snaps open his *Wall Street Journal,* tries to read. Tough to concentrate; holds the newspaper in front of his face, but his mind keeps drifting to his objective, that drawer stuffed with his "client's" cash.

He's ticked off. This entire effort has turned into a GD fiasco. Started out okay, but quickly collapsed, mostly due to those two friggin' women. It was a sweet deal until they got nosy.

He can't understand how they put two-and-two together to figure out what he's really up to, then collaborated to uncover his strategy. The CEO has been quite happy with their agreement, the

CFO is upset, but so what! But those broads -- the CEO's wife and his administrative assistant -- they've screwed up everything.

Bottom line, he has two choices: dump a lot of his own money into the company, which is against his religion! Or, scoop what he has already stolen from their bank account and beat a hasty retreat before anybody even knows he's back in Rhode Island. *That's* his religion!

He's very concerned about those vendors in North Providence, the other side of 95. They might discover he's local, vulnerable, theirs for the picking. It never occurred to him that the people he's screwing might have those kind of connections; never ran into this in any of his previous "opportunities."

+ + +

Pat has pulled off similar scams several times before with other companies in other cities, mostly hotshot startups founded by techies who didn't know crap about the stock market. Pat knows that market well, plays every angle, but never with his own money.

That's been his "wealth strategy" for ten years, ever since he landed in the U.S. from Australia. He's come a long way from the sheep ranch where he'd been raised, seventy-five miles northwest of Sydney: (*"Had to get the hell out cuz sheep stink and the friggin' fleas were enough to drive you nuts."*)

Hit Sydney at nineteen, studied a little economics, relished a course on market growth and the role of stock exchanges. He tended bar in a down-and-out pub which smelled of stale beer and an over-flowing urinal, saved his salary and tips until he could buy passage on a freighter bound for Los Angeles.

California was magic. Sunshine, gorgeous women hoping to find someone to make them famous. And money, lots of money. It flowed like sweat, oozed out of California's every pore, waiting for some shark to wipe it up. Hello, Pat!

All he needed was what the Aussie's call a scheme, their word for "plan" but American for "uh-oh!". The scheme had to sound entirely legit, a plan to make those entrepreneurs trust him with their livelihood, their dreams, their checkbooks! It took awhile to perfect, but between voracious reading, over-heard conversations in a swanky Hollywood restaurant where he landed a waiter's job, plus his crafty imagination, Pat finally devised his scheme. It was amazingly simple.

He began by phoning a leading London bank, engaged a Vice President *("Everyone in a bank is a VP!")* in a lengthy discussion about international business, the Australian and US economies, and his high-tech clients *("they must remain confidential for the moment")* who were eager to expand their business by entering the UK and selected European markets. What was involved? Licensing fees and regulations? Banking regulations, capital deposits, import structure and regs, employment laws, legal representation?

By the end of the phone call, Pat had what he needed: a name, email address and phone number of an executive, Geoffrey Blair, at the Commonwealth Bank of London. And he had enough information about British business regulations to sound knowledgeable, well connected, a savvy financial advisor.

Next, he phoned a Hong Kong law firm, one with a reputation for representing a portfolio of leading corporations in countries on several continents. Again, he passed himself off as an international institutional investor *("on assignment")* for a leading British bank with clients anxious to commence manufacturing in China. By the end of that conversation, he had the particulars he needed to claim his legal representation was in Hong Kong. But it included a promise to visit the law firm and his contact there, Ian Gilbert, within the next two months. That was a trip Pat vowed never to make.

Then there was his wardrobe. He had saved enough cash to have a suit, shirts and tie made by British and Hong Kong tailors who advertised in the *Los Angeles Times*. The shoes and leather folio waited until he accumulated some additional cash; he used the down time to refine the essence of his "wealth strategy."

He began by scanning local newspapers and one or two professional journals, even phoned a couple of trade magazine editors pretending to be a newly-arrived institutional investor in the hunt for "opportunities" that would interest his primary financial backers in the UK. Of course, he had no backers in the UK or anywhere else, but who was to know!

His line of palaver was well rehearsed, his delivery superb, and even the Aussie accent helped convey the impression that this dude had been around the world of international business, knew what he was talking about. Once he identified what appeared to be an ideal target -- a company with an interesting product or service, a firm which clearly needed an infusion of cash to expand its business and, hopefully, position itself for a listing on a U.S. stock exchange -- Pat would make his move.

+ + +

It took three months before he approached his first target. SmartApps, Inc. was a one-year-old privately held company in San Francisco, owned and operated by a young entrepreneur and his wife. Pat had read about their company, their proprietary software product, their ambition to market it to large companies in the U.S. and, ultimately, Canada.

The couple was hungry to enhance their business reputation, improve their company's balance sheet and earnings statement, then maybe sellout to a bigger firm, lining their pockets with gold. They were, to put it mildly, Pat's perfect target, and he wasted no time aiming for a bullseye.

He began with a telephone call to the principles to introduce himself; followed up with an email extolling his credentials, his "bankers" in London, his international legal "advisors" in Hong Kong. The couple could hardly believe their luck at suddenly playing in the big leagues with the guidance of an experienced international investment manager, an expert interested in meeting with them to explore the possibility of investing in their company so they could achieve their commercial ambitions.

Pat flew to San Francisco a day later, pulled up to the couple's small offices in a nondescript building in Oakland (not San Francisco) in a chauffeur-driven Cadillac.

Jeff and Penny Marigold were an interesting couple, both in their late 20s or early 30s, smart but not particularly market savvy. Jeff stood six-five, shoulder-length blond hair, ready smile, dressed in jeans and a T-shirt blaring "Sperm Donor". Penny was about five-three, tangled black hair hanging to her waist, brains, horn-rimmed glasses, wearing an ankle-length denim skirt, plaid blouse, sandals. They both held MBA's from Stanford in information technology.

They clearly understood the bits and gigs of their new software product, had worked hard with no staff on a shoestring budget. They admittedly didn't know how to price it, or sell it. They were techies, eager to create, proud of what they had achieved, but with limited understanding of how to move what they created into the market; didn't know how to position their product or company. What they lacked in know-how they made up with enthusiasm.

Their fondest hope was that Pat would solve their marketing problem, put their product on the map, fatten their bank account.

They had a brief introductory meeting, then Pat suggested they join him for lunch at a local restaurant. The negotiations began in earnest over drinks. Before lunch was digested they had reached an agreement whereby Pat's "bankers" would "invest an initial $25,000 of a $100,000 preliminary commitment" to their business.

Pat would move into their offices, collect a weekly consulting fee of $3,000 and -- at the insistence of those London backers -- have joint signature rights on their business bank accounts to protect his UK "colleagues".

Pat also "promised" he would work with his "British associates" to guide Jeff and Penny through the London bank's extensive due diligence maze, "a time-consuming process which will drive you bonkers if you don't understand how to deal with it." He was surprised, but not shocked, that the couple did not ask why they had to look overseas for investment dollars, why they couldn't deal locally with a resource in Oakland or San Francisco.

The most tantalizing aspect of Pat's proposal was that he help them structure a plan to issue stock in their company, a maneuver he assured them could funnel lots of greenbacks into their pockets. His game plan was to strongly emphasize that this was an extremely complicated process, requiring his intimate knowledge of the stock market and government regulations. He succeeded: the complexity he described blew Jeff and Penny's minds; they never considered doing anything remotely like this, but here's this big-shot financier telling them it can happen! Wow!

"Can we really do that?" This came from Jeff.

"No! You can't, but I can. I have experience dealing with the market. I know the pros and cons, Jeff, and they can be quite complicated."

Pat assured them he could arrange the initial public offering and get them listed on the penny stock market, a simplified beginning of what could surely lead to a listing on one of the big boards once their company had achieved a sufficient level of capitalization. He did not share with them that the world of penny stocks was a notorious haven for con men and hustlers; a market the FBI termed "rife with fraud."

He said Jeff and Penny could issue, say, 200,000 shares at a buck apiece, keep some shares for themselves, and of course Pat would need 30,000 shares as his take for handling the deal. It was a step intended to serve as a sure-fire sign they were in this as a team.

Of course, Pat never mentioned anything about restricting his shares to prevent him from selling them whenever he wished. If restricted, he (theoretically) would be required to hold onto the shares for several months or years, depending on the restriction clause. "Theoretically," because Pat knew he could transfer his shares to a contact in Canada, where stock restrictions did not apply, and sell whenever his shares reached an attractive price.

He did, however, make it clear to Jeff and Penny that if the shares doubled or tripled in price, which he predicted would happen relatively quickly, they would earn a bundle. And Pat, of course, would direct the effort to make certain the stock price did move upward fairly rapidly. He deliberately neglected to describe how he would do that *("better left unsaid!")*.

To cement his importance with SmartApp, he embarked on a long and intricate discussion of the imperative do's and don'ts associated with having their stock traded publicly on any stock exchange. He placed great stress on the prompt and broad disclosure requirements of the Securities & Exchange Commission, and the potential legal ramifications and financial penalties if they didn't obey the rules.

"Lord, this sounds risky!" This was Penny. "Should we really be attempting this?"

"Just relax, Penny. It sounds worse than it is as long as we play fair." *("Interesting choice of words!")*

Pat emphasized that he would handle everything, making certain information about the firm was released immediately to the appropriate news outlets so no one could ever accuse Jeff or Penny of tipping off friends or relatives with inside information. He also made clear the disclosure of proprietary information -- information, good or bad, which might impact a stockholder's decision to buy or sell the company's shares -- had to be announced promptly.

"Bad news! We have to announce bad news?"

"Yes, Jeff, if we feel it is proprietary, meaning a shareholder or potential shareholder most likely would not invest in your stock if they were aware of the bad news. But not to worry, that does not crop up often, and *we* decide what is proprietary. That requires some delicate decision-making, but again, I will oversee that."

It was part of his con, a strategy designed to make the stock idea sound so complicated, so fraught with legal pitfalls that his targets would bow to his professionalism, put him in complete charge. And it clicked with Jeff and Penny: to them, the whole idea was overwhelming, but they relaxed knowing they had a pro with extraordinary backers to guide them.

Pat knew his 30,000 shares would be worth a small fortune if he succeeded in playing the charade to its logical conclusion. All he had to do was balloon the shares to four or five bucks and he'd earn

$120,000 to $150,000: eight bucks would earn him almost a quarter million because he was free to sell anytime he chose. That plus his monthly retainer and whatever he could swipe from the company's bank account with his signature rights . . . well, shucks, all of that would keep him happy for several months.

To make that happen, Pat would require a title -- Chief Operating Officer would do -- business cards, a private phone line, a private office. He would move to Oakland the following week, after he had squared the deal with his London and Hong Kong "associates", wrapped up "other business" he had on his books.

Even the chauffeured Cadillac, which Pat used daily to commute to work and back to his rented condo, did not fail to register with Jeff or Penny until later, when they got past-due collection notices from the car service and the owner of Pat's rented condo. That was a nightmare neither Jeff nor Penny had anticipated, but by then Pat was gone. At the outset, they remained starry-eyed about playing in the big league and possibly realizing their financial ambitions.

Things went smoothly for almost three months. Pat invested a minor amount of his own money in the company as a show of good faith. He said the balance of the UK bank's first $25,000 was to arrive by wire after bank officials had completed due diligence on the company, its owners, and the validity of their product and its market potential. But that never seemed to be happening.

Meanwhile, Pat drew $3,000 a week out of the company's bank account, writing the checks himself in an amount several times his modest up-front "investment." Of course, the balance of the London bank's $25,000 "obligation" never arrived; when Jeff and Penny began asking questions about the delays Pat knew it was time to move on.

He entered the office early a few mornings later, wrote himself a check which cleaned out the firm's checking account, cashed it when the bank opened, drew several thousand out of the business savings account, and grabbed a cab to the airport. He left behind a stack of unpaid invoices assigned to SmartApp and insufficient funds in their checking account to pay them all.

By the time the couple figured out what had happened to their company's money, Pat was at 35,000 feet on his way to Chicago, a favorite stomping ground he first discovered a few years earlier. He intended to lay low in the Windy City, scout opportunities to pull a similar scam on another unsuspecting entrepreneur. He carried a fat wallet, still held 30,000 shares of SmartApp stock he planned to dump immediately. Word of the firm's financial problems was sure to get out in a few days, and their stock would crash.

He sold out before any of that happened, pocketing an additional $230,000.

+ + +

Pat fell in love with Chicago, the vitality and pace of the city, it's architecture, museums, jazz clubs, the waterfront magic of Lake Michigan. He set himself up in a room at a fancy hotel smack in the center of the swishy, upscale neighborhood renowned for its high fashion retail outlets catering to young and not-so-young up-and-comers.

He also found the young women alluring as they strolled or walked briskly along Michigan Avenue, window shopping, moving on to office jobs or meetings with business associates, their skirts billowing in the breezes which whipped ashore from the massive ocean-like lake.

Chicago, he discovered, was a marvelous city in which to fall in love, not permanently, of course, but for an evening or even two. The jazz clubs were a spectacular source of attractive women looking for a good time. Pat used his Australian accent to maximum advantage, as well as his good looks, his fat wallet, a chauffeur-driven Cadillac or Lincoln Town Car, his hotel room landscaped with bouquets of flowers, ice cold champagne, room service shrimp, lobster or caviar. Occasionally, he found he had overdone it and the young lady was reluctant to leave, necessitating his most cordial persuasion.

Initially, he spent his days relaxing, joined an athletic club to keep his body in shape, read *The Wall Street Journal, Chicago Trib* and BLOOMBERG BUSINESS WEEK to quench his thirst for news of the economy, devoured issues of WIRED to scout possible targets for his next venture. He was in no hurry, had plenty of cash from the SmartApp caper, lived extremely well. He was not particularly anxious to jump on a new opportunity until he had done his own due diligence and was comfortable the prospect was ripe for picking.

Pat felt Chicago was a lot easier to get lost than in New York City. That place was an enormous worldwide financial center, anyone looking for him would begin their search there, especially since he always claimed to be a Manhattan resident.

Chicago was somehow not as focused, or at least he perceived it to be so. He was much more comfortable assuming he could disappear in the Windy City, and so far that had worked; none of his victims had found him, he wasn't in jail or being sued, he felt secure he could remain free to pounce when the time was right.

He operated out of the hotel for several weeks, scouting potential targets and moving on unsuspecting start-ups in St. Louis, Atlanta and Kansas City. In each case he used the same modus operandi he had with SmartApp, but he escalated the financials to impress the "suckers" and substantially increase his own take on every scam.

He was amazed so many smart people could be lured into his line of bullshit, leaving them shocked and dumbstruck that they had been ripped off by a smooth talking bastard who, on the surface, appeared to be a terrific guy, talented in ways they were convinced was in their best interests to engage.

He disappeared from St. Louis with a take of more than $750,000 in cash plus salable stock, his "reward" for helping a start-up company find its feet, so to speak, in the mammoth world of international commerce. The owners had said "Yes" to Pat's recommendation that he serve as a go-between for the firm and Pat's financial "resources" in London, and the bank fees "just kept piling out of sight." They escalated into Pat's pocket, something the principals didn't realize until they couldn't find him any more.

Atlanta was more of the same, almost a mirror image of what he pulled in St. Louis, but his take was a little smaller: $540,000 plus stock. Still, he had no right to complain; just disappeared, leaving the client to feel like he was waking from a nightmare.

Then came Kansas City, the Heartland of America. He loved that city, hung out for several months, much longer than he had planned. But, the deal he conjured up was too lucrative to cut short. He was paid a ridiculous monthly consulting fee -- for nothing! He kept generating intricate monthly performance reports, optimism personified, hope eternal, and it had taken the management months to understand that hope is not a strategy.

Pat had not done one-tenth of what he claimed, and when the owners got suspicious and started making phone calls, Pat suddenly came down with a rare sickness that necessitated his hospitalization in a specialized medical center overseas. Adios, and thanks for an easy $1,270,000.

He blew his cover, though, when he decided to take on a company in Evanston, a sizable city north of Chicago, also bordering on Lake Michigan. The job had gone well for about two months, then management got edgy, lawyers began sniffing around, and Pat made a decision to grab his football and get the hell out of Dodge.

He left with his leather folio stuffed full of six-figure cash, decided he'd be smart to explore London for several months before trying his skill at another score in the U.S. It was in London that he first met the CEO of Fabricated Structures, Inc., but that's a story for later.

+ + +

The traffic eased on 195 as Vince approached the Route 24 exit to Aquidneck Island, and he shifted the Town Car into the right lane. Like 195, 24 is a four-lane divided highway so Vince goosed the car to seventy or seventy-five MPH, making good time toward Newport.

Everything so familiar to Pat: the rusted old Tiverton bridge which the State grumbled about demolishing, the change from four lanes divided to four lanes undivided as Route 24 became 114, the view of Fabricated Structures assembly plant as they passed through Portsmouth.

There's the McDonald's and Kentucky Fried Chicken across from the shopping mall in Middletown, then the sprint down Broadway passing Newport city hall on the left, the police station on the right, and finally the turn toward Washington Square and Fabricated's offices.

All the while Pat's glancing at his *Wall Street Journal* but is really absorbed in plotting his movements within the Fabricated offices. He plans to double-time the stairs to the second floor, load bundles of cash from his locked desk into his briefcase. He'll casually wave a greeting to a few employees as if this is a normal visit, then exit the building quickly and re-enter the Town Car so Vince can drive him back to T. F. Green Airport for his flight to JFK, where gorgeous Cecily will be waiting for him.

He opens the leather folio to check the only two things in it, his plane ticket back to LaGuardia and a connecting flight from Kennedy to Rome, his next R&R location. Tickets are safe and sound, now all he needs is less than ten minutes in the Fabricated Structures office, and the prize is his: $300,000 in cash. His earlier take from the company's bank account, plus his 50,000 shares of stock, are carefully banked abroad or stored with his friend Kyle in New York. Plus, he's been drawing a $5,000 monthly retainer for the past five months. All in all, not a bad haul.

He really wondered how much longer he could keep this up without somebody catching on and nailing his ass to a cross before he could flee the scene. This is his sixth caper since he hit the U.S., and he has an uncomfortable feeling he may be pressing his luck.

This episode with Fabricated Structures has been the most difficult he has ever attempted, largely because the GD treasurer is no pushover; first time Pat has ever had to deal with a company staffed by a guy who knows just as much as Pat about the workings of the stock markets, a guy who did not fall for the line about "my bankers in London." This guy isn't impressed, doesn't care one iota about "my lawyers in Hong Kong."

And then those two damned women!

Might be time to sit in Rome, learn Italian, tour a few cathedrals, let the whole scene cool off for awhile. He's saved plenty of dough to keep living his preferred lifestyle for at least two, may three years. Probably ought to sit tight, learn to love pasta, pizza and good wine, soak up sun in southern Italy, maybe scoot over to Sicily for beach time, visit Florence or Venice for an injection of art and culture.

Vince brings the Town Car to a stop in front of the office building. Pat had earlier told CEO Tom Mulholland that for reasons of "prestige and image" Tom should vacate the small office space he had been occupying downtown and rent two floors of this building.

He had also convinced Mulholland to refurbish the building's offices and construct an attractive reception room and board room. Pat hired and supervised the contractor, painters, lighting firm, and temp secretarial staff. He has been receiving their monthly invoices, but never pays them. He draws cash, enters a payment into the firm's check register, and stashes the cash in his locked desk.

Today's the day to jump ship with that cash.

Pat pulls the wrapped three-hundred-thousand out of his desk, stuffs it into his briefcase, and strides across the large central office toward the stairs when someone calls his name. He freezes, turns to see Steve Johnson approaching with some papers.

Johnson is the ticked off CFO, the smart ass who has darned near blown Pat's cover. He does not like the fact that Pat can sign company checks just because he's sunk a little money into the company as a bridge loan; damned little actually, because Pat's "L.A. people" always seem to be too busy to wire all of his promised funds to the firm's bank account.

Pat is not eager for a conversation with Steve while holding a briefcase loaded with ninety percent of the company's cash.

"Pat, good to see you. I thought you were in New York."

"Yeah, I was, Steve, but something came up, so I stopped in here to gather some files and I'm on my way to a meeting. How can I help you?" Pat's heart is beating fast and loud. He can feel sweat beginning to bead on his forehead.

"I have some invoices here from the restaurants where you and Tom entertained clients last month, plus several others from a florist, your car service, the carpenters and painters, stuff like that. Should I pay these, some are 60, even 90 days out?" There's an edge of sarcasm in Steve's voice, a reflection of his distress at being subordinated to this outsider who now controls the company's money.

"Go ahead and pay them, Steve. You're still listed on the bank account, and I'll tell Tom I authorized you to do that. Thanks for being on top of this." There's no sarcasm in Pat's voice, just relief.

He waves to some others busy at their desks, hits the stairs for a quick exit of the building. Settled into the back seat of the Town Car, he instructs Vince to return to T. F. Green Airport. Pat peers into his folio to admire the bundles of $100 bills.

The car does a loop out of Washington Square, quickly moves west across the Pell Bridge, reaches Route 95 North, where it has to slow because of the heavy commuter traffic. Vince eases the car off at an exit just before the airport, approaches a traffic light and interrupts Pat's focus on his stolen money.

"Mr. Clauson, Sir, I am going to pull off into a car wash at this next traffic light," Vince says. "I hope you don't mind. My boss asked that I get this car washed, and it will only take a few minutes."

"Well, dammit, OK," Pat replies, "but let's not kill a lot of time. I have to catch a flight to New York and I don't want to miss it."

"No problem, Sir. Thank you, Sir."

Pat grumbles beneath his breath, glares out the window as the Town Car turns left to the car wash. Vince waits for a vehicle ahead of him before he can drive into the building, pays the attendant who brushes the vehicle with soapy water, pushes a control button.

The Town Car moves slowly along the track, drowned by powerful soap and water sprays that cloud the windows, automatic brushes banging and clattering, loud piped-in music blaring from wall-mounted speakers. Pat remains staring at the side window, lost in thought about the end of the Fabricated Structures deal and his decision to lay low in Italy for awhile, perhaps a long while, with Cecily as his arm candy. Probably best to let the U.S. market cool down before he re-enters to sniff out another opportunity.

He hears rustling in the front seat, turns to look at Vince, finds himself starring at the wrong end of a huge handgun.

He freezes, his eyes wide with panic, his gaze shifting from the gun to the menacing grin on Vince's face. Pat presses himself back into the seat, his left arm extends with his palm in the "stop" position. He tries to speak, even yell, his throat locks shut, no sound will pass through it.

Lots of noise in the car wash, machines humming, brushes banging and dragging, automatic water sprays hitting the car, loud music, no one can hear him anyway. Nothing to do but close his eyes, hope to God this is some sort of bluff or a stick-up for his cash-laden briefcase.

Pat lets out a deep breath and waits, terrified, for Vince's next move.

2

LONDON
FIVE MONTHS EARLIER

The weather in London was magnificent, bright sun, crystal clear, no fog or rain. Emerald carpets of grass dotted the city's many parks, trees in full bloom, gardens a canvas of bright colors: hundreds of tulips in red, yellow, blue, rainbows of roses, flowering bushes. Sidewalks crowded with tourists shopping and sightseeing, business execs dashing between appointments, streets a sea of red double-decker buses, black London taxis.

The city was humming.

This was his first visit to the capital city of the former Empire, and London quickly won his heart: historic, extraordinary buildings, amazing architectural sites, history on every corner, superb restaurants, pubs and more formal bars.

Pat had been in London for several weeks, fled the States following his last "victory" over that medium-sized company in Evanston, Illinois. He barely made it out of town before lawyers began closing in. He jumped a flight to New York, then London, his briefcase stuffed with a bundle of the company's cash, a stock certificate for 35,000 shares safely stashed with a Canadian operative instructed to sell at twenty bucks a share.

He debated whether to phone that fella Geoffrey Blair at the Commonwealth International Bank; thought better of it because Blair and/or his colleagues would probably ask too many questions Pat wouldn't have good answers to. They might become suspicious that he wasn't all they had been led to believe. Besides, he hadn't contacted Blair since their original telephone conversation when Pat first arrived in California, but he bandied the guy's name around as "my London banker" in every deal he negotiated.

He set himself up with a suite in a five-star luxury hotel on Park Lane overlooking Hyde Park, had a battleship grey four-door Bentley at his beck & call. His favorite driver was Lionel (like the trains), always dressed in an immaculate suit and tie, a chauffeur's cap covering his greying hair, mustache, appealing British accent; not the stiff lockjaw delivery of an Eton snob who never moved his upper lip. Lionel was a regular guy, kept to himself, never spoke until spoken to, never if Pat had company in the car, especially a woman.

Pat enjoyed the companionship of a pretty woman, soft skin, ruby lips, sculptured body wrapped in high fashion, flowing long hair. He fancied long hair. It was easy, he discovered, to find the best places in the city to run across an assortment of available women; not pros, just good looking women eager to have dinner, perhaps a show, then whatever.

For a £10 note, the hotel's concierge would sell ninety percent of his intelligence. So evenings when Pat was in the mood, he took advantage of his good looks, engaging personality, seemingly unlimited cash, to find a warm and willing companion. The chauffeur-driven Bentley didn't hurt, nor did the hotel suite if the young lady was willing to be escorted that far. His "sexy" Australian accent was a plus.

Tonight, though, was *not* one of those evenings. He was booked on a flight to New York in two days, opted to stay in the hotel, slipped into the lobby bar for a quiet drink or three.

The place was dominated by mahogany woodwork, polished brass fixtures, lots of flowers, subdued lighting. It was an ideal place to get lost: upholstered love seats and living room style chairs, muted conversations occasionally marred by a burst of laughter, tuxedoed bartenders and waiters. Soft music emanated from a corner piano, ivories tickled by a fella willing to play a favorite song for cash dropped into his brandy snifter.

Pat settled onto one of the high-back upholstered bar stools, ordered a Chivas Regal on the rocks, became absorbed in his thoughts about returning to the States, the process he would go through to identify his next target. He was interrupted by the guy sitting next to his left elbow.

"Hi! What brings you to London?" American accent.

"Oh, I'm just killing some time to re-group. Also had a couple of meetings with my London bankers." The lie rolled off Pat's tongue like olive oil.

"May I ask what business you're in?" The guy looked to be in his mid-thirties, Hollywood handsome, solid build, probably a football lineman in college, had a habit of frequently adjusting his glasses.

"Yeah. I'm an investment manager," Pat lied.

"No kidding! That's gotta be fascinating . . . dealing with so many well-known outfits."

"Not really. I focus on small to medium-sized companies, mostly in the States," Pat said. He went on to explain that his primary "customers" were outfits looking for investment funding to expand their business, perhaps take it public. He could see the stranger's eyes light up, turned slightly on the bar stool to face the guy more directly, asked "How about you?"

"I run one of those medium-sized companies you're talking about." He explained that his firm had developed a process for laminating carbon fibre panels into a thin sandwich, panels in virtually any size or shape, lighter and stronger than anything made with aluminum or other metals.

"Who uses them?" Pat inquired.

"Well, we're pursuing the aircraft industry to see if they will consider them for wing structures, rudder and stabilizer parts, things like that. Most anything can be made from them: large household appliances, automobile fenders or doors, and so on."

"That's very interesting," Pat said, trying to prevent *his* eyes from lighting up.

"How big is your firm?"

"We're two years old, do almost two million a year, U.S. dollars. We're running ourselves ragged until we can expand our reputation and our manufacturing capacity. We're eager to enlarge the footprint of our customer base. I'm just stopping here for a couple of days, heading back home."

("Jumping Jesus! I may have found my target!")

"Where are you guys based?"

"We're headquartered in Newport, Rhode Island, and our primary manufacturing operations are a couple towns over, in Portsmouth," the fella said. "We're actually thinking of looking for larger manufacturing space; want to keep it fairly close to home so we can keep tabs on everything. Thought of China, but that's a zoo and too far away. Plane fares and phone calls would kill us. Besides, we'd like to keep the jobs in Rhode Island."

"Yeah, I can understand that." Pat extended his right hand: "My name is Pat Clauson."

"Tom Mulholland, Pat. Nice to meet you." His grip was athletic firm.

Their conversation continued over a couple of additional drinks, then moved to a table in the dining-room: more mahogany, more flowers, more brass, crystal chandeliers, sparkling white tablecloths, waiters in tuxedos, soft music and muted conversations.

They discussed their respective businesses over cocktails and steak, mostly Tom's business with occasional comments from Pat, who asked a litany of questions about Tom's plans for manufacturing, market expansion, financing. As the drinks and dinner went down, Tom became more talkative about his hopes for his company and, as luck would have it, his desire for additional capital and professional handholding to take his firm public.

"I really don't know how or where to begin to accomplish that," Tom said.

Pat was careful not to come on too aggressively, did not want to frighten the guy off. But he did suggest they meet again the following day for lunch at a restaurant quiet enough for a business discussion. Pat named a pub in Knightsbridge, close to Harrod's Department Store.

They shook hands at the elevator bank, confirmed their lunch appointment. Pat retired to his room, stayed up half the night plotting his approach to Tom:" (*"Gotta prove I'm his guy, don't go overboard, remain a little distant, lots of client work awaiting me in New York... yeah... OK, I can give you some help, I'll meet you in Rhode Island on Monday."*)

That's exactly how Pat played it at lunch the following day, slow, easy, friendly. By the time they had swallowed their fish and toasted with after-dinner drinks, Pat had himself an appointment in Newport, Rhode Island, wherever the hell that was.

+ + +

He landed in New York, checked into a Fifth Avenue hotel, began plotting his strategy to impress Tom Mulholland and his colleagues at Fabricated Structures, Inc., when he met up with them in Newport.

He first called a car service in Providence, RI; wanted to make an impression by showing up at the Fabricated offices every day in a chauffeur-driven car. He phoned three firms before he connected with an outfit with a fleet of "presidential" black Cadillacs and Lincoln Town Cars; Here-to-There (*"Damn stupid name for a car service"*). He explained his need for a chauffeured vehicle six or even seven days a week, got a sweet monthly package deal including his choice of a dedicated driver on call. And, Yes! They would invoice him at Fabricated Structures.

His second call was to a Newport real estate firm which specialized in expensive properties, the kind he chose for impression as well as creature comfort. He laid it on thick, waxing enthusiastic about his professional credentials, international bankers and lawyers; told the agent he wanted a six-month lease on a four bedroom home with maid and cook, a large dining-room, tiled patio with a swimming pool, long or circular driveway leading to the front entrance.

Impression was critical. The view wasn't as important because he would be entertaining clients in the evening. The patio and pool were for his own enjoyment; even at night, with the pool lights on, it would shout Wow! Price: get serious! The agent, Candi Sommers, was excited by the time they completed their conversation; showings scheduled for the day Pat was to arrive in Newport.

He had never been to that city before, never even thought about the place. He knew Rhode Island was the smallest state in the union, made even less significant because it was cut almost in half by a large body of salt water called Narragansett Bay. The Ocean State couldn't have a lot going for it that would interest a guy eager to pluck some entrepreneur clean, taking his company (if possible), his money, his dream of financial and commercial success.

Or would it?

As planned, Pat flew to Providence four days later, was met by a black Town Car courtesy of Here-to-There, an older man named Phil behind the wheel, uniformed and polite as a British servant.

Phil drove like a bat out of hell, screaming south on 95 to a left exit onto Route 4, swung right onto 138 to pass over two bridges across the west and east passages of Narragansett Bay. Heck of a view of Newport from the top of the second bridge, the Navy War College, hundreds of colonial homes, a big church. Spring weather, sunny, temp in the mid-70s.

Pat peppered Phil with questions about Newport so he'd have some feel for what he was being led into. He was assured Newport was a beautiful, historic, quaint New England city of about 25,000 people, ballooning to about 80,000 with the summer influx of tourists, sailors and yachtsman.

"This was home to the America's Cup for decades, ya know," Phil said. "In 1983 the Aussies won the Cup and it hasn't been back since, but there are still dozens of regattas and international races held here every summer, both in Narragansett Bay and the waters just offshore."

"Yeah, I know about the Aussies winning the Cup," Pat said. "I'm Australian, born and raised on a sheep ranch near Sydney."

"No kidding! You sure are a long way from home."

Phil went on to list the highlights which made Newport such a popular destination city: oldest ballpark continually in use; oldest lending library in the US; oldest Jewish synagogue in the U.S.; home of the U.S. Naval Academy during the Civil war; home of the U.S. Naval War College; more 17th- and 18th-century colonial homes than any other city or town in America; lots of extravagant mansions built by wealthy folks like the Vanderbilt's now open to public tours; on and on as if Phil were reading from a Chamber of Commerce brochure, which he wasn't.

Phil pulled up in front of a small nondescript building on a side street one block from the water. Offices on the ground floor, condos on the second, no off-street parking, small sign beside a door whispered Fabricated Structures, Inc.

Not very impressive, but way ahead of what Pat encountered once inside: soiled and torn dull grey carpeting struggling to support several well-used grey metal desks commonly found in low-level government offices. People crammed into small spaces, no walls, lots of phones and computer screens, fake wood table housed a coffee pot and stack of Styrofoam cups, piles of documents everywhere, some on the floor beside desks. Nothing in the large room said "Great Future."

A door at the far end of this jungle suddenly opened and Tom Mulholland stepped out carrying a stack of papers, yelling "Martha!" He stopped short when he saw Pat, moved quickly toward him and stuck out his hand.

"Hi, Pat. Welcome to the Land of Oz! Sorry for the mess, you're earlier than I expected, but even if you weren't this place would still resemble a leftover convention site!" They both laughed as they shook hands.

A middle-aged woman appeared at Tom's side (Martha?), took the bundle of papers from his hand, never said a word, disappeared into the chaos, perhaps never to be seen again. Tom grabbed Pat's arm and steered him toward what appeared to be the firm's only office door, offered Pat coffee from the steaming pot on the table (Pat declined) and they entered what passed for Tom's office.

It was no better than the general floor out front: same torn and soiled carpeting, same beat-up metal desk drowning in scattered stacks of paper, computer and phone, grey metal filing cabinet in one corner. Blueprints were tacked to at least three walls, the fourth adorned with broken laminate panels of various sizes, each tagged with hieroglyphics of some sort, a window too dirty to see through. It was an upholstered sewer!

"Do you really run your business from this place?" Pat couldn't help asking.

"I know, Pat, it isn't really impressive."

("Impressive! It's a shit house!")

"Frankly, I'm amazed you've done as well as you have working in this environment. I can't believe you bring customers into this . . .whatever." Pat was incredulous, and it showed.

Tom graciously accepted the insult, recognizing that every word was true. He and his management team had been discussing a move to a better location but had not found the time, money nor motivation to actually pursue the idea. They had grown accustom to the chaos and clutter, were proud of it . . . actually proud of it!

He waved Pat to one of two metal folding chairs facing his desk, slipped into his well-worn office chair, leaned both elbows on his desk after shoving several documents so far into a corner some spilled onto the floor. He left them there.

"Pat, let's talk first about how you might help us, how we work together," was Tom's opening. "Then I'd like to move to our manufacturing facility so you can meet my management team, they are all based there because we have no room here, and you can see what it is we make and how we make it."

"That sounds good, Tom, but why don't you begin by telling me where you are today and what you would like to achieve over what period of time."

Pat's response was calculated to draw as much detailed information from Tom as possible so he could tailor his own proposal, especially with regard to the company's financials and potential stock listing. So far the game was being played just as he had hoped.

Tom proceeded to wax enthusiastic, very proud of his company, its achievements in bonding and laminating carbon fibre into thin but extremely strong and durable panels that could be molded, cut and shaped into whatever was required for the particular application of their customer. Fabricated Structures did the manufacturing to specs submitted by the customer or developed jointly between the customer and Fabricated, which also handled whatever sanding, finishing and polishing the customer's application required. The completed panels could, on average, be produced in three-to-five weeks, delivered in finished condition, ready for immediate use by the customer.

But Tom didn't stop there. He traced his company's history back to its very beginning, when he and another fella (his current manufacturing VP) spread a bunch of worksheets on Tom's kitchen table, sketched out not only how to achieve the laminations quickly and economically, but also the equipment, space and people they would require to get the business launched.

That planning and the hunt for space required the better part of eight months, the investment of both their savings, signatures on equipment leases and commercial real estate contracts, federal, state and local government permits and licenses, ad infinatum. The entire experience was a "Tylenol high but worth every headache because look at what we have achieved."

"But we're stuck, Pat," was his closing remark. "We do not have the resources to take this company to the next step. We need twice our manufacturing space, more and better equipment. There is no room to do that in our current location. We need help," Tom said, "and that's why you're here.

"So tell me what you can do for us." That last sentence was a command, not a request.

Pat took a deep breath, slid his chair closer to Tom's desk, leaned forward and commenced his sales pitch with a compliment.

"Tom, you obviously are very proud of what you have accomplished, as well you should be. You have formed a company with a unique product. You've been remarkably successful after being in business only two years. And, you have reached a plateau which hundreds of other companies also have experienced: gang-buster growth initially, then resources become insufficient to support further potential. You are not alone in wrestling with this quandary."

Pat sounded very knowledgeable, intimately aware of Tom's concerns, appeared to have helped others with the same frustrations. He shifted on the uncomfortable chair, continued his preamble.

"Your solution is reasonably simple: you require an influx of capital so you can secure larger manufacturing space, more modern equipment, and in your case, a much more impressive showcase office complex. You really need an office environment which shouts success, growth, smarts." Pat's eyes never left Tom's, a presentation technique intended to convey confidence in his ability to accomplish all that he would propose.

"And if I correctly recall our conversation in London, you also would welcome professional guidance on how to take your company public, when that is a feasible option for you." Pat could see Tom nodding slightly as he spoke. "I think I have the experience and capital connections to achieve your goals. Let me tell you how." Pat was on a roll, could tell he was winning.

He began with a discussion of what would be required for "his London bankers" to commit to a three-million-dollar commercial loan, possibly higher, to help Tom lease a new manufacturing facility and more modern equipment. Pat emphasized that he would represent the London bank to encourage their consideration of Pat's company as a business opportunity. The bank would conduct extensive due diligence of the firm as well as Tom personally before committing to such a large loan, and Pat was in a position to guide Tom and the bank through the prolonged and sometimes frustrating process.

As a reflection of his confidence, Pat would agree to loan Tom's company $10,000 per month for the next three months until London approved and executed its loan. He would give Tom his first $10,000 check upon the signing of their cooperative agreement.

Additionally, and most importantly, Pat would need signature rights to the company's bank accounts as protection for the London bank! *("This a possible deal-breaker, I know. But I have got to make him understand it's important. Without it, I won't have access to his cash!")* This was a *must*, Pat insisted, or there could be no deal.

And Pat, himself, would require a $15,000 monthly retainer for his work on behalf of Tom's company, including negotiations with the London bank, coordinating the due diligence minefield, finding and retaining an underwriter for the company's stock offering, hiring an investor relations specialist to take a company "show" on the road to gain market support for the company's stock offering. Without that, the IPO (initial public offering) wouldn't fly.

It was a complicated business, Pat stressed, which required very delicate maneuvering to make certain it was handled expeditiously and within the letter of the law.

And, upon securing the three-million-dollar commercial loan, Pat was to be paid a $300,000 "advisory fee".

Finally, he urged Tom to issue non-public, restricted shares of stock to himself, his key management people, and to Pat, of course. Pat would require 20,000 shares as the bank's on-site representative, ten percent of the 200,000 shares Pat recommended in the IPO.

He explained that the issuance of restricted shares to Tom and his management insiders was an excellent method of rewarding key employees. They must be restricted, he said -- that is, bound under an agreement that prohibits them from being sold for several months, or years, if appropriate -- so no employee could flip them for cash as soon as they were issued. It was a good way, Pat stressed, to keep important employees married to the company.

Tom's eyes began to gloss over. He shifted in his seat.

"It all sounds interesting on the surface, Pat, but I'd like us to meet with my treasurer this afternoon at the plant. He knows more about this than I do, and we can work through the details together with him when we meet."

"That's a sound idea, Tom," Pat answered. "But can we put off that meeting until tomorrow morning? I have some real estate appointments this afternoon to find myself housing."

He really wanted time to think about how he would handle the meeting with Tom's treasurer. (*"What does the guy know? How smart is he, really? Will he ask penetrating questions that'll shoot holes in my proposal. I'm shocked Tom didn't gag at giving away ten percent of his company!"*)

+ + +

Candi Sommers assumed her client had money so she was not surprised when he arrived at her office in a chauffeur-driven car. The man who stepped out before the driver could open the rear door was tall, slim, handsome, dressed in an impeccable blue suit and bright red tie, carried a black leather envelope-style briefcase.

She felt a slight twinge vibrate through her body as she rose from behind her desk to greet Pat Clauson when he stepped into her office.

"Good afternoon, Mr. Clauson. I've been looking forward to meeting you."

"Good afternoon, Ms. Sommers. May I call you Candi? Please call me Pat." He enjoyed looking at her: five-nine frame, maybe thirty, beautifully sculptured body, fashionably attired in a sleeveless green dress, blonde hair that hung below her shoulders, ruby lips, no wedding ring.

"Yes, certainly. Thank you, Pat. Are you enjoying Newport? We're really proud of our city."

"Well, I haven't seen much of it yet. Maybe you can change that." He smiled warmly, she smiled back.

"Please have a seat and we can discuss the properties I've selected to show you. I'm sure at least one of them will meet the requirements you described to me."

Pat settled into an upholstered chair at an oak conference table. Candi grabbed a stack of brochures, drawings and listing sheets and settled into an identical chair next to him. She began her presentation with photographs and a layout of a micro-mansion on Rhode Island Avenue, a neat residential street in the heart of Newport. It had most of what Pat was seeking for his own comfort and to impress Tom Mulholland and his senior managers. The rent was quite doable.

Pat smiled again: "Good find, Candi. What else have you got? Why don't you go right to the best you have to offer. It'll save both of us some time, and we can think about getting out of here so you can take me someplace where we can enjoy a drink or two and discuss something other than real estate. My treat."

Candi shifted slightly in her chair in response to that twinge again. She gave Pat a big smile, placed her hand briefly on his forearm, shuffled the documents in front of her, grabbed a color brochure of a mansion on Ocean Drive with a magnificent view of Block Island Sound. It met all of Pat's specifications: size, number of rooms, large dining-room and exquisite living-room, both with high majestic mahogany-paneled cathedral ceilings, large patio overlooking an enormous circular swimming pool, outstanding ocean views.

The full-time staff included a cook, maid and gardner who also handled a few minor household repairs. The driveway, while short, was circular and surfaced with manufactured cobblestones creating exactly the image Pat wished to convey to Tom and his people. *("It appears I've got money; stick with me, just stick with me!")*

"That's the one, Candi. Let's take a drive by it on our way to a libation." Pat again gave her one of his best smiles.

"Okay, but don't you want to see it? The rent is $9,000 a month."

"Sounds right on target. Bring the contract with you so we can execute this deal. We'll ride in my car outside, if that's alright with you." Pat stood up to leave, briefcase tucked under his arm.

Candi was flabbergasted, the easiest rental she had ever handled, silently prayed nothing would screw it up. She gathered some papers, her pocketbook, a leather-bound note pad, locked the office door behind her as she and Pat approached the Town Car and slipped into the back seat.

Phil closed car the door, got behind the wheel, waited. Candi had been looking at Pat, suddenly became conscious that only she knew the address, told it to Phil, and the Town Car began to move at a leisurely pace.

The house was certainly everything Candi had described: sprawling, natural rock exterior, architecturally beautiful, sculptured gardens, discreetly hidden from the traffic on Ocean Drive. A two-pillared portico encased the front door three curving steps above the cobblestone driveway.

Candi had a key -- she explained that the owners were skiing in Austria, then spending several months touring Europe and the Far East -- so entry was easy. Pat was hoping entry into Candi might be just as easy, took her arm as they walked through the front door into a large paneled vestibule.

She led the way, gave Pat a walking tour of the home. Very large living-room, concert grand piano, several settees, upholstered easy chairs, floor-to-ceiling windows on two sides with terrific views, enormous flat-screen TV with stereo sound, sliding glass doors opened onto the patio and pool; large dining-room with hand-carved wooden table surrounded by twelve chairs, two matching sideboards, full bar, more sliders onto the patio.

She walked Pat into a large paneled library with floor-to-ceiling shelves on three walls laden with an an enormous collection of books, many first editions, dozens leather bound; then into an ultra-modern kitchen (which he would most likely never enter again!). Three guest bedrooms, each with private bath, completed the first floor.

They climbed a wide, curving, carpeted staircase to the second floor, which led them into a huge master bedroom with his-and-hers walk-in closets, two large bathrooms with showers and jacuzzi tubs, mirrors everywhere except on the ceilings. Walls throughout the house were covered with expensive artwork, pricey antiques in every room. Pat was surprised the rent was *only* $9,000 per month.

"What the heck do these people do, Candi?"

"He's into high-tech, has sold a couple of companies, and she's an interior decorator. Lovely home, don't you think?" It was really a statement, not a question.

"Absolutely. It's perfect. Let's find a quiet corner someplace. I'll sign the paperwork."

Candi smiled, relief on her face that the deal was a deal, and they headed for the front door and the Town Car. Phil quickly opened the rear door for them, then slipped back behind the wheel.

"Where to, Mr. Clauson?"

"Where to, Candi?" Pat repeated Phil's question.

"Do you know the Patriot's Tavern?" Candi addressed Phil.

"Yes, Mam." The car moved slowly along the circular drive.

The Tavern stood on a corner in the center of Newport, a red clapboard beacon of ages past, a very old colonial tavern. The atmosphere inside was warm, friendly, very early American. Old wooden beams boxed the smoke-stained white painted ceiling in every room, rustic wooden walls and worn wooden floors, subdued lighting, cozy fireplaces throughout the two-story structure.

Pat spotted a quiet corner of the ground-floor bar, led Candi toward a small table. A lighted candle graced the center of the polished wood along with two place settings of silver cutlery and white linen napkins. They both ordered drinks -- Chardonnay for her, Chivas on the rocks for him -- and settled back to admire the early American environment.

"This is a neat spot, Candi. Do you come here often?"

"Only with special people," she replied, laughing.

"Wow! Am I special?" Pat asked laughing in return.

"We'll see!" She was smiling.

"Well, I'll drink to that!"

They talked and laughed through a second round of drinks, Pat providing a heavily edited version of his background, the Australian sheep ranch, the raunchy pub in Sydney, what he does for a living. He exaggerated his contribution to the "success" of his clients, skipped over the shady stuff, made for an interesting, somewhat exciting, fairy tale.

Candi spoke mostly in response to questions from Pat, prying but not uncomfortably so; native born Newporter, graduate of URI, backed into real estate by accident, doing well, eager to open her own agency, nervous about the risk. Pat was very encouraging, urged her to take the plunge. They clinked glasses a few times, clearly enjoyed each other's company, had discharged the rental contract quickly.

"Candi, I'm not going to give you a check this evening. I don't yet have a contract with the company I'm courting, but that should be accomplished within twenty-four hours."

"Okay, Pat, but I can't process the signed rental contract until I have your check for one month's rent plus the security deposit."

"Right. That's fine with me."

Pat glanced at his watch, 8:25; looked into Candi's eyes, smiled and asked: "So, how am I doing?"

"What do you mean?"

"Am I Special?"

She thought for a few seconds, her middle finger and thumb sliding slowly up and down the stem of her wine glass in a motion Pat recognized instantly. "Well, you're damned interesting. I guess that's special," she replied, looking directly into his eyes. *("And you appear to be loaded with m-o-n-e-y! That's VERY special!")*

"Super!" He put down his drink. "We have a choice: dinner here, or you take us back to *my* house so we can relax!"

"It's not your house yet!" Candi was smiling.

"Well you know it's going to be."

"No, I don't, Pat, and I'm not able to process the lease until I have your check and it clears."

"Come on, Candi!" Pat paused. "Listen . . . hear that? It's that king size bed calling out to us: 'I'm all alone here!'"

Candi laughed, took a sip of her wine, looked at Pat rather coyly, half smiled as she lowered her glass to the table. "Let's not rush, Pat. You're smooth as silk, very handsome, fun to be with. But give me an opportunity to think. Let's have dinner."

"I'm crushed, but optimistic!" Pat replied smiling but disappointed, signaled the waiter for a menu.

Dinner was excellent, accompanied by an outstanding wine, rambling conversation that continued to touch on their respective businesses, social interests, former attachments or lack thereof; easy-going, non-threatening, not really very revealing.

Both were laughing as they exited the Tavern and headed for the Town Car. Phil had the back door open, Candi stopped, held out her hand to shake with Pat.

"Good night, Pat. and thank you for a lovely dinner, and for what I suspect will be a very satisfying piece of business for us both."

"God! You're deserting me in a strange city! Maybe I oughtta rethink this whole thing."

"No! I don't think you should, Pat. You never know what tantalizing opportunities may await your future." She wasn't smiling, but Pat sensed a special look in her very blue eyes.

"OK! I'll dream about that!" He smiled, shook her hand, climbed into the car to head for the hotel on Goat Island. Candi turned and walked toward a taxi in the restaurant parking lot.

3

FRIDAY

Pat rose at 7:30, entered the bathroom, stared into the mirror, pleased with the reflection staring back. He shaved, showered, dressed, phoned room service for a huge breakfast. Felt ready to whip a tiger.

He pulled a pad from his leather envelope, began making notes for his meeting this morning with Tom Mulholland and the firm's chief financial officer. He was both curious and wary of what that guy might be like, how much he knew about market trading. Grabbed his cell phone around 9:15, dialed Fabricated, connected quickly to Tom.

"Hi, Tom. It's Pat Clauson."

"Good morning, Pat. Did you find someplace to live?"

"Yes, I think I have. I'll confirm the details once you and I have a contract."

"Well, that's good. Pat, I suggest you go straight to the plant in Portsmouth. I've set our meeting for 10 o'clock. See you then."

The Fabricated Structures manufacturing facility was a long, single story brick building, an architectural style commonly referred to as "box store" construction. A sizable parking lot protected the front door, embraced by narrow glass panels on both sides. It opened into an unimpressive lobby furnished in early Salvation Army, paper notices of one sort or another taped to the walls, magazines and newspapers on a low table surrounded by more metal folding chairs. The metal reception desk was staffed by a matronly woman, reading glasses dangling from a gold chain around her neck. She was partially obscured by a computer and multi-button phone.

Pat approached her wearing his best smile.

"Good morning. I'm Pat Clauson, and I have an appointment with Tom Mulholland."

"Yes, Mr. Clauson. We've been expecting you. Welcome to Fabricated Structures. Please have a seat and I'll notify Mr. Mulholland that you're here."

Pat parked his frame on a metal chair, lay his briefcase on the floor beside him, looked up at the suspended fiberboard ceiling panels stained brown from water leaks. A day old *Providence Journal* stared at him from the low table along with the back issue of a national trade magazine.

A door opened behind the reception desk and a vision entered the room. She was about five-ten, her height exaggerated by four-inch heels. She was slim but well endowed, her figure sheathed in black skin-tight jeans. A designer scooped-neck sleeveless blouse accentuated her sexuality.

What really caught Pat's attention was her long, glistening black hair and her eyes: dark eyes, penetrating eyes, eyes that looked *into* you, not just at you. He was mesmerized.

She walked straight toward him, one foot planted exactly in front of the other, like a runway model. She extended her right hand as she drew close.

"Good morning, Mr. Clauson. I am Colette Dubois, Mr. Mulholland's administrative assistant. It's a pleasure to meet you." Her smile was beyond charming, red pouting lips, teeth white as ivory. And those eyes!

"The pleasure is all mine, Colette. Please call me Pat." Her grip was soft, warm.

"If you will follow me (*"Anywhere Colette, anywhere!"*) I'll show you to the conference room where Mr. Mullolland and Mr. Johnson are waiting." They passed through the door she had entered, walked down a hallway with offices left and right inside metal partitions topped by frosted glass. They entered a conference room at the end of the corridor. Colette announced his arrival and disappeared.

The room was drab, light grey walls, no windows except for a long horizontal clear glass pane on the far wall which revealed the manufacturing floor beyond, people in white hazmat suits scurrying between large machines. A dirty suspended ceiling with fluorescent lighting hung over a ten-foot metal-trimmed Formica topped conference table surrounded by metal chairs meant for efficiency, not comfort.

Tom sat in one at the head of the table; another occupied by the guy Pat figured had to be the treasurer, Steve Johnson. Both were wearing white shirts but no ties, no jackets. Steve stood to shake hands.

"Hi, Pat. I've been looking forward to meeting you, heard a lot about you from Tom." Johnson was younger, late twenties maybe early thirties, tall, slim, another athletic build, dark hair and ruddy tan.

"Hi, Steve. Likewise."

Tom rose, walked toward Pat, right hand extended. "It's good to see you, Pat."

"Thank you, Tom. I've been anticipating this meeting since our discussion yesterday, and I look forward to the opportunity of working with you." He settled onto one of the chairs. "Where would you like to begin?"

"I want Steve to hear all the details we discussed yesterday about how we might collaborate, Pat. He is our treasurer and has a vested interest in the financial ramifications you outlined for me, including your idea of issuing restricted stock, the due diligence by the London bank, and so on. We should confirm all of the details so that, hopefully, we can sign an agreement and get moving."

("Oh, man! This where the rubber meets the road! This Steve Johnson is going to choke on some of my proposals . . . my signing checks, grabbing a chunk of stock, my advisory fee . . . lord knows what else. Gotta move slowly, anticipate questions, above all keep my cool!")

Pat stood draped his suit coat over the back of his chair, loosened his tie, settled in for a protracted conversation.

He began his song-and-dance by again complimenting Tom and Steve on all they had accomplished in just over two years, hit the "proud" button hard, dragged out the discussion of "so many" other young firms facing similar obstacles and concerns as Fabricated. He described it all in language framed to suggest that Pat had played a significant role in turning those firms around with the assistance of his financial and legal colleagues in London and Hong Kong. His prelude was a masterful performance.

"Can we talk to any of them?" Wham-o! This was Steve.

"What do you mean?"

"Well, I think it would be interesting to speak to one or two of your clients to see how well things turned out for them. Might even help us avoid some pitfalls."

Pat began to sweat.

"Well, Steve, the nature of my business is quite confidential and I don't think any of my clients would appreciate me sharing their business problems with a third party. I'll check with a couple, if you'd like *("don't count on it!")*, but I'm not certain they'll agree to permit my sharing confidential information."

"Let's keep moving." This was Tom.

Pat quickly switched to a discussion of Point A: his ability to help the company secure a three-million-dollar commercial loan, possibly more, from his London bankers. He emphasized the importance of his role as facilitator between the company and the bank to help Tom and Steve deal with the complex due diligence which would be performed by the bank before it would agree to a loan.

He closed Point A with his offer to pay Fabricated ten thousand a month out of his own pocket until the Commercial Bank of London wired the agreed loan amount to Fabricated's bank account. This would demonstrate his confidence that he could secure a sizable commercial loan because of his strong ties to the bank.

Steve interrupted.

"Pat, why can't we talk to the bankers in London?" Wham-o #2!

Pat paused before answering.

"You can, Steve, but they won't discuss this kind of international activity over the phone. They will insist that you fly to London. I can arrange such a meeting if you'd like." Pat swallowed hard. *("Jesus, this will blow my entire plan! Don't you dare tell me you want to go to London or even talk to the bankers!")*

"Steve, let's not do that," Tom cut in. "Either we trust Pat can do what he claims, or we don't. And we'll know our comfort level before lunch today. Let's not forget Pat has offered to pay us ten grand a month until the commercial loan comes through."

"Yeah, how's that gonna work, Pat?" Steve asked. "Is that out of the kindness of your heart? What's our bottom line regarding your cash investment?"

Pat laughed, although he was developing a dislike for Mr. Johnson.

"No, Steve, it is not out of the kindness of my heart. As part of our agreement, I will charge Fabricated a monthly retainer of fifteen thousand dollars."

"You give us ten a month and we pay you fifteen. That's no deal." Wham-o #3! Steve looked directly into Pat's eyes, bit of a smirk on his face. "Our net cost to retain you is five thousand a month. Let's settle that and forget the swap, which doesn't make sense because, in effect, you're not lending us anything. We're just swapping dollars."

"We never spoke about that yesterday, Pat."

"Yes, I'm sorry I overlooked that, Tom. But, actually, my retainer is cheap given all you want me to do to help you out. We're talking about some very complicated negotiations; what I understand you folks to be looking for isn't going to come easy. You might as well be aware of that. And, in my view, my ten grand investment should ease your cash flow."

"It will if we don't pay you fifteen to get your ten," Steve said.

Pat's guts were churning; he hadn't even touched on the three most controversial issues yet to be raised.

"We'll just pay you five thousand instead of fifteen. That will have the same effect on our cash flow."

"True, Steve. My offer was simply to demonstrate my sincerity in partnering with you as we move forward." *("Damn! My plan was to collect the fifteen, but go slow on paying them the ten, blaming the delay on the bank or my 'people' in California.")*

"I appreciate that, Pat, but let's keep the math simple. You keep your ten, and we'll pay you five each month."

Tom: "Let Pat keep going, Steve. We'll get to the fine points after we understand all he is proposing."

"Yeah, we should look at that closely, Tom." Turning to Pat:

"When are we likely to see the Bank's loan money, and what's your cut for making it happen?"

Pat was struggling to control his voice.

"Well, Steve, we're shooting for a three-million commercial loan, maybe even more, which is doable if the bankers come out of their due diligence giddy with delight. Whether the loan is three or more, my fee remains fixed at $300,000. That's only ten percent, and it is a very fair fee.

"Yeah, but it sure cuts into our proceeds from the loan," Steve observed. He had been scribbling on a pad and proceeded to read his notes. "We'll have to pay interest on the fee we pay you, and we'll lose some of our purchasing power as we shop for new equipment.

"Would you be willing to accept a staggered fee payment over twelve or twenty-four months so we can pay you out of current earnings, avoid interest on our payments to you, and have more cash available to solve our equipment problems?" Wham-o #4!

Tom: "That sounds very reasonable, Pat."

Pat leaned forward, his arms resting on the table.

"I really can't do that, Tom. I don't plan to be around here for twenty-four months because I can't believe you'll need me for that long. And, I have other firms asking for help," Pat lied. "I think if you were me, you also would want to be paid once the banking deal closes. I'm sorry about the interest, Tom. Perhaps you can pay me partially out of retained earnings and the balance from the loan."

Steve leaned forward, bearing in. "That's just not going to work for us, Pat." He paused. "How about increasing your personal investment?"

"It's your company, not mine, Steve." Pat was beginning to show just a touch of frustration, his voice rising slightly, told himself to back off.

"Look, the only way I could justify that is if you folks agree to issue stock to the three of us, perhaps some of your senior managers as well, and you give me a number of shares so I can benefit from my security sales."

Tom: "We haven't even discussed the stock idea with each other, Pat. It's something we've been thinking about, but we're not close to a decision." He looked to Steve for confirmation, Steve nodded.

Pat leaned back in his chair.

"Well, Tom, we touched on that yesterday, and it's the only way I can see for justifying an investment in your company. That's the only road open, because you have nothing else to offer me."

"I understand, Pat. Steve and I will discuss that idea this afternoon, in fact we'll want to discuss this entire proposal in some detail and get back to you perhaps tomorrow."

"That's fine, Tom." *("Damn it, Steve is screwing it all up!")*

"How many shares do you think we should issue, and what's your grab?" It was Steve again, pressing the subject.

"That bears some discussion, Steve. I would recommend nothing less than 200,000 shares, maybe 500,000, and my 'grab', as you put it, would be 25,000."

Steve looked shocked. "Jesus, Pat, you planned to invest about sixty thousand in our company and walk out owning over five percent of it, with another three-hundred-thousand in cash from a loan on which we pay interest! And 200,000 shares aren't enough to build a significant market. Come on, Pat, this is nuts!"

Wham-o #5! Pat could see his entire deal collapsing.

"He's right, Pat." Tom was now leaning his forearms on the table. "We really cannot agree to this proposal. I personally would welcome an opportunity to do business with you. I think you can help us achieve some of our goals. But this package your describing is beyond our serious consideration."

Pat sat back in his chair, arms extended and spread on the table. *("Well, shit! Can't allow the negotiations to end here. Gotta counter, gotta think, gotta keep the dialog rolling.")*

Steve, of all people, suddenly came to his rescue.

"Look, Pat. Suppose we forget about the London bankers. We have our own bankers here, and we are quite capable of negotiating a larger commercial loan with them. Our credit is good, they know we are growing and succeeding financially, and I believe they would give us a good audience if we ask for a hearing."

Steve continued. "Absent that, why don't you think about two things. One, you increase your proposed investment in our company at a reasonable interest rate, with the principle paid back to you over a short period of time, open to negotiation.

"Second, let's focus our attention on the possibility issuing stock in the company, including you for a number of shares. And let's get that done as quickly as possible."

Steve had verbally passed the baton back to Pat. Salvation?

"OK, Steve. I'm willing to consider that. I need to consult with my associates in California *("what associates")* to determine how much we can invest with you. And if we're going to move quickly on the stock subject *("thank god!")* I suggest we avoid the major exchanges and focus on the so-called penny stock market. This will give us a chance to float shares, help them increase in value, and profit from our sales."

Tom: "Who the hell is interested in penny stocks?"

"You'd be amazed, Tom. There are a lot of companies like yours, just starting out with a good initial track record. And there is a solid population of investors. While the return can be small per share, there are normally no dividends paid, it can be huge if you have big enough holdings and the shares are actively traded. The investment cost is low, and so is the risk, so the penny stock market appeals to a certain class of investor." No mention of con men or hustlers (like Pat)!

Pat was smiling. This wasn't the deal he wanted, but it was a deal. And if he hyped the stock sufficiently he'd make some good money. Besides, these guys would never see the amount of money he proposed to invest; he'd delay writing them checks, blame that on his own cash flow or the inefficiency of his so-called California associates, and walk with his stock profits, monthly retainer, plus . . .!

"Another possibility, Tom, longer term, is to grow the value of this initial offering, and your company's capitalization, until they've reached the point where it makes sense to approach one of the major exchanges. That is a huge step, you can make your stock more attractive by paying a small dividend. And raising the dividend in small increments over time, assuming you remain profitable, will enhance public interest in your company's shares.

"It's not a bad investment strategy." He was on a roll, really wound up.

"You also could create a private performance share program for valued employees you want to keep happy as you grow. You could pay a dividend on those shares because there is no market value, it's just a performance bonus." Pat could tell Tom was interested.

"How many shares would you want for helping us to make all this possible? Anything more than the 25,000 you've mentioned?"

"I'm not sure, Steve. It will depend upon how you structure the stock offering."

Tom stood, indicating the meeting was over. Steve and Pat did the same.

"Well, you've given us a lot to think about, Pat. Let Steve and I noodle all that you've said this morning, and we should get together again -- let's do it in an afternoon early next week -- to see if we can arrive at an agreement. We are anxious to put things in motion." He extended his hand to shake with Pat; Steve did the same.

Pat grabbed his coat, picked up his briefcase, led the trio out of the conference room. Tom stuck his head into office.

"Colette, would you check my schedule, and Steve's, and book us into a meeting with Pat early next week. And please show him the way out." He stuck out his hand to again shake with Pat, confirmed interest in meeting to get things settled. Steve had disappeared into his own office.

("Well, *that didn't go at all like I planned, but there's still hope; gonna take some extra work, but the payoff should be good. Still need to get my hands on their checkbook, that won't be easy; Steve, damn Steve.*")

"Mr. Clauson?" *("That voice! It's that vision, Colette!")*

Pat turned, stuck his head into her office as she rose from her desk, calendar in hand. "How does two o'clock on Tuesday sound?

Both Tom and Steve are open for a couple of hours at that time. Tom has a four in his office."

"Sounds great, Colette. Two o'clock it is. And remember, it's Pat, not Mr. Clauson." He was smiling, so was she. She turned and headed for the reception room, Pat following like a lamb.

("Is it too soon to ask her out? Even for a drink? Yeah, yeah, yeah. Play it cool; don't get Tom or Steve thinking the only thing I want out of them is Colette! But if all else fails . . . .!")

+ + +

Pat slid into the back of the Town Car, instructed Phil to head for the hotel on Goat Island. He gazed out the car window but saw nothing, his mind lost in the details of the morning's meeting. He vowed to park his ass in his hotel room, pencil and notepad in hand, to sketch notes and rebuttals for the sore points already raised by Steve.

He arranged a pickup with Phil at seven o'clock for a dinner date, then realized he didn't have one! He phoned Candi, could he pick her up about seven-fifteen. Nope, she would leave her office early, show up at the hotel.

He sat at the desk in his room contemplating the Tuesday meeting: didn't expect it to be easy, more jabs likely from Steve, needed a smart response to every objection the guy raised. He felt comfortable Tom wanted to pursue an agreement, but Steve . . . didn't like many of Pat's terms; appeared suspicious that perhaps Pat didn't have all the fire power he claimed; seemed dubious about Pat's "relationship" with a British bank'; didn't give a damn about Hong Kong lawyers, either.

Pat's focus would remain on his own promised investment *("that will never happen in full")* and his recommendation about issuing stock. Those steps appealed to both Tom and Steve. Pat knew how to hype the stock price to make a quick payoff possible. Add in his retainer, plus his determination *not* to pay out-of-pocket expenses, including rental checks on that house *("sorry Candi, tough lesson")*, and he'd have a good haul.

And, if he succeeded in convincing these guys to give him signature rights to the firm's checking account -- *("just to protect my investors!")* well . . . the apples were ripe for picking.

Candi wrapped on his door about four o'clock. He was stunned when he saw her standing there. She looked delicious.

"What's up, Big Guy? Are you relaxing?" She entered and plopped into an easy chair.

"Nope, I'm making notes for another meeting with my prospect on Tuesday afternoon."

"How did today go?"

"Tough. The treasurer is too damned smart for his own good. But the CEO is interested in retaining me, so I hope we can sign a deal on Tuesday."

"Great. But no rental check yet, right."

"Right."

"Well, don't be a bore. I came here to play."

Pat packed up his paperwork, winked at Candi, reached for her hand and pulled her upright. They locked eyes for several seconds, then kissed long, passionately. Kissed again, walked hand-in-hand toward the king-size bed and spent the afternoon wrestling, finally dozed off wrapped in each other's arms.

They showered and dressed for dinner in the hotel's dining room, shared a chilled Veuve Clicquot with their appetizer, a marvelous dry white wine with their lobster and salad, coffee and aperitif with a cold chocolate mousse.

Their conversation was relaxed, their mood warm, familiar. Pat suddenly turned serious, had an idea he considered brilliant.

"Candi, do you handle commercial real estate?"

She hesitated, his shift to business so unexpected.

"Purchase or rental?" she finally asked.

"Rental. Office space, but a lot of it."

"Sure do. What are you looking for?" She straightened in her chair, her face also serious, pushed her aperitif and coffee aside to clear the tablecloth in front of her.

"Oh, it's not for me, but the company I'm consulting with has its CEO and support staff in the ugliest hunk of crap you can imagine. I want them to upgrade, and I'm pretty certain they'll listen to me, in fact, I know they will."

Pat went on to describe Fabricated's so-called corporate headquarters, used a variety of adjectives to help Candi appreciate the commercial squalor Fabricated occupied versus the more comfortable, appropriate, up-scale office environment Pat felt was needed before bringing potential or existing clients into a meeting. He spared no expense in conveying his impression of the reception room or conference facility at the manufacturing plant.

"The whole shebang looks like it's been assembled from the ruins of a bombed out neighborhood," was Pat's closing.

"We'll we can sure do better than what you're describing, Pat. I'll slip into the office tomorrow morning and check some of our commercial listings. I recall seeing something come in the other day in Washington Square, which is a very nice area, but I don't recall the details. And I'm sure we have several other listings, as well, that might interest you."

"We'll, it isn't just me, Candi. I, or we, have to do a sales job on the CEO, a local guy named Tom Mulholland. He seems eager to improve the company's image, but his treasurer might not share Tom's enthusiasm. He's a bit of a prick, may try to sabotage the idea, so we have to have our ducks in order."

"Okay, I copy."

"Check your office records tomorrow and give me a call. I'd like to see these places before we show them to Tom. That way I can help direct him to the space which I think would best meet his requirements, and mine!"

"Easily done, Pat. I'm in the office Saturday mornings anyway. I can't guarantee we'll be able to view all the commercial stuff on a Saturday, but I'll see what we can accomplish. The rest will have to wait until Monday, is that okay?"

"Yeah, I don't see these guys again until Tuesday afternoon, so that's fine. I think it will help me enormously if I go into the Tuesday meeting excited about a potential office relocation that will help Tom showcase his business as forward-thinking, fast-growing."

They finished their coffee, pushed away from the table, and Pat held her hand as they walked toward the elevator bank and bed.

4

THE WEEKEND

Candi slipped out of bed early, grabbed a cab in front of the hotel, hit her office by 7:30 and began pouring through commercial real estate listings to locate a few she felt might interest Pat and his client. Pat's comments the previous evening made it clear he was looking for an interesting building in an attractive part of the city, a building which would accommodate a number of executive offices, a general administrative office area, a comfortable reception room, a sizable conference room.

Pat's feet didn't hit the floor until 9:30. His reflection in the bathroom mirror was a guy six hours short of a good night's sleep. He showered, dressed in his underwear and a soft robe hanging in the bathroom, retrieved *The New York Times* and *Providence Journal* from the hall, phoned room service for a hefty breakfast and settled into an easy chair to digest the news.

With the newspapers and breakfast behind him, he stared out the hotel window, not really seeing the sailboats moving up and down Narragansett Bay propelled by a light wind under bright sunny skies. His mind focused on the meeting he had concluded with Tom and Steve yesterday, and the upcoming meeting at two o'clock Tuesday. He was upset that Steve had shot down his plan to grab a hunk of cash as he "negotiated" a loan from the British bank.

That left his retainer, plus whatever he might secure from a potential stock offering, plus his skill at sucking cash out of the company's bank accounts before disappearing. Meanwhile, he was expected to invest some of his own money into the company, something he was damned certain he would *not* do -- or at least not all he'd promise -- come hell or high water.

So this Fabricated Structures "opportunity" was not shaping up as he had hoped when he first met Tom in London. Then it seemed like a sure thing, even now Tom seems more amenable to Pat's suggestions than that damned treasurer.

Pat realized he would have to work harder, focus on the details to influence Tom, apply more clever thinking than he had in previous deals. *("Ignore Steve; keep hammering at Tom, Tom is the pivotal actor, Tom controls the power, Steve dances to Tom's tune, so make sure Tom likes your music.")*

He grabbed a pencil and his notepad, began sketching more notes for the Tuesday meeting. He hoped to open with the news that he had found what looked like a good location for new offices, with an invitation to Tom to tour the new facility as soon as the real estate agent could make the appointment. He would not use Candi's name, never mention that he and she had "become involved."

Next, he would agree to increase his investment in the company. It didn't matter what he promised because it would never happen; he'd delay and stagger payments over several months, demanding interest payments on the total mount from the get-go. He'd also push hard to make the stock issue a priority. The toughest sell would be getting signature rights to the firm's bank account. *("I might be able to sell Tom; Steve will burst a gasket!")*

In the midst of his preoccupation, he looked up and for the first time focused on sailboats streaming north toward the huge bridge across East Passage, others heading south toward the open ocean.

("That's it! Why didn't I think of this earlier! When I talk with Colette, I'll ask her if she'd like to go sailing, maybe for an afternoon next weekend. It's gotta be easy in this town to rent a boat and crew for three or four hours.")

His revery was interrupted by the telephone.

"Hi, Pat. It's Candi."

"Hi! How's it going?"

"Not well, Pat. I have been out flat all morning with some real estate showings. I did make some calls regarding commercial avails, but none of them impress me as what you are looking for."

"Why waste your time calling them?"

"I'm trying to be helpful, Pat. Please don't get huffy. I really want to show you that Washington Square property. It was a bank, but it sounds like it has the potential to be converted into exactly what you want. Unfortunately, I can't find the owner or his estate agent so we can't get into it until Monday."

"That's not a problem, Candi. My meeting with my clients isn't until Tuesday."

"Ah, that's great. I have to run, but can I see you this evening?"

"No, I'm sorry, Candi. I have to fly to New York this evening *("a fat lie")* to meet with two associates tomorrow in the City *("another fat lie")*. I'll be back here Monday morning and will give you a call."

They said their good-byes and hung up. Pat had lied about the New York trip because he felt Candi was closing in on him. The sex yesterday and last night had been sensational, but he needed breathing room before his pecker developed callouses!

Having lied, he decided on the spur of the moment to actually head for New York. He phoned Phil requesting a pickup ASAP for an afternoon tour of some of Newport's highlights, with Phil as his guide, before he left for New York. He didn't dare not go to the City now that he told Candi he couldn't see her until Monday, didn't want to run the risk of being caught in Newport because she was too valuable a resource for locating suitable office space for Fabricated Structures.

Phil's first stop was a popular local spot for lunch in a homey cafe next door to the police station. Pat sat at the counter, enjoyed Jammie's Shrimp Roll with a side of fries and an ice coffee while he ogled a gal behind the counter named Beth: super friendly, attractive, seemed ripe for . . . well, maybe next time! He learned the guy seated next to him was a city councilor, quiet reserved fella with not much to say. Seated alone at a corner table was a jovial state rep who spent his time teasing the waitresses while his lunch got cold.

Back in the Town Car, Phil took Pat to one of the world famous mansions constructed in the 1890s by wealthy execs history labeled "robber barons". That was in the days before Teddy Roosevelt blew holes in the synergy between politics and industry by convincing Congress to pass effective trust-busting legislation. These palaces were only used for a few weeks in the summer anyway, then the one-percenters of their day moved on to their other lavish estates on Long Island or in Bar Harbor, Maine. The Newport estates had been turned over to a charitable organization as public attractions because heirs to the robber barons could not possibly afford the maintenance, heat, nor real estate taxes.

Pat also toured the military museum at the Naval War College, admired scores of model ship exhibits, uniforms, weapons old and new (mostly old), several dioramas, and the ugly Enigma machine which the British had recovered from a captured Nazi submarine, de-coded and used to intercept German Wolfpack attack plans.

His final stop was the Redwood Library, the oldest lending library in the U.S., its charter signed by King George III in 1747, more than twenty years before the American Revolution. Pat admired the Library's enormous collection of antique leather-bound books, its huge vaulted reading room with hundreds of best sellers from the present and decades past, a wide assortment of current magazines and newspapers, and the Museum's vast collection of rare and beautiful early American art and modern sculpture. He felt he could hibernate there for months and never get bored, vowed to return for another visit.

It was closing onto six o'clock when Pat told Phil to head for the airport, meet him again late Monday about ten for a ride back to the hotel. Pat had held his room in reserve.

Since New York had been a spur of the moment decision, Pat had no specific plan on what he would do once he was in the City. He did manage to get a room at a five star hotel on Park Avenue, vowed to hang out in the room, work a little, and get some rest. That plan lasted less than an hour before he took the elevator to the lobby floor, stopped at the bar for a nightcap prior to retiring.

The place was hopping with a thirsty Saturday night crowd, including a platoon of men wearing convention name tags. They were loud, half in the bag, rambling on, joking about customers incapable of providing them with repeat business. Turned out they were undertakers! Gave Pat a quiet laugh, never thought of undertakers as party animals.

He was three sips into his Chivas when the empty bar seat to his right was suddenly occupied by a stunning blonde, dressed to the nines, long blonde hair tumbling down her back, makeup looked like it had been applied professionally. She set her handbag on the bar, label facing Pat: Hermes. *("Okay lady, I get it. You're expensive.")*

She ordered a glass of champagne by label, Sir Winston Churchill, and shot Pat a quick smile.

"Did it ever occur to you that undertakers are party animals?"

The woman looked at Pat as if he was nuts, saw his smile, smiled back. "Are you serious?"

"Yeah. Those guys over there seem to be undertakers. I've never thought of undertakers as party dudes. I'll bet they're from some jerkwater towns in the Dakotas; don't get to the big city often."

The woman gazed at the men across the bar, then turned back to Pat, smiling broadly, a warm twinkle in her eyes. "I take it you are not an undertaker?"

"Lord, No! The only thing dead about me is this evening. I just flew down from New England. I've had a brutal week, looking forward to a respite before I enter the lion's cage again on Monday."

She was laughing, turned on her bar seat to face Pat a little more directly. "What do you do, if you don't mind my asking?"

"Don't mind at all." He was putting on the charm, Australian accent in full throttle, for whatever reason it was a siren call, shrimp on the bar-bee, kangaroos! "I'm an investment manager, help companies secure financing or stock exchange listings, stuff like that, to help them grow and make the owners rich." *("Mammoth lie!")*

"Wow! That's a mouthful." She sipped her champagne, her wrist wrapped in a gold and diamond bracelet. "And you're not American, or are you from the Dakotas?" She laughed again.

Pat's turn to laugh. "No! I'm from Australia originally, been living in this country for several years. Started my business here, doing quite well."

"How do you like living here?"

"Love it. It's the land of opportunity, as they say." They both sipped their drinks.

"So what's your story? Where're you from, what do you do?" *("I bet I can guess your answer!")*

"I'm from a jerkwater town, to use your phrase, in New Jersey. And I am in the entertainment field."

("I'll bet you are! This should be interesting.")

"No kidding! The entertainment field is a very broad industry. What segment are you in?"

"I entertain gentlemen like yourself so they are relaxed before they have to enter the lion's cage on Monday." She was still smiling. "Do you need to relax?"

Pat did some very rapid mental calculations, figured he'd have to invest twenty or thirty grand in the Fabricated project, maybe more. He didn't normally believe in paying for sex, but this gal looked extraordinary, and what the hell . . . . He laughed before replying.

"Do I ever!" They clicked glasses, she began that thumb-and-finger slide up and down her champagne flute. *("Jesus, they must teach that in high school!")* "But I haven't had a bite to eat. Are you hungry?"

"Are you staying here?"

"You bet!"

"How about room service." It was a statement, not a question.

"My name is Pat."

"Cecily, Pat. Nice to meet you."

"Cecily! I like that. Well, Cecily, I don't believe in trying to walk on one leg, so why don't we both have a re-fill, then retire to my room and relax together."

The bartender quickly responded to Pat's signal for another round, seemed delighted to pull away from the drunk undertakers and have a chance to look at Cecily. They nursed their second drinks, engaged in harmless conversation about New York, New Jersey, Australia and other subjects which did not require either of them to share much personal information. After 20 minutes, glasses empty, they headed toward the elevator bank and Pat's floor, the hell with dinner!

Once in his room Cecily suggested Pat order a bowl of fresh strawberries and a bottle of Sir Winston Churchill champagne. He also opened the locked bar, retrieved two nips of Chivas, phoned room service for the fruit, champagne and ice. Cecily, meanwhile, had disappeared into the bathroom.

Room service was quick to respond to his call. Pat was unwrapping the stopper in the champagne bottle when he announced through the closed bathroom door: "The goodies are here. Come and get 'em!"

Cecily emerged from the bathroom tall, slim and stark naked. She walked over to the room service tray, lifted a flute of champagne Pat had just poured. "Cheers!"

Pat was too dumbstruck to reply, stared at her gorgeous body to the point where she laughed.

"Are you relaxing?" She was teasing, very sexy.

"Jesus, Cecily! Relaxing isn't the word for it!"

"Now! Now! Let's not be hasty. You said you were hungry, so grab some strawberries, lift your glass of whatever, and let's relax for a while."

"How long is a while? How long does that have to be?"

"You'll know when it's up. Meanwhile, get rid of that tie, open your shirt, kick off your shoes, get with it, Pat." She was laughing again.

Pat did better than Cecily suggested, hastily removed his shirt and trousers, sat beside her on the bed, could not keep his hands off her body or his lips away from hers. It didn't take long before they lay back on the bed, Cecily determined to make sure her prediction about relaxation came true. It was an exhausting hour, the strawberries left to spoil, the champagne to get warm.

+ + +

Pat awoke about nine Sunday, found a note pinned to his tie: "til next time" with a local phone number. He dropped it into his briefcase for future reference.

He shaved, showered, dressed, called room service for a hefty breakfast. He was not only relaxed, he was starving, the shriveled strawberries just didn't appeal. He needed eggs, bacon, home fries, juice, toast, pot of coffee, devoured all when it arrived, settled back with the Sunday *Times.*

He grabbed his cell phone mid-morning, dialed the number for Kyle Mullen. Kyle was a retired investment banker (the real thing) whom Pat had met early on and used as an advisor. He was a big strapping guy with mucho smarts, brusk personality, rough sense of humor. He called a spade a spade and if you didn't like it he'd tell you where to stick it. He answered the phone after only two rings.

"It's your nickel."

"Hi, Kyle. It's Pat Clauson."

"Christ, I know it's you, nobody else I know sounds like you! Where are you and how much is your bail?"

Pat laughed. "I'm in the City. Thought I'd call to say hello and pick your brain about something."

"My brain's still asleep, has nothing to do with the fact that I'm talking."

"Well, wake the damn thing up. I don't wanna waste my money talking to the dead air hibernating in your skull!"

"Smart ass! Okay, it's awake. What kind of free advice can I dispense to you on this otherwise gorgeous Sunday morning?"

Pat took a good ten minutes to spell out in detail everything he had been discussing with Tom Mulholland and Steve Johnson. He described his impression of the company, its management, their office disaster, his desire to find them more impressive space, the commercial loan idea which went nowhere, the issuance of penny stock, and so on.

The only part of his proposal he chose not to discuss with Kyle was his desire to get signature rights to the company's bank account. That would be a huge red flag, would tip Kyle off to what Pat was really after, as if he couldn't figure it out.

"Lemme ask you a couple of questions. Why do you care what their offices look like?"

"Lord, Kyle, if you could see the dump you wouldn't be asking that. They get a fair amount of customer traffic, apparently. Some of the meetings are held in a conference room at their manufacturing plant, another dump, but somewhat passable. But the offices . . . I cannot imagine anybody walking away with a positive image of this company."

What he didn't say is that he'd offer to hire the renovation contractors, suggest he pay from the company's bank account . . . but he'd pocket the cash instead. That was an easy scam.

"Okay. Talk to me about the stock idea. What's your angle, what do you want to achieve?"

Pat described his plan in detail, an internal issue versus public, restricted versus tradable, non-dividend versus dividend, penny market versus a major exchange. He stressed his interest in making it all happen quickly, rocketing the price for a quick profit. How many shares to issue? What should his cut be?

"Wow! Pat, is this a sincere effort or a scam? Do these guys understand what I think you're really up to?"

"Kyle, it's not really a scam, but I do want to make some quick dough."

"'Not *really* a scam!' You're talkin' the penny market! Am I gonna share a cell with you?"

"Don'cha love me?" Laughter.

"Like tooth decay!" More laughter.

"Look, Kyle, these guys have been thinking of a public issue for some time, but they don't understand how to do it without incurring horrendous expenses from people like you. I want to get them on the market fast, start the stock growing so I can cash in my shares for a quick payoff, and move onto something else. I have no desire to stick around Fabricated any longer than necessary."

"Yeah, I get that. Okay, three things. One, forget the major exchanges. The whole package you're describing is too small. None of the majors will even look at you, and listings are very pricey. You will have to look at the penny stock market, which on the surface appears to be not all that bad. On the surface!

"Second, recommend they issue 500,000 shares, minimum, maybe even one million."

"A million! Jesus, I don't want to frighten these guys!"

"Look, Pat, you have got to have sufficient shares available to the brokers so they can create a market. The publicly traded shares will earn you money when you sell. A million gives you plenty of shares to spread around the management team and still have a viable public market. You inside guys can help move the price, but you have to be damned careful not to go overboard and run afoul of the SEC. Got that?"

"Yes, I do."

"That's very important. If you screw up, jail is waiting, or lawyer's fees that will put you all in bankruptcy. I recommend you demand 50,000 shares. That increases your share count, but drops your percentage of the offering to five percent or less so it looks like you're doing those guys a big favor. You can still net a bundle when you sell."

"Yeah, okay, I got that, too."

"And you know where to sell restricted shares, right."

"Yes! Canada, because restrictions don't apply there."

"Atta boy!"

"That's where I've been selling every time my client gives me stock, which is mandatory or I blow them off!"

"How safe is your guy in Canada?"

"He's okay, but it might make sense to give someone else this shot. Do you know someone?"

"Yes! I'll give you a name, will phone you this week. Do you have some kind of institutional investor type who knows his way around the brokers that deal in penny stocks. You can't do that because you don't have the contacts, and you'll drive yourself nuts."

"Yeah, I know. That's what I've been trying to do."

"Well, you don't need a road show, but you do need somebody to call on the penny stock brokers. That'll save you a lot of time, and sweat!"

"Good advice. Do you know anyone I could call?"

"Yeah, one guy comes to mind. Name is Daniel Grady, goes by Danny-Boy. He's reasonably sharp, and cheap. His biggest failing is he's a fan of John Jameson, likes his Irish neat, if you catch my drift. Call him on Monday, here's his number in New York."

"Thanks, Kyle. I appreciate your counsel and Danny-Boy's name. I'll let you know how I make out."

"Nah, don't call me. Just send a large check, like I can hang in the wind until I see it." Laughing.

"Kyle, you're a natural wonder. In fact, I *wonder* why I consider you a friend!" Both guys laughing.

"Okay, take some friendly advice: try not to contract any sexually-transmitted diseases."

"You mean like yours?"

"Screw you!" Both guys were laughing as they hung up.

5

MONDAY

Back in RI, Pat spent the better part of Monday morning on the phone with Danny-Boy arranging a meeting in Newport for the first of next week. He expected Tom to have secured by then everything required to get a penny stock plan in motion, registration with the SEC, printing of share certificates, and so on. He'd advise Tom and Steve of Kyle's recommendations regarding the number of shares to register when they met again tomorrow at two.

He also phoned Candi to see if she had luck contacting the realtor or owner who had keys to the former bank building she felt would address Pat's requirements. He was eager to check out its potential before his Tuesday meeting. Candi told him the walk through with the owner's real estate agent was scheduled for three this afternoon.

Candi also agreed to join him for lunch at the hotel so they could get their dialog nailed down before they met the other realtor. She showed up about 1:15 dressed for a date.

"Man, you look terrific, Candi. Who are you impressing today?"

"You'll do." She gave him a quick kiss. "Besides you have a little Sean Connery look yourself." He was dressed in slacks and a white polo shirt. They both laughed as they moved to chairs abutting the room's circular dining table.

"So, Cowboy, how was the Big Apple and your meeting?"

"I didn't get to see much of the Big Apple, but my meeting was memorable. I learned a lot *("like several ways to achieve orgasm!").*

"Well, that's good."

"Candi, what have you got I can look at? I'd like to see photos of the former bank building so I know what I'm walking into."

She extracted a listing sheet and brochure with photos from her brief case, walked him through the interior first pointing out existing offices, a large general secretarial area capable of handling several desks and file cabinets, an adjacent but smaller area right off the elevator which would serve as a reception room.

"All this space is on the second floor?"

"Right. The first floor is dominated by a huge walk-in safe, and the former teller stations which could be ripped out and converted to the conference room you're after."

"What the hell do we do with the walk-in safe?"

"Close it, or leave the door open as an interesting talking point. That's what I'd do. You could even put one chair in the center so it looks like an execution chamber!" She was smiling.

"Maybe I should tie you to the chair, complete with a gag!"

"No! I don't look good in jailhouse orange." Laughing.

"Who said anything about having you dressed?"

"My, God, Pat, you are incorrigible . . . but special!" Both laughing.

They continued working over lunch, discussing the merits of the interior layout on both floors: the location and size of Tom's office, Steve's office, Pat's office between the two, offices for others on Tom's management team *("I don't know how many people that is")*, adequate wiring for phones and computers, restrooms up and down, the size and shape of the proposed conference room, improved lighting, window treatments, *ad infinitum*.

As they talked Pat become more and more excited about the building's potential, the marvelous intro it would provide him as he began his pitch to tomorrow afternoon.

Candi shifted her emphasis to the building's exterior. It was imposing, large columns on either side of a thick double door with massive brass handles, several locks, minimum barred window exposure onto Washington Square. There was a drive-through window on the left side -- "useless for your needs, Pat, but it leads directly into the rear parking lot" -- a side door entrance on the other side -- "strictly a fire exit with a set of stairs from the second floor." The entire structure composed of sand-colored concrete blocks, the building less than 20 years old.

"It looks perfect, Candi. It'll need interior work to bring it up to snuff, but it is fantastic."

"Thank you, Pat. I think you'll be even more impressed when we see it this afternoon."

Candi pulled some additional papers from her briefcase and spread those next to Pat's empty lunch plate.

"This is the financial stuff," she said. They discussed the rental price, lease details, deposits, maintenance costs, occupation dates, Pat's need for the names of a reliable contractor, electrician, painter, furniture rental firm.

"I can handle that for you, Pat. I know people in town whom I think you will find reliable, affordable, and very professional. They will do a good job for you. I'll give you their names and phone numbers."

"Okay, let's talk about our meeting this afternoon with the owner's real estate broker." Pat's demeanor had turned very serious. "I want you to call me Mr. Clauson, not Pat, and I do not want to convey the slightest impression that we have anything more than a professional relationship. The same goes for any time you meet Tom Mulholland or any of his associates."

"Right. I understand. Can we hold hands?" She was smiling.

"Candi, get real!" Pat was not smiling. "I'm *not* kidding."

"What kind of relationship do we have?" She was still smiling.

"For chrissake!" Candi burst out laughing.

The real estate showing went extremely well, Pat even more impressed than he had been when looking at Candi's photographs. He was convinced he could sway Tom to lease the building, especially once Tom saw the facilities and Pat walked him through the improvements which would make the place an impressionable, and efficient, up-scale corporate HQ for Fabricated Structures, Inc.

Pat also would tell Tom he would willingly assume responsibility for retaining the contractors, would also agree to supervise their work since both Tom and Steve were too pre-occupied with running their business to handle that chore. That alone was a good reason to give him access to the firm's checking account!

With their tour of the property over and the owner's real estate broker gone, Pat suggested he and Candi hit the bar at the colonial tavern for a celebratory drink. Pat vowed to himself that one drink was it; he'd plead prep time for tomorrow, drop Candi at her condo, then head back to his hotel.

But, he insisted they have a second drink, then move to a table in the ground floor dining room for yet another, followed by a leisurely dinner amid the early American decor, dim wall lights, lots of candles, a bottle of Pinot Noir.

After they slid into the back seat of the Town Car, Pat turned to Candi.

"Where to?"

"There's a spot at the corner of America's Cup Avenue and Thames that has a neat bar and a dance floor. Let's go dancing. Do you know the place I mean, Phil?"

"Yes, Mam."

The music was deafening, not a genre which appealed to anyone over thirty. A deejay wore jeans with no knees, a ripped T-shirt, and head phones to keep his sanity. The crowd was collegiate, drunk, jammed so close together it was impossible to move. No one danced, the entire mob just swayed, yelled, clapped, laughed, one guy in the corner was puking.

"Is this your idea of entertainment?"

"What?"

Yelling into her ear: "Is this your idea of entertainment?"

"What?"

"IS THIS YOUR IDEA OF ENTERTAINMENT?"

"DOESN'T APPEAL?"

"LET'S GO!"

They stepped outdoors, walked a few yards down the street, Pat struggling to stop the ringing in his ears.

"Mother of God, do you go there often?"

"I never go there!" Pat stopped dead in his tracks, a shocked expression on his face as he looked at Candi in disbelief. Both burst into raucous laughter, Candi doubled over, Pat holding her arm.

"You devil, you! Let's find Phil and the car."

"I've got an idea, Pat."

"You had an idea an hour ago that almost cost me my hearing!"

"This will be less painful. Let's go back to your hotel."

"Candi, I'd love to, but I've really got to get some rest. I have a make-or-break meeting with Fabricated's senior management tomorrow. I can't afford to be less than fully prepared."

"Well, Pooh!" She wasn't laughing or smiling any more.

"I'm sorry, Candi." He pulled her close, hugged her. "I really am, but I know if you and I stay together tonight neither one of us will get much sleep, and I just cannot afford to play that hard. I have to be at the top of my game, so to speak."

"Well, I understand, but I'm going to miss you, you bum." Now she was smiling. He smiled as well.

"I'm going to miss you as well, you know that." He kissed her quickly. "Now let's find Phil and the car and we'll give you a lift home before I head for my house."

"Actually, let me take a taxi. There's one parked right there in front of the music jungle. I'll call you tomorrow." She turned and walked toward the cab.

+ + +

Pat ate breakfast in his room Tuesday morning, browsed the daily newspapers, lingered over coffee. At 10:00 he decided to begin his work day with a phone call to Colette Dubois, ostensibly to confirm that the two o'clock meeting was still on. The receptionist transferred him immediately to Colette's line.

"Good morning, this is Colette Dubois." Her voice was like honey.

"Good morning, Colette. This is Pat Clauson. I'm just checking in to make sure my meeting with Tom at two is still on."

"Yes, it is, Sir."

"Please, Pat not Sir. Do you know if Steve is joining us?"

"No, Pat, I don't believe he is. He has a meeting in Providence this afternoon."

("Thank you! Oh, thank you!")

"Okay." Pat paused for a moment before continuing. "Colette, do you like to sail."

"Well, I like boating, but I don't know anything about sailing."

"Would you be interested if I charter a boat for a few hours on Saturday afternoon with a guarantee you will not have to do anything but sit back and relax?"

"Yes, sure, that sounds like it could be fun."

"Okay, I'm delighted. I'll make the arrangements and call you with a time and place, or I can pick you up."

"Why don't I meet you at the dock? Thank you for the invite."

"My pleasure. I'll see you at two this afternoon." He was disappointed he could not pick her up next Saturday, had hoped to learn her address, get a chance to scope out her digs.

Phil dropped him at the Fabricated plant just before 2:00, same receptionist, same uncomfortable chairs, sports section from today's *Journal* on the coffee table, still the out-dated trade magazine.

Then she appeared, splendid in a bright red sheath dress that accented her figure *("How do these guys get any work done?")*, the same sexy walk, the same warm welcoming smile, the intense eyes.

"Good afternoon, Pat."

"Hi, Colette. Did you miss me?" They both laughed.

"Tons! But here you are." She turned for the door to the hall-way and he dutifully followed her to the conference room, Tom again seated at the head of the table.

"Good afternoon, Tom. How are you doing?"

"I'm well, Pat. How was your weekend?"

"Not bad. I went to New York Friday afternoon, had a couple of meetings in the City."

"Hope they went well." Tom cleared his throat, opened the meeting.

"Pat, we like some of what you recommended last week, but other aspects of your proposal just don't meld with our preferred method of operating."

"Tom, let me interrupt for a couple of minutes. I think I have found a terrific location for corporate headquarters offices that will knock your socks off."

With that, Pat spread out the color brochure Candi had given him, walked Tom through a detailed tour of the former Washington

Square bank building, including his thoughts on renovations, the financials, renovation costs and leasing details. He also included a description of the neighboring businesses, the park in the center of the Square, ample parking behind the building, other benefits of the location.

Tom was floored, impressed that Pat had taken it upon himself to scout for a better headquarters location. He was excited to see the building, Pat would arrange a tour for the next day. They then got back to the business at hand.

"I understand, Tom, that you have reservations about some of the ideas I proposed. I think Steve's idea of forgetting involvement with my UK bankers makes sense, especially if you already have good connections with your bank here. I've phoned London *("another lie")* to say we will not be knocking on their door. They'll get over it!"

"Good. That's one item we want to dump." Tom shifted in his seat. "Now, let's talk about the amount of your investment in our company until such time as we begin to benefit from our stock offering. We have agreed to move forward with that idea quickly. Did you consult with your colleagues in California?"

"I did, Tom *("lie")*, and here's what we propose. We have a lot of irons in the fire *("another lie")*, so our capital base is spread pretty thin until such time as a few of them reach maturity *("a huge lie")*. How-ever, we are prepared to invest up to $100,000 in Fabricated *("like hell!")*, with a couple of provisos.

"First, we cannot provide all of that funding up front. We can invest thirty thousand over the next ninety days in ten-K increments, another thirty thousand ninety days from now, and the balance -- forty grand -- in six months. *("This is just smoke! If you think I'm going to invest $100,000 of my money in this enterprise I can also sell you a swamp in Florida.")*

"Well, Pat, that's a hell of an improvement over what you were talking about last week." He was scribbling on his notepad. "What are your terms? What interest rate? What payback schedule? Any penalties if we pay back early?"

Pat sat back in his chair. This was going well. Tom was asking the right kind of questions, not harping about the offer.

"We're looking at eight percent on our money. You pay interest on the full amount immediately, but principle payments don't commence until the stock is issued. Then you start paying us principle. If your stock soars and you want to pay us back early, that's okay with us."

Pat had strategized that when making his first ten grand investment, he'd offer to hire and supervise contractors to get the new building ready for occupancy. He'd negotiate with the contractors to cut improvement costs but he'd charge Fabricated the full estimated amount and pocket the difference. That was step one.

Step two: once things were progressing smoothly, he'd tell Tom the contractors wanted to be paid in cash. He'd enter cash with-drawls in Fabricated's checkbook, but pocket the money by delaying, or avoiding altogether, paying the contractors.

Step three: he'd hedge on subsequent monthly investments, blaming delays on his people *("what people")* in California. He figured he could stall the Fabricated people long enough to avoid a second, or surely a third, ten grand investment. Meanwhile he'd be collecting eight percent on the full $100,000 "promise", plus his retainer, plus the squirreled cash, plus whatever he got selling his shares.

This was going to be a win-win!

"Why would we pay interest on the full amount if you're making it available in ten grand increments?"

"Because we will be accumulating $100,000 on our books, designated for delivery to you as quickly as possible, Tom. Eight percent is a fair rate; promissory notes will guarantee the principle balance on the transaction dates I specified *("there won't be any promissory notes!")*."

"That's a pretty strange way to secure $100,000, Pat. We could go to the bank and get a regular loan for the full amount delivered immediately."

"Not if you're also asking the bank for a three-million-dollar commercial loan," Pat countered. "And you'd still be paying interest on the $100,000 you pay me off the top. The bank won't like that. My way, you get $100,000 *("whopper of a lie")* to expand your business while you're plotting an equity offering and hitting your bank for the commercial loan. It may be strange, but it's the best way to have your cake and eat it, too!

"Also, Tom, you should not carry the full amount of our investment on your books at the outset, and don't show it as a loan. That would be a red flag to your bank, signifying increased debt."

"Jesus, Pat! Are you suggesting we cook our books?"

"You're not cooking them, Tom. You're only warming them a little, and it's perfectly legal. Even your auditors won't smell a rat, because there is no rat. It's not really a loan. It's an investment, paid back with a combination of stock and cash." Pat was smiling broadly.

Tom looked hesitant. "I think perhaps I should check with Jerry Watling at our bank to get his impression."

Pat was beginning to sweat, could feel the dampness under his arms, soaking his back, didn't dare shed his suit coat.

("Dammit, they have GOT to believe I intend to invest in their company. That's the only leverage I have to insist I be given signature rights on the company's bank accounts. Even then, my demand is going to be met with some hysteria, and if I fail this entire episode will have been a waste of my time; they will be turning the tables and whipping me at my own game. Not gonna let that happen. Who the hell do they think they are!")

"Tom, it's my understanding that you already carry a sizable commercial loan with the bank. I don't think you should tip your hand that you're looking for additional money so you can float a stock issue. The bank will want part of the action, and there's no point in further diminishing your own equity."

"Let's discuss that idea. How many shares should we issue, and what's your take?"

"In New York over the weekend, I took the liberty of phoning a good friend of mine who is a retired investment banker. I outlined what I think you're looking for, and he suggested you issue 500,000 shares, possibly even one million . . . enough to spread around your management team, with plenty to put into the marketplace." He turned, began pointing in the air to emphasize the security payoff.

"That's where the stock will grow in value, Tom, and I will work hard to increase the share value. Giving shares to some of your management people is a good morale builder, but it will not impact the share price.

That can only happen with shares for sale by the brokers. You should restrict the stock you offer employees so it cannot be flipped for cash right after it's issued, make people wait a few months, even a year."

"Yeah, that's a good idea." Tom was warming to the subject.

"I also have the name of an institutional investor type who would be helpful in calling on brokers who specialize in penny stocks. I will work with him to build a market for your shares."

"That's good, but tell me, Pat, what you're expecting your cut to be, how many shares do you expect if we go through with this?"

"I'll need some security to protect my investment, Tom. My partners (*"who?"*) will insist on it."

"Yeah, I understand. Give me a number I can think about."

"Fifty-thousand shares, if you issue 500,000."

"Good lord! Why so many?"

"Well, as we've discussed, Tom, I'll be investing $100,000 in your company (*"like hell!"*), and any protection for our investment is months away in the form of shares of stock with a minimal initial market value. We've got to have something to protect our investment." Pat kept saying "we" and "us" as if there were actually some kind of team behind him. It was an act he'd been polishing for years.

"That is not an unreasonable request, Tom. It's ten percent if you issue 500,000 shares, only five percent if you issue one million."

"Man, that's a lot of stock!"

"It's only paper, and you have to give the brokers enough to build a viable market so the stock can grow in value. A million is probably the number you should settle on, because that will provide the brokers with a number sufficient to build the market. Growth is the key, Tom. The number of shares you issue has to be based on how fast you want the street to establish a viable trading market in order to increase the value of those shares.

"We're talking a penny stock, Tom, so you have more than sufficient capitalization to pump a million into the market, less whatever you want to hold for internal distribution to yourself, key employees, and me." Pat was smiling.

"Anything else, Pat?" Tom was smiling just a little.

"Our second proviso, Tom, is that I be given signature rights on the company's bank accounts." *("Here's where the wheels may fall of the wagon!")*

"What? Why the hell would I agree to that?"

"Tom, I understand this is a very unusual request."

"No kidding!"

"I completely understand your feelings. But we have *got* to protect our investment in your company. We cannot do that on the basis of a stock offering which may, or may not, develop a good return. You don't know that yet, and we certainly don't. And, frankly, you don't have anything else to offer us as surety.

"And, I'll be paying all of the contractors who renovate your new office building. I'll be pumping money into your account to handle the building renovations, so in effect, I'll be writing checks on your account against my own funds. What the problem?"

"Steve may give birth to a set of dishes!"

"Look, I don't want his job, nor any part of it. But I insist on protection in the event things don't go in the direction we're planning."

"How about a legal document specifying our payback?"

"Tom, if we get lawyers involved in this we'll be sitting here for a year. It's up to you, but we're anxious to move forward or move on. Your choice."

"Okay, Pat. Steve is out of the office this afternoon. He's actually meeting with our bankers in Providence. Let me speak with him in the morning, see how he's made out, and tell him all that we have discussed this afternoon. I think we can move forward, but I value his input. I'll phone you no later than Thursday morning, earlier if possible"

"Thank you, Tom. I also hope that before this week is out we can come to an agreement and begin to move forward. Meanwhile, I'll arrange for you to see the Washington Square property tomorrow or Thursday?"

"Actually, I'd like to do it tomorrow, Pat. Can you arrange that for the afternoon?"

"I'm sure I can, Tom. I'll phone Colette with the particulars."

Pat left the building, found Phil with the Town Car and climbed in, thought the meeting had gone reasonably well. Tom's interest in touring the bank building as soon as possible was a good sign he wanted to proceed with an agreement. Hopefully, Steve would not say anything to jinx the deal, although he will be rip-shit about the bank account thing. *("Screw 'im!")*

Pat was humming as he sat in the back seat, Phil directing the car back to the hotel.

"Good to hear you singing, Sir," said Phil. "I take it your meeting went well. Congratulations."

"Yes, Phil, I think it did go well, but hold the congratulations until I have a signed contract. Hopefully, that will happen Thursday."

6

THURSDAY

The call came promptly at nine o'clock. Pat was dressed, sitting with the newspaper, awaiting room service with his breakfast. But it wasn't Tom Mulholland on the phone, it was Steve Johnson, the Treasurer.

"Good morning, Pat. Steve here. Are you sitting down?"

("This isn't good. Steve on the phone, not Tom, and he's asking me to sit down!")

"Pat, I want to apologize for my rough demeanor during our meeting last week. Frankly, what you said opened my eyes to a number of things we should have been pursuing but were reluctant to undertake."

"Well, that's good news, Steve. That's what I'm supposed to do, rattle your cage a little, help you overcome your lethargy, not only you, but Tom as well."

"You did it in spades, Pat." He laughed, Pat joined in.

"Mind sharing the specifics with me?"

"Not at all. First, I understand you took it upon yourself to find us a potential new headquarters building. Tom and I saw it yesterday. He's signing the lease agreement this morning. It's terrific space, Pat. A huge improvement over the slum we're currently in."

"Thank you, Steve." *("This going better than I had hoped!")*

"Second, you offered to supervise all of the renovations so Tom and I can focus our attention on running our business. We'll set you up with signature rights on our bank account to facilitate that, and so you can deposit your agreed financial support. Contractor and vendor invoices will come to you, okay?"

"Absolutely, Steve! I'll gladly handle that for you, under your supervision, of course."

("Damn!! I cannot believe this! No gun fire from Steve!")

"Third, Pat, we're moving forward quickly with an IPO on the penny stock market. We're meeting our attorneys today to structure that deal and secure whatever okay's or licenses and registrations will be required to begin executing our plan as soon as possible."

"Ah, Steve, that's good news. You won't regret it."

"We're initially going to hold the shares pretty tight. Tom and I will each get a bundle, a few other people in the company as well, and of course you will get your shares for opening our eyes to the benefit. And, we'll ask you to retain and manage the institutional investor type you mentioned to Tom on Tuesday."

"I'd be delighted, Steve. This is all very exciting."

"Yes it is, Pat, and the other exciting news is I have secured a four-million-dollar commercial loan with our bankers in Providence, so we can begin to look for larger manufacturing space and more modern equipment."

"Congratulations, Steve!" Pat was grinning so broadly he almost couldn't talk, had begun dancing in place while speaking on the phone.

"Pat, please swing by Tom's office tomorrow morning so we can all initial a simple letter of agreement. No fifty-page legal thesis, just a friendly letter spelling out our points of discussion, the arithmetic you and Tom agreed to, and so on."

"Wonderful, Steve. How about ten tomorrow morning."

"You got it. See ya then. And Pat, thanks, again, for waking us up!"

Pat dropped his phone on the carpet and began marching around the room, pumping his fist, yelling "Yes! Yes! Yes!" He sat on the couch, pounded his right fist into his left palm, rose and walked around the room again, continued yelling "Yes!! I don't believe it!"

He scooped up his cell phone, dialed Candi, screamed into the phone when she answered:

"Gimme my house keys, I'll get you a check, I'm moving out of this hotel within the hour! There really is an Easter Bunny, Candi, and he just left me a basket of goodies!"

She began laughing.

"I take it you got your contract."

"You won't believe it! Let's celebrate tonight in *my* pool at *my* house and then see where that takes us!"

"Probably upstairs, Pat. What do ya think!"

She was laughing, he was delirious!

"Candi, I'm gonna hang up; have to call Phil and get him here with the car. Can you meet us at the house?"

"Right on, Cowboy. See you soon."

It didn't take an enormous effort to move: a suitcase and his envelope-style briefcase. Candi was standing in the front doorway when Phil drove up.

Pat was out of the car in a flash, bounded up the front steps, grabbed Candi in a bear hug and swung her around in a circle, planted a long kiss on her lips. They parted when Phil dropped Pat's suitcase on the front steps, whispered a soft "Congratulations, Sir!"

"Thank you, Phil. I have a ten o'clock meeting at the Newport offices tomorrow. Can you pick me up, please?"

"Certainly, Sir. My pleasure, Sir"

Phil was back in the car and gone. Pat picked up his suitcase and led Candi into the house.

"Man, I can't believe this, can't believe all that has happened since my feet touched the floor this morning." He was giddy with laughter.

"Pat, I want to hear all about it, but I must get back to my office. I'll call you later, and perhaps we can meet this evening."

"Perhaps? Come on, Gal. We have to celebrate. After all, you are responsible for some of the good news. Tom was blown away when I said I had found him potential office space. He and his treasurer looked at it yesterday, loved it, and Tom is signing the lease today. So, congratulations to you, as well!"

"I was there, Pat! I arranged the showing, remember! Okay, I'll be here with bells on, and we'll rattle the windows in this house."

"Good deal. Don't be late -- please, don't be late."

She wasn't, and they did!

+ + +

Pat woke a little after eight, darn near delirious with today's pros-pects. He was still excited about his deal with Fabricated, agreement signed during a quick meeting with Tom yesterday morning, start date on Monday. Pat could not believe Tom was accepting the deal he had proposed. Even Steve seemed to be on board with the plan to give Pat signature rights on the company's bank account, "protection" for his promised investment dollars as well as his agreement to hire contractors and supervise renovations to the new office space.

He was convinced Tom and his manufacturing chief, whom he had not yet met, had to be over extended to get their company started. They most likely mortgaged their homes, drained their personal bank accounts, were up to their necks in personal debt. Why else bite for Pat's very unconventional proposal to get the company into a classy corporate headquarters building, using his staggered investment deposits to fund the renovations, interest paid on the entire "promised" amount from the git-go.

Tom also agreed to Pat's strategy of orchestrating an IPO to raise thousands through the stock offering so Tom and the other guy could retire some or all of their personal debt, probably allow them to get a good night's sleep for the first time in god knows how long. And they gave Pat five percent of their company! His shares would be restricted but he didn't give damn, had a quick way around that obstacle.

Pat had to control himself, could not waste time adding up his anticipated take from Fabricated Structures; to do so was tempting, but focus had to be on whatever it might take to semi-legally hype the stock, escalate the price as high as possible as quickly as possible so he could bail out.

The second reason for Pat's excitement was that Colette was meeting him at 11:00 this morning to go sailing. He had chartered a 45-foot Beneteau with captain and mate so they could take a cruise in Narragansett Bay. The boat was owned by a young live-aboard couple, who would provide lunch and soft drinks, Pat to supply his choice of wine and/or liquor or both. Cast off from the Goat Island Marina was set for 11:30. Colette was meeting him at the boat.

The thought of spending several hours alone with Colette in an environment free of interruptions (the crew would confine themselves to operating the boat) was a dream come true. He would put his Australian accent on full charm, fondest hope being dinner this evening followed by . . . well, who knows!

Pat arrived a half-hour early dressed in shorts, nautical collared polo shirt he purchased the day before, a white, lightweight sweater casually draped over his shoulders, his cap emblazoned with the words "Sail More, Work Less." Captain Bob and the mate, Paola, were busily removing the mainsail cover, spreading cockpit cushions, otherwise preparing the boat for departure. Pat paced the dock awaiting the arrival of his dream.

Colette arrived a few minutes early dressed in bright red short shorts, a white sleeveless top, broad-rimmed straw hat, fashionable sunglasses. She carried a large canvas shoulder bag, smiled broadly as she approached Pat, her sandaled feet placed one in front of the other like the runway walk he had seen each time she met him in the office.

They each extended a right hand to shake, but Pat pulled her close to give her a brief hug, friendly but clearly unexpected.

"Well, hello!" She grabbed her hat prevent it from falling off.

"Hi, Colette. I'm very glad to see you, and really appreciate you're joining me for a sail today. I wasn't anxious to sail alone."

"Well, there's always the crew." She smiled, those eyes looking at him coyly.

"Yes, well that's what they are, and you're not! You're a companion, pleasant company, perhaps even a date!"

"A date! Well, I guess so, hadn't really thought of things that way."

Pat helped her aboard, stashed her shoulder bag below. They settled on opposite sides of the cockpit, each accepted a tall cold non-alcoholic drink handed up from the galley by Paola.

"Welcome aboard, folks." It was Bob, the captain. "We have a gorgeous day for a sail up and down the Bay. We'll go north first, passing under the Newport Bridge, up the east side of Prudence Island, and will anchor in Potter's Cove, a pretty little harbor for lunch and a swim, if you like.

"After lunch, we'll swing around the north end of Prudence, sail down the west side, pass under the new Jamestown Bridge. We'll sail West Passage along the coast of Conanicut Island, round Beavertail Point, and work our way back to this marina. We should be back at this dock about five this afternoon."

"Sounds great, Bob. Please let Colette and me know if there is anything we can do help you or Paola."

"Just sit back and enjoy yourselves, Pat. Feel free to sunbathe here in the cockpit or sprawl out on the foredeck. Paola or I will shout a warning if we're going to come about so you don't get whacked by the genoa as it sweeps the foredeck."

"That's good thinking." Pat and Colette laughing.

"And if you have any questions about what you're seeing on shore, just ask and Paola or I will narrate."

"Not a problem, Bob. Colette is a local. She'll whisper into my ear whatever it is I should know!" All three laughing.

"Well, you're a very lucky dude, Pat!"

Bob started the diesel engine, left it running to warm up while he and Paola cast off lines which she coiled, tied to the stern pulpit.

Bob slid behind the binnacle, took control of the wheel, eased the boat out of its slip into the waters of Newport Harbor. They motored for about ten minutes around the foot of Goat Island and into East Passage before Bob headed into the wind, turned the wheel over to Paola and moved up to the mast to raise the mainsail. Paola swung the bow towards the bridge, Bob set the genoa, Paola killed the engine and they were sailing, light southwesterly, bright sun, blue sky, the hull slipping lazily through the blue water.

They passed under the bridge and Pat moved over beside Colette on the port side cockpit cushion, asked her to describe the landmarks they were passing along the coast of Newport and Middletown: Navy War College, Alden Boat Yard, New England Boat Works, sixth fairway and green at Wanumetonomy Golf Club, a large Middletown waterfront condo community.

Colette finally stood, announced she was going below to change and sunbathe on the foredeck. She came topside a few minutes later in the skimpiest bikini Pat had ever seen. It didn't conceal much of her gorgeous body. Pat swallowed to avoid panting, hurried below and emerged in his own suit plus two towels and a bottle of tanning lotion. He lay on a towel beside her.

Colette rolled slightly, saw the bottle of suntan lotion.

"Oh, would you rub some of that on my back?"

"Absolutely!" *("Would I?! Can I take all afternoon?")*

Colette untied her bikini top so Pat had unobstructed access to her entire back. He did take his time, asked if she'd like him to do the back of her legs -- "Sure!" -- which enabled him to massage those portions of her posterior protruding from the bikini bottom. He kept his hands moving quickly so she would not think he was trying to cop a feel, although that had to be obvious. She didn't flinch.

Once he had his own chest, arms and legs coated, he lay on his back next to her, pretended he didn't have a thought in the world, could not get her body out of his mind. He was concerned he might be showing his emotions. That would be awkward.

They anchored in the quaint cove Bob had described on the north end of Prudence. Colette sat up, her bare breasts staring at Pat as she searched for and found her bikini top. She put it on backwards, attached the strap, then swung it around so the cups at least partially covered what they were designed for. She was not at all uncomfortable with her breast exposure, behaved as if it were nothing unusual.

Pat had difficulty standing up.

Colette was first in the water. He followed her quickly, stayed as close to her as possible without appearing too forward. Bob and Paola stayed onboard to prepare lunch, set the cockpit table with places for four. Post-lunch, Bob suggested a one hour break, Pat and Colette could relax while he and Paola cleaned the lunch dishes.

The two charter guests spread out on the foredeck again, this time Colette rubbed suntan lotion on Pat's back, a pleasure he found stimulating. *("God, forgive me for what I'm thinking!")* After they enjoyed another quick dip in the salt water, Bob hoisted anchor and they were off.

Pat and Colette sat talking and laughing on the foredeck throughout the afternoon cruise, shared a chilled bottle of white wine.

They exchanged a few comments about Tom, Steve and Fabricated Structures. Colette revealed that she had been with Tom since the company's founding, enjoyed the people and the work, and was interested to have learned the specifics of Pat's proposal as she prepared Tom's letter of agreement for his signature.

"One thing I don't understand, Pat." Colette had stretched out on her back, her full figure revealed by the bikini.

"What's that?"

"Why are you doing this?" She looked at him, those eyes, even through sunglasses, were hypnotic.

"You mean sailing with you?" He knew that was not what she meant.

"No! No! I mean, you're an intelligent guy, but what are you getting out of this deal with Fabricated? You put ten grand of your own money in the company's bank account already, and you're using it -- your own money -- to renovate a building for our corporate offices. Why?"

"My responsibility to Tom is to help him build his business, Colette." He remained sitting; Colette remained lying on her back. "I'm not a salesman, or advertising guru. I'm really in the strategic positioning business.

"If you'll pardon my language, the company's so-called headquarters is an upholstered dump. There's no way any customer or prospect can walk out of that mess with a favorable impression of Fabricated as a sharp, with-it, 21st century success story. I've seen junk dealers with a better image."

"So, what does a fancy headquarters building do for you? What do you get out of it that's worth a lot of your money?"

"Opportunity."

"Opportunity for what?"

"Money. I'm in it for the money, Colette, plain and simple. And if your company has a showcase headquarters, that is very likely to inspire more business and it will definitely prompt investors to consider buying your stock. And if -- when -- I am successful in helping your company grow and profit from its stock sales, that will permit me to expand my own business with other firms."

"From where I sit you're putting money in but not getting much out. A five grand monthly retainer isn't going to buy you much. It just doesn't make a whole lot of sense to me!"

"I know, but the real payoff will come from the stock issue. That will be a payoff for all of us, you included."

"Only if the price goes in the right direction."

"Right, and I'm confident it will. You know I recommended to Tom that he issue one million shares so there would be enough to water the inside garden -- people like him, Steve, you, me, some of the other heavy hitters -- and still leave a large amount to be traded publicly. That's where the dollar growth will come from, and I'm going to retain an investor relations guy to call on selected brokers, so they push the stock." He was on a roll, showcasing his knowledge of the stock market.

"That guy and I will speak almost daily, Colette. He'll give me a report on how the stock is moving and who's moving it, and I'll fill him in on company information so he can make the place sound like it's on a rocket ride."

"Yeah, well the firm is definitely growing, but it's not a rocket ride."

"Leave that to this other guy and me. Our job is to make the firm's growth appear to be a rocket ride, and we'll get that done. He will hold some of the stock, too, so it will be in his interest to get the price up. And frankly, we'll do a good job. I think it will list at two bucks and in short order it will be trading at six and still climbing."

"Keep it legal, Pat. I don't look good in stripes."

"Not to worry. We know what we're doing, and besides, you're a sideline observer, not responsible for impacting the stock price." He stopped talking, realized he had said more than he intended.

"So, if I understand correctly, this entire episode -- the long, involved pitch to Tom and Steve, the idea of borrowing from a British bank, all that stuff . . . it was really a kind of charade to convince them to issue stock, which you intend to hype for a massive payoff when you sell your shares!"

Pat sat bolt-upright. He was furious.

"'Charade' is an insulting word to use as a description of what I do, Colette. I hope to hell Tom and Steve don't feel that way!"

"I'm sorry, Pat." She was looking at him, sunglasses in her hand. "Poor choice of words; I didn't mean to insult you. I'm sorry, and No! I have not heard Tom or Steve say anything like that."

"You have a very superficial impression of what I do, the strategic recommendations I present to a company's management." Pat was choosing his words carefully.

"In all honesty, Tom and Steve were sitting on their asses hoping they could find an answer to their cash problems, but they were afraid to take the first step. Steve even admitted that to me in a phone call.

"I've taught those two how to walk in the financial world, for christssake. They were *petrified* to take the first step. I really did believe I could help them secure a substantial loan from my British bankers *("lying again")*, but Steve preferred to go to your bankers in Providence, and Tom agreed. At least Steve finally got out of his chair, met with the local bank, and secured a loan. And I'll take credit for getting him off his ass!" Tom's anger was intense, clouding his thought process, taking control of his tongue!

"As for the stock issue, Tom and Steve *both* were anxious to make that happen. But they didn't know how to go about it without spending a lot of money on underwriters. I got it done for them, at a fraction of the price. It's the best way for the company to obtain an influx of cash without piling on debt, and it's a darn good way for them . . . and you and I, by the way, and others . . . to line our pockets, as well.

"So 'charade' my ass! The whole fucking lot of you would be lost in the woods if I hadn't shown you the way out!"

"I said I'm sorry, Pat" She wasn't looking at him "It's just that, to me, on the surface, that fancy strategy you conceived seemed a little . . . well, overdone. But I'm just a working gal, and high finance is not my thing. Let's just relax."

Colette stretched out on the foredeck, replaced her sunglasses, looked as if she was planning to fall asleep. Pat continued to sit up, sip wine, ogle her body, and think! *("Fuck it! If she's reflecting anything close to what Tom and Steve feel, I better watch my ass!")*

Docking back at the marina was quick and easy, Bob doing most of the legwork while Paola handled the wheel and throttle. Handshakes and thank you's were quick. Pat and Colette stepped through the yacht's lifeline gate and onto the dock itself, walked toward cars in the parking lot.

"Colette, can I interest you in a drink to quench your thirst?"

"Yes, that would be nice."

"Where should we go? You know the town better than I do?" He was praying she would not say the old colonial tavern, didn't relish bumping into Candi if he could avoid it.

"There's a nice restaurant and bar off the beaten path on The Point, called Jefferson's. Why don't I meet you there?"

"We could go in my car, if you wish. It's that Town Car with the driver waiting by the doors."

"I think I'll drive my car over there, Pat, but thank you." She gave him directions which he didn't need; Phil knew the way, he was sure. This was not going the way he had hoped.

Colette was first to arrive, he saw her waving from a bar stool as he entered the restaurant, walked all the way to the back. He gave her another hug, suggested they sit at one of the small round tables hidden from the restaurant's main floor. They both ordered red wine, Pat made it a bottle, Frog's Leap Pino Noir. They clinked glasses.

"That was a wonderful afternoon, Pat. Thank you for inviting me to join you."

"My pleasure, Colette. I hope you enjoyed the day half as much as I did."

"Pat, please forget my unfortunate choice of words awhile back. I did not mean to diminish in any way all that you are doing for Tom's company, and I assure you I have not heard either Tom nor Steve say anything like I suggested."

"Forget it, Colette. I have."

They chatted for another half hour or so, when Colette suddenly turned as someone called her name.

+ + +

Her name was Ione Jontile. She'd tell you point blank: "Don't pronounce the 'e' in Ione, it's like 'I own.' And the last name is 'shon-teel', not the American bastardization 'John Tile'".

She was gorgeous, five-eight, long glistening black hair cascading down her back almost to her waist, dark sparkling eyes, light brown complexion, both her name and complexion a gift of her heritage from an Antiguan mother and French father. She wore a bright yellow sleeveless dress, magnificent against her dark skin, the scoop neckline graced by a gold necklace.

She made her living dueling with fashion designers, fashion photographers, and stick-skinny models who strut along runways before crowds of drooling women's magazine editors, retail womenswear buyers, cosmeticians, and assorted fashionista hangers-on.

She organized the elaborate "shows" designers used to launch new clothing lines, which necessitated that she spend half her life on jets between New York and Paris, occasionally Italy. She maintained a condo in Newport and her family home in Antigua, the only two spots where she felt "safe" from the demands of a world infested with people who began sentences with "Dahling!".

She recognized Colette, shouted her name from 20 feet away.

"Ione!" Colette said, quickly stood, they embraced. "How wonderful to see you! It's been much too long. Where have you been keeping?"

"Paris, Colette. The city is so delightful. I regretted leaving but, frankly, I got sick of working!" They both laughed.

"Oh, forgive me, Ione." She turned to Pat. "May I present a friend and colleague, Pat Clauson, Pat, this is Ione Jontile, one of my oldest and dearest friends."

Pat stood, offered Ione his hand, her wrist encased in a gold bracelet, a gold Rolex watch on her left forearm. "Very pleased to meet you. Won't you join us for a refresher?"

"I hesitate to interrupt."

"Oh, please, Ione," implored Colette. "We'll move to a larger table in the dining area, and you're not interrupting anything."

They settled at a table for four. Ione joined Pat and Colette in their red wine so Pat ordered another bottle.

"So, Colette. Where did you catch this attractive specimen?" Ione looked from Colette to Pat, who blushed ever so slightly.

"Actually, Pat's a consultant to the firm where I work. He is helping the company go public with a stock issue."

"How interesting." Turning to Pat: "You don't appear dressed for financial meetings."

"No, I'm not." Pat laughed. "Colette agreed to go sailing with me this afternoon and we just returned to shore an hour or so ago. It was a wonderful day to cruise the Bay."

"You own a boat, too?"

"No! No! I just chartered one for the afternoon."

"Ahhh, do I sniff a touch of romance in the air, Colette?"

"No! Ione. Not at all. We're colleagues who work in the same office area."

"Too bad, Colette. Isn't that how things start? I was about to compliment your taste!"

Colette blushed, Pat laughed.

"God, Ione, you're nothing if not forward! You haven't changed one bit!"

"I cannot help it, Colette. I am French heritage, as you know, and I have just returned from the City of Love, so what do you expect of me!" She laughed and winked at Pat, placed her hand on Colette's and gave it a friendly squeeze.

"What were you doing in Paris, Ione?" Pat asked.

"Well, Pat -- may I call you Pat? -- I am a fashion show coordinator, and I met with a designer to commence plans for next season's unveilings. They require an enormous amount of planning and handholding, the darlings. Much more than you would guess from seeing models strut the length of a runway looking like they are about to cry because their feet hurt or they have pins stuck into places pins should never be stuck. And they're all so thin they are anorexic."

They all laughed as she continued.

"Paris is such a beautiful city, but when you are confined to offices and studios all day, wrestling with fashionista czars and demanding photographers, you really don't know where the hell you are and the desire to flee is overwhelming. So I fled!" More laughter.

"I have the impression, from absolutely no experience, that it can be difficult."

"You have no idea, Patrick. But I am a screaming bitch on steroids once I get rolling, so to speak!"

They all laughed; Colette interrupted the humor.

"Listen, you two, I hate to do this but I really have to run. Ione, I'd appreciate it if you remained to keep Pat company, and I want to see you again as soon as possible." She stood to leave.

"What's your rush, Colette?" This was Pat. "Your best friend just arrived, we are having a wonderful conversation. You can't hang in a little longer?"

"I'm sorry, both of you. But I have another engagement I cannot ignore."

("Another engagement? What the hell does that mean? With whom? Male or female? Damn, I was hoping . . . .")

"Pat, thank you again for a marvelous day. I'll see you in the office on Monday. And Ione, please call me Monday so we can set a date to re-connect, soon." She leaned over, pecked them both on the cheek, then turned and walked toward the exit. Ione and Pat watched her leave.

Pat raised his wine in a toast. "Well, that leaves us to play."

"I enjoy playing. Do you?"

"Oh, Yes! I'm a player."

"I kind of thought so." She took a sip of her wine. "Do you prefer Pat or Patrick? I assume that is really your name?"

"Yes, but nobody calls me Patrick."

"Then I shall be the first, Patrick. I think it is a very masculine name, and you look very masculine."

"Thank you, Ione. I like your name as well. Are you originally from France?"

"No, Patrick, I am from Antigua. My mother is Antiguan and my father was French. I still have my family's home in Antigua, plus an apartment in New York and a condo here. I love Newport, it is so relaxing compared to the bustle of Paris or the hustle of New York or Milano. I travel to those cities for work, but I replenish my energy here in the summer, and in Antigua when it gets too cold in this corner of the vineyard!"

"Well, you certainly get around."

"Yes, I am fortunate. And you, Patrick, you are not American?"

"No, I am originally from Australia, moved to America several years ago and like it here very much."

"And what is it you do besides play?" She gave him a mischievous wink.

Pat winked back and delivered a short, very edited rendition of the "assistance" he provided to companies like the one Colette works for. He referenced his British and Hong Kong "colleagues" to impress Ione that he is well connected, a world traveler. She was less than impressed, asked several questions about his background, his Australian heritage, his client experiences.

As that discussion began to wane, Pat invited her to join him for dinner.

"That would be lovely. Thank you." A waitress brought menus, within a few minutes they had given her their orders: oysters followed by grouper filets for Ione; shrimp cocktail and steak medium rare for Pat. They sipped their wine, continued to chat, dinners served in short order. Ione lifted an oyster in its shell.

"Do you not like oysters, Patrick? They can be invigorating, raise all sorts of emotional cravings!" She winked again; Pat's reaction: *("Jesus! This may turn out alright!")*

"I honestly cannot bring myself to try one. They look like . . . ."

"Something that fell out of your nose!" She was dangling the oyster above her plate.

"Yes!" He made an ugly face. "I wasn't going to say it, but Yes, that's it! Snot!" He laughed.

"Some people close their eyes and try to forget that!" She swallowed the oyster she had been dangling.

"You eat them raw, correct? What do they taste like?"

"Sperm!"

Pat was stunned! "WHAT! SPERM?" He struggled to compose himself, glanced around to see if he had been over-heard. "Is that what you said? God, I can't believe you said that! I shouldn't ask, but how do you . . . never mind, I can't ask!" He laughed nervously.

"Patrick! I am a French woman, at least partly, and we French woman know how to play, how to make a man very happy!" She was laughing at his embarrassment, placed her hand over his as if to calm him down. He needed calming.

"Boy, Colette was right when she said you're 'forward'!"

"Patrick, it is no secret that one of the pleasures in life is sex for both men and women, is that not so!" She slurped down another oyster.

"That's been my experience, Yes!" Pat laughed, sat mesmerized as Ione lifted each oyster shell to her ruby lips, swallowed the crustacean and its "liquor", his mind not thinking of oysters.

When dInner was done, the waitress cleared their table, Pat and Ione were enjoying coffee and cognac.

"Do you enjoy swimming, Ione?" Pat decided to make his move; what did he have to lose, Colette had disappeared.

"Yes, I have been known to dip, although I prefer fresh water to salt!" Another wink, another smile.

"Well, you're in luck. So am I if you say 'Oui!'" They both laughed at his effort to speak French. "The house I'm renting comes complete with a heated pool, ocean view -- which will be hard to see tonight -- but the house itself is magnificent. How about an after dinner date?" Fingers crossed, figuratively speaking.

"That sounds like fun, Patrick, but I must decline." She reached for his forearm. "I am very tired from traveling, and wish to go home and rest. Perhaps another day, Patrick. I will look forward to it."

Pat was disappointed, and it showed.

"Well, I will hold you to that promise. May I give you a ride home?'

"No, thank you, but my car is right outside."

They both rose, shook hands, did the kiss-cheek bit so popular in Europe, and she departed. Pat sat back into his chair, lifted his glass, and drowned his disappointment with wine.

+ + +

Colette exited Jefferson's, climbed into her BMW 650 convertible, top down, and drove to a Thai restaurant in a small shopping plaza. Her engagement was sitting in a booth next to the front windows.

"How'd it go, Colette?" It was Tom.

"Well, the sailing was wonderful, but that guy is an operator, Tom. He's very charming, suave, slippery as grease. You better keep a very close eye on him."

"I knew that bastard was sleazy, Tom. We never should have given him access to the company bank account."

"Calm down, Steve. All he's going to do is building us a nice, modern corporate headquarters, and he's using his money to do it."

Addressing Colette: "What do you mean slippery?"

"Just what it implies, Tom. As the three of us agreed, I pumped him on what he's getting out of this deal. I pushed especially hard on his initial investment in the company, money he's using to renovate our new office building. I asked him why he would do that?"

"What did he say?"

"He said 'Opportunity!'"

"'Opportunity?' What the hell is he talking about?"

"Money, Tom. All he wants out of this deal is money. He could give a shit less about strategic planning, or marketing. Zippo! Money is his only goal. He agrees that his retainer is squat. He's looking for a very large payoff, and I have the impression he'll do anything, legal or otherwise, to get our stock price up considerably. That much he did say, but not in those exact words." She sipped the drink Tom ordered for her.

"I also told him I thought his pitch about London bankers and Hong Kong lawyers was a charade just to get his hands on the company bank account."

"Good god, you actually said that, 'charade'"!

"Yes, Steve, I did!"

"What was his reaction?"

"He pitched a fit, swore all over the place, and was not flattering in his remarks about your knowledge of the financial marketplace or your hesitation to initiate an IPO . . . both of you."

"Shit! That self-important S.O.B. He better not cross the line or the S.E.C. will be breathing up our ass, and that won't be any fun!"

"Yeah, well it's your job to make sure he *doesn't* cross the line, Steve. You're Treasurer."

"Pat doesn't think so! At least that's the way he behaves."

"Uh, come on, Steve. That's nonsense!"

"So why did you agree to let him sign checks, for chrissake? I'm still not at all comfortable with that."

"You just keep an eye on our checkbook, and if he goes over about twenty or twenty-five grand without talking to both of us first, we'll slam the door."

"He's still holding fifty thousand shares of stock!" Steve was beet red.

"Hell, that's just paper, and it'll most likely be months before that penny stock is high enough for him to recoup all of his one-hundred-grand investment in our company. Anyway, it's restricted."

Steve was boiling mad. "We've only seen ten percent of his so-called investment, and I'll eat your shoes if we ever see it all! And, by the way, he told me he's retaining some guy to bounce between Boston and New York calling on brokers to push the shares and get the price up, fast!"

"He brought that up with me," Colette added. "He apparently plans to talk with that guy every day about who's moving the stock and how many shares they're moving. Pat and that guy are developing a joint strategy to portray the company's growth as a 'rocket ride'. Those were his exact words; 'rocket ride'."

"Aw, god, Tom, we've got to be damned careful what we permit this clown to say about our business."

"I agree, and I'll talk to him about that. You should be doing the public talking, Steve, not Pat. I'm aware of the outside guy, name is Danny something. You should know what that fella Danny is going to be telling brokers."

"So, what if Pat doesn't deliver the balance of his $100,000 investment? I wouldn't put it past him to 'forget' it, if you catch my drift."

"I catch it, Steve."

"Tom, I still worry about the bank accounts. I'll bet that guy knows exactly how to skim the cream without us catching on, and I'll bet when he gets out of our hair he'll be taking our scalps with him."

"Steve, for the luvva Mike. We'll know in a few weeks if he's stiffing us and if he is, Colette's friend will take care of him."

Steve wasn't sure what Tom meant by that, but it didn't sound good.

Colette spoke up.

"My impression: Pat is a real bullshit artist, but he does have some talent. The trick is to separate the bull from the talent, and that's not always easy."

"Leave that to Steve and me, Colette."

"OK. But help me understand . . . If you're willing to give that sleaze fifty thousand shares, what are you prepared to give me? I'm operating like one of 'Charlie's Angels' and may be called upon to fix a mistake. What's that worth to you?"

"You've already got a healthy chunk of our stock, Colette. We made certain of that," Tom said. He looked serious, no smile, no grace. "As for the rest . . . it depends. Steve will give you a check for a grand on Monday for what you've learned for us today. I'll make judgement calls moving forward based on what we ask of you. You will *not* be underpaid, I assure you."

"I don't object to being your 'Charlie's Angel' but I will not sleep with Pat. That's what he wants, but he makes my skin crawl. He spent most of the afternoon undressing me with his eyes."

"Who can blame him!" Tom and Steve laughed, Colette looked annoyed.

"Look, Colette, I don't want you to do anything that makes you uncomfortable. If you want to bag the 007 bit, just say so."

"I'm okay with that, Tom, but nothing else. And I really do appreciate your support."

"I appreciate what you're doing for us, beyond the call of duty. If things get hairy or uncomfortable for you, just tell me and it's all over. Now, let's dine and celebrate. That slimy bastard thinks we're a bunch of hicks, but we'll string him along and then snap the trap shut, and break his balls doing it."

"I'll drink to that," Steve said. Colette merely smiled.

7

MONDAY

Steve couldn't believe what he was hearing. He was pacing in Tom's office, first thing Monday morning, as the CEO detailed the various elements of the agreement he had reached with Pat on Thursday and confirmed with him on Friday in Steve's absence. Steve was really ripped over the clause which gave Pat signature rights on the firm's checking account.

"What the hell were you thinking, Tom?"

"Calm down, Steve. You're still going to have control and oversight to make sure he plays us straight."

"Oh, bullshit, Tom. I'm the CFO of this organization and you've now handed the firm's checkbook to a clown we don't really know a lot about. What kind of logic is that?"

"He demanded it, Steve. Said his investors need to protect the money they will be investing in our company. And as you know, Pat gave me his first check for ten grand on Friday."

"Hell, he'll recover half of that with his retainer this month."

"Steve, he's using his own money -- not ours -- to renovate that bank building so we have a decent office complex for the first time ever. He's even hiring the contractors and supervising the work so you or I don't have to. And, he's got us an IPO on the cheap, and an investor type to call on brokers and push the stock."

"Oh, for god's sake, Tom, that guy has to be controlled to make sure he doesn't say anything we don't want said, or which isn't true. And I suppose it's my job to make sure that doesn't happen!"

"Damn right! You just said you're the CFO!"

Steve continued pacing, scratching his head, turned and looked at Tom, flame in his eyes.

"Let me make certain we are both on the same page, Tom." He stopped pacing, leaned across the desk, his face no more than a foot from Tom's.

"You have given Pat a significant slice of my responsibility as CFO. You have authorized him to hire some financial whiz to call on brokers to hype our stock, which is a dangerous exercise at best. And I'm supposed to keep my eye on both guys -- Pat and this other guy I never heard of -- to make sure none of us land in jail. Is that about the sum of it?"

"Steve, please! Give things a little time to work out. You are definitely still CFO of this company. Nothing I've done changes that. Yes, I've complicated your life a little . . . ."

"'A little!'"

"Yes, dammit, a little! Now let's calm down and get back to work."

"Well, Tom . . . ."

"NOW!"

Steve froze, stared at Tom for a few seconds, stood and walked hurriedly out of the office. He was boiling mad, avoided seeing Tom for the balance of the day; actually left the office early to head home and rant to his wife, Robin.

+ + +

Steve wasn't the only one ticked off. Pat also wasn't at all happy.

He'd spent Sunday noodling the Fabricated agreement he signed on Friday, discovered it wasn't anywhere near the lucrative deal he'd been planning. He'd basically screwed himself!

First, he lost the opportunity to hit Fabricated for a hundred grand fee for "arranging" a multi-million-dollar commercial loan with "his" British bankers. Steve shut that down, then negotiated a larger commercial loan with Fabricated's Providence bankers.

Also, Pat had given Tom a check for ten grand when they executed the letter of agreement Friday as the "first" installment of his "promised" $100,000 investment in Tom's company. Then he had agreed to use his own ten grand to provide the company with newly renovated office space, paying contractors out of his money now sitting in the company's checking account!

And ten grand wasn't about to cover all of the work required, so he was certain Tom would demand a second, or even a third, ten grand investment before the renovations were completed and Pat could stop shuffling his own money.

His real plan was to withdraw money from the company account, ostensibly to pay the contractors. But he'd screw them, lock the cash in his desk until he had satisfied his greed, then blow town. But that was like stealing his own money! *(Damn! What a screw up!)*

And fourth, Pat learned late in the game that his fifty thousand shares of Fabricated's stock were restricted for *six months* from the date of issue. He had the share certificate in his hands, but would need to trust some guy in Canada, recommended by Kyle, when he wanted to sell; couldn't just phone some local broker.

And Colette's comments during their sail on Saturday were still drumming like a sore tooth, adding to concern that all was not blissful within Fabricated's management.

He was pulling a five grand monthly consulting fee, but that was chicken-shit compared to the cash he really wanted, and it would likely be months before the stock price was high enough to justify bailing. Even worse, the stock pay-off depended upon how well Danny-Boy, the so-called institutional "expert", succeeded in convincing brokers to hype the stock, and Danny-Boy couldn't even show up for a meeting on time! Granted, he was flying up from Manhattan.

Pat's face was contorted into a scowl as he drummed his fingers on the table. He kept looking through the cafe's large front windows. He had had two, maybe three, telephone conversations with Danny-Boy, had arranged this lunch date in the last call, set for 11:30 at this cafe because it would keep Danny-Boy away from the Irish whiskey. Pat wanted the guy sober so he would understand Pat's marching orders.

Pat had already downed three ice coffees, felt like he was going to float, growing madder by the minute. If this slush-bucket was going to be responsible for calling on brokers to get momentum behind the Fabricated penny stock offering, he was going to shape up, lay off the sauce, follow Pat's instructions to the letter. Pat wanted a stock price increase, and he wanted it quick.

He intended planned to "support" Danny's effort by issuing press releases about Fabricated's "rapid growth", releases which narrowly crossed the line between fact and fancy. He was very good at that, but he needed Danny to barn-storm the brokers. Where the hell *is* the guy?

All-in-all, Pat was boiling at himself because he had allowed so much to go foul in his agreement with Tom.

So where the hell was Danny-Boy? Pat initially had been chatting and joking with Ashley and Iuliia, the cute blond from the Ukraine, but as the minutes ticked by he became irritable and rude, so the waitresses left him alone to stare out the window.

Danny-Boy finally showed, apologies galore, blamed his tardiness on a late flight arrival, traffic from the airport, and lack of a parking space. He wore wrinkled slacks, a wrinkled dress shirt, no tie or jacket. His hair looked just-out-of-bed messy, his glasses were dirty, his smile too wide to be sincere.

"You must be Pat," as he slid onto the upholstered bench against the windows. "Glad to meet you. Sorry I'm so late."

"Hi, Danny. Is that how you prefer to be addressed? Or is it Danny-Boy?"

"Ahhhh, Kyle told you Danny-Boy, huh! Nobody calls me that, except Kyle and some of his friends. Danny is fine."

"Okay, Danny it is. Let's order lunch. I can't hang out here much after two, and we have a lot to cover. We can talk and eat."

They spent the next ninety minutes discussing Danny's market credentials, his connections with penny stock brokers, his experience promoting previous stock issues similar to that being floated by Fabricated. He stressed his success rate in doubling, tripling, or quadrupling the initial offer price over a brief period of time. How brief?

Pat was impressed with all Danny had to say, was reasonably comfortable he was not being led down a yellow brick road.

"Those brokers are in the business to make money, Pat. They are not going to sit on their hands and hope a penny stock grows because the price is low. They will push customers to buy, and buy big, because the investment cost is trifling. My job is to give them the ammunition they need to push. Your job is to give it to me."

"I see." Pat liked Danny's enthusiasm, commitment, and language as he explained a host of strategies he employed to motivate the brokers. This was all contrary to Pat's initial impression of the guy, didn't fit at all with Danny's wardrobe of the day!

"Look, Pat. You're not gonna pay me to sit on my ass and make a few phone calls. You want me on the street, knocking on doors, nursing the brokers, taking them to lunch, drowning them in specifics about how fast Fabricated is growing, yadda, yadda, yadda. *That's* what it will take to get that stock off the ground in a hurry."

"I agree, Danny. That is exactly what I'm looking for."

"Okay! And I assume you hold a substantial portfolio of the shares, and you want the price to move into the twenties so when you sell you'll pocket a bundle. Right?"

"Right!"

"Are your shares restricted?"

"Yes, for six months."

"Well, we should get the stock into the twenties before that, and if you want to sell early, move your stock to someone in Canada because restrictions don't apply there."

"Yes, I know that, and I have the appropriate connections."

"Good. That'll save you a lot of aggravation."

"Correct me if I'm wrong, but I sense that you have played this game a few times before."

Danny hesitated, sipped his ice coffee.

"Pat, I make it my business not to do anything illegal, nothing that will attract attention from people I don't really want to talk to."

"I understand."

"However, we're dealing with penny stocks here. If you're Gramma Brown you can sit on your shares and wait for them to grow in price. But if you're like you and me and hundreds of others, you want a quick payoff and a way to cash out, screw the restrictions. I make my business in penny stocks and I don't intend to wait months for a payoff if I hold shares."

"I understand, and I agree completely."

"Okay, Pat, let's talk turkey and discuss exactly what you want me to do, when you want me to start, and how much it's going to cost you to keep me happy."

They spent two hours, well past Pat's two o'clock deadline, discussing Danny's specific objectives, his start date, negotiating his weekly performance fee. Weekly? "Yes, weekly. Payable in cash, not interested in stock."

"That's not gonna fly, Danny. I want you to own some of this stock as an additional incentive to have you break your back getting the price up to where I want it. Let's say I pay you seventy percent in cash and thirty percent in stock."

Danny set down his ice coffee, wiped his lips with his napkin, looked Pat straight in the eye.

"I don't like it, but I'll work with you if you pay me the cash weekly and issue me *unrestricted* stock at the end of each month." That demand took Pat by surprise.

"Why unrestricted?"

"Because I don't wanna be shifting shares to Canada on a weekly basis. That wouldn't look good."

"So don't. Move them every other month. You're smart enough to deal with that. You just told me that's now you run your business. So it's a seventy/thirty split, cash and stock, or I'll find someone else to help me."

"Yeah, alright." Danny didn't look happy. "And you keep saying 'I' and 'me' but you're not my client, right. Mulholland is! So are we talking about what he wants, or do you have the right to negotiate on his behalf?"

"I have that right, and you are free to call him if you wish."

"No need. I just want to know who I'm working for."

"Tom is the CEO, and I am the guy authorized to hire you, supervise your work, and negotiate your fee. Checks will come from the company, signed by me."

"Okay, Pat. I understand. Do I start tomorrow?"

"You can start this afternoon, as far as I'm concerned. I assume you wear a different wardrobe when you visit brokers." Pat laughed, Danny only smiled.

"I hope I've convinced you, Pat, that I'm not a fucking idiot."

Pat paused, reflected on the guy's balls; tough way to talk to a client!

"Let's be clear, Danny. I want a daily telephone call from you yelling me which brokers are moving the stock and how much they're moving. I'll follow the market on line, but I want to know exactly how many shares are trading each day, and what the brokers think of the outlook for Fabricated."

"I got ya, Pat, and I'm going to need from you every little bit of whiz-bang info about Fabricated you can provide so I can feed it to the brokers. I don't want bullshit, but paint Fabricated as best you can within common sense."

"Okay. I'll actually put that stuff into press releases on line, and I'll be sure to email you copies before they go public."

"I mean everything, Pat. You said they're moving into a brand new, sexy corporate headquarters building. Gimme the details and I'll milk that, position it as a need because the firm is growing so fast, yackity-yack. Anything like that will be helpful."

He stood, they shook hands, Danny left with a promise of daily phone calls, and a "guarantee" that he knew how to kick up the price of a penny stock.

Pat ordered another ice coffee from the blond, who said something in Russian and began laughing. He laughed as well, but assumed what she said wasn't really polite or funny because anything said in Russian sounded to him like an insult.

He was proud of himself for having found a guy he was now certain could put the Fabricated stock on the map. Money. Money. Money. Had to get that stock price somewhere in the clouds.

He made an executive decision: he would send his stock certificate to Kyle Mullen with power of attorney to sell in Canada upon written instructions from Pat, or at his own discretion if the price should reach or exceed $20.00 per share. At that price, Pat would pocket a minimum of a million dollars on his shares alone, plus whatever cash he could milk from Fabricated's bank account and by screwing contractors and other vendors.

+ + +

Tom Mulholland was lost in his Tuesday morning newspaper, hardly conscious of eating breakfast, mechanically reached for his coffee, ignored his wife Alice seated across the table.

She broke the silence.

"Tom, put down your newspaper for a couple of minutes."

He looked at her across the top of the page, admired her face and figure, folded the paper and lay it next to his coffee cup.

"What's up?"

"I've had a very distressing call from Robin yesterday after-noon."

"Robin?"

"Yes, Robin. Steve Johnson's wife, Robin!"

"Oh, Yes, Robin." He smiled in embarrassment. "What's her problem."

"*You* are her problem. She said Steve is extremely upset with you, is actually on the verge of quitting, because you apparently gave that consultant guy signature rights on the company's bank account and Steve is rip-shit."

"Oh, for chrissake!"

"Never mind 'chrissake'. He is very important to your firm. He's been with you from the start. You're friends, for god's sake, and whatever you've done has got him roiling. You're going to lose him if you don't come to your senses and treat him with respect."

"Dammit, Alice, I'm running the company, not Robin, and not Steve. This fella Pat brings a lot of expertise to the table that we haven't had, and he's doing it on the cheap. He's delivering new office space at his own expense, and he's finally got us moving on an IPO which has the potential to give us all a terrific financial return.

"Yes, I put Pat's name on our bank account because he said he needs collateral so his backers have adequate support for their investment in our firm, a hundred grand, Alice." Tom's face was red he was so mad.

"Well, apparently Steve feels this guy is impinging on his responsibilities and has your blessing to do so."

"Aw, god. I've told Steve a thousand times not to be concerned. This is a temporary thing, and we're watching it -- Steve should be watching it -- very carefully to make sure it doesn't get out of hand."

"Well, you've created a firestorm in the Johnson household. I don't know what Steve's like in the office, but at home he's a screaming dinosaur! In fairness to Steve, and in fairness to our friend Robin, I want you to do or say something to Steve that will calm him down. *You* pissed him off; now *you* calm him down, because Robin doesn't know how.

"Whatever you've done, it's apparently not fair to Steve and it sure as hell isn't fair to Robin." Alice was almost as mad as Tom. "Now choke on your coffee and go act like a CEO!" She stood and stomped toward the bedroom.

Tom also stood, left his dirty dishes on the table, grabbed his briefcase and slammed the front door as he headed for his car.

He hit the office like a tornado. He was scarlet with rage, really hopped that Alice and Robin would interfere with the way he chose to manage HIS company. And Steve! (*"Was he really thinking of quitting? Was his paper on the street? Damn, maybe Alice is right! I better calm down and sooth Steve's ego!"*)

He pressed the intercom button on his phone and asked his secretary to have Steve join him. He showed within a minute.

"Have a seat, Steve. We need to talk."

They both sat in chairs around Tom's conference table.

"I understand your wife and mine have been conversing, and that you are far more upset than I realized about my decision to give Pat Clauson signature rights on our corporate checking account."

Steve shifted uncomfortably in his seat.

"Yeah, I'm pretty upset, Tom, but I was not aware that Robin was venting to Alice. That's embarrassing."

"Well 'venting' is too strong a word, Steve. They're friends, and they talk. Frankly, I'm glad Robin spoke to Alice because she made it clear to me this morning exactly how upset you are. I sure as hell didn't want that to happen."

"Yeah, well . . . ."

"Alice says you're thinking of leaving the company! Is that true, Steve? Is your paper on the street?"

"No, it's not, Tom. And I have no immediate plans to resign. I want to wait and see how this all plays out, and I'm really sorry Robin said that to Alice."

"Steve, we go back a long way, and I do not want to lose you under any circumstances." Tom shifted in his seat.

"Let me make it perfectly clear to you, Steve, that Pat is in no way going to sabotage your responsibilities as Chief Financial Officer of this company. His name is on that account because that's the security he says his California backers need to protect their investment in our firm."

"That's all well and good, Tom, but I don't believe for a second that Pat has any investors, nor do I believe he intends to invest $100,000 in this company."

"You may be right, but let me finish." Tom leaned toward Steve, his elbows on his knees. "We do have ten grand of his money in our account, which he's using to renovate our new office space, as you know. He's using his own money, Steve.

"Now, I don't believe ten grand will do the job, so he's going to have to deposit another $10,000 of his own money to cover the renovation costs. And once the renovations are complete and we move into that new space, his name comes off the account!

"So, what I'm really doing is giving him signature rights to spend his own $20,000, or more, to renovate our new office complex. So tell me who's stupid, Steve!" Tom was smiling.

"Are you serious?"

"Absolutely! You think I want that guy on our team instead of you! God help us!" Tom was laughing.

"Tom, I'm very sorry. This has been a gross misunderstanding, and I'll make sure Robin understands that when I see her this evening. In fact, I'll phone her now so she can relax, just like I am!"

"It's my fault, Steve. I was not very forthcoming with you when this arrangement was initiated. I'm very sorry."

"Forget it, Tom. Really, let's forget it and get back to work." He stood, stuck out his hand and they shook.

"Thank you, Steve. By the way, I'm sure you folks got Pat's invitation to dinner this Saturday evening. What's that all about?"

"Beats me! I'd like to think its just social, but something tells me it's show-off time. He wants us to see the McMansion he's renting so we'll come away thinking he's made of money. But maybe I'm just a doubting Thomas, no offense intended."

Tom burst out laughing. "None taken, Steve. One way or another, it'll most likely be an interesting evening."

Steve had no sooner left Tom's office than the senior exec hit his intercom button again and asked Colette step into his office. Like Steve before her, she was prompt in arriving.

"Hi, Colette."

"Hi, Tom. What's up?"

"I assume that, like the rest of us, you got an invitation from Pat to attend a dinner party at his digs this coming Saturday evening."

"Of course! I think I'm being romanced, sort of!" She smiled.

"That I can believe." They both laughed. "Look, is there some way . . . I hate to ask this of you . . . is there some way you could talk to him, maybe by phone, and pump him diplomatically to find out what the hell he's up to? I don't want a bunch of us walking into some kind of setup without knowing what we're facing."

"Not a problem, Tom." She was laughing. "Actually, Pat has asked me to join him Saturday afternoon for a swim in his pool. I have accepted, but I have no intention of playing his game."

"What's his game?"

"I'll bet you any amount he'll ask me to stay overnight after the dinner so we can wrestle in that bed of his. It ain't gonna happen, Tom, but I don't mind using my time with him that afternoon to pick his brain . . . that's not even a challenge. All I have to do is wear my bikini and his brain will vomit whatever we want to know!"

Tom burst out laughing.

"Colette, I'm very glad you're on our team! I'd hate to be in the other corner!"

"I'll do my best to learn whatever I can, Tom. I don't think it will be too hard an assignment."

"Many thanks, Colette. I'll make it up to you."

She stood, shook hands, and left laughing.

+ + +

Pat was beside himself, upset that he'd had to deposit thirty grand of his own money into Fabricated's checking account to pay for renovations to the Washington Square building. He found it difficult to believe he had allowed himself to waltz into that part of the deal with Mulholland just to gain access to the company's bank account.

Well, he had access, but so far all he was able to do was withdraw his own money; cash he was supposed to be paying to the contractors, but which he was hiding in his desk drawer . . . hiding his own damned money! What a screwup.

He decided to bail out of the office early, have Phil pick him up and bring him to building. He wanted to see firsthand what *his* money was producing for Tom. The contractors would be gone for the day, he could make his own private tour.

He went immediately to the second floor, and was blown away. He entered a large reception area, recessed ceiling lights, wall sconces, the floor awaiting carpeting. A clear glass wall with glass doors opened to a general secretarial area, offices lining three walls. Large office windows admitted bright sunlight, walls were painted, doors, door and window trims, baseboards, crown moldings, all stained a rich brown mahogany.

He walked into an end office, visualized sitting behind his desk, Colette in her office to his left, then Tom, then Steve, then whomever else comprised Tom's management team.

He found a note from the contractors, two brothers, Guido and Gabriele, whom Candi had recommended as quality builders. She sure as heck was right. The brothers had said initially the entire renovation project, upstairs and down, could be completed in little more than two weeks, at a budget of $23,000-to-$28,000. Tom had okayed the estimate, which meant Pat had to drop more of his own money into the company bank account.

("I didn't plan on that, dammit! When I raid that account for cash I'm pilfering my own money, for god's sake! This isn't how it's supposed to work!")

The contractors' note did assure Pat they were on target for the completion timetable. The note also said the carpet would begin laying forty-eight hours, rental office furniture would begin moving in next Monday. *("That means I'll be on the hook for another ten grand before I can begin rifling Tom's money instead of reclaiming my own!")*

On the plus side, Pat was eager to advise Tom that his new corporate headquarters was just about ready to be occupied. When he broke that news he'd be carrying some champagne to share with the management staff and, he hoped, Colette, since she seemed privy to everything going on in the firm.

He took the elevator to the first floor, walked past the closed door of the former bank safe, entered the newly finished conference room. The brothers had salvaged all of the brown mahogany used by the bank, covered the existing plaster walls floor to ceiling, stretched a narrow chalk shelf along one wall just below a large blackboard.

Another wall contained a pull-down projection screen with a ceiling-mounted projector fed by an electrical hookup so computer generated presentations could be projected with the click of a hand control. Recessed ceiling lights also could be dimmed, brightened or extinguished completely with the same hand control.

Pat leaned against a saw horse, thought again of his plan to stiff the contractors, electrician, plumber, carpet firm, furniture rental outlet and any other vendors by not paying them at all, or feeding them a minimum of cash to keep them quiet, while he stashed the balance in his "escape fund." *("Let 'em scream! I'll be long gone! It'll be Steve's problem!")*

Back at the house he changed into shorts and polo shirt, phoned Candi to tell her how much progress had been made in the building. Then he shifted gears.

"Candi, I stopped on the way home to pick up lobsters, corn and salad makings. Can you join me for dinner? Please say 'Yes'! If you don't, I'll cry and Nora, the cook, will have a stroke!"

"Well, we can't have Nora doing anything like that," Candi said laughing. "So Yes, I will gladly join you for dinner. What time, and make it early enough for us to skinny dip in your pool."

"Nora's telling me she'll have dinner ready about seven, needs that much time to chill the wine. I bought a couple bottles of a special wine, Far Niente chardonnay. If you haven't tried it, you'll shout

'Hallelujah'!" He was laughing.

"I don't know about shouting 'Hallelujah' but I can think of something else that would make me shout!" She was not laughing, just teasing.

Pat caught his breath. "Oh, god! Please don't talk like that until you're actually here or I'll have to lock myself in the bathroom! And remember, the pool is heated and lighted, so we can skinny dip any time of day or night."

"Well, forget locking yourself in the bathroom and I'll see you shortly." They both were in hysterics as they hung up.

Dinner was beyond delicious, fabulous wine, the setting positively spectacular, the sky speckled with a million stars and a bright half-moon.

They had started dinner in wet bathing suits under a canopy of bright stars. Conversation drifted around the Washington Square building, probable move-in date, and Pat's intent to announce all that to Tom with a spontaneous office champagne party. Should Candi attend? *("Probably not! I sure as hell don't want her and Colette in the same room.")*

Nora served a chocolate mousse dessert and disappeared. Candi removed her string bikini, carried her mousse to a chaise lounge, stretched out, beckoned to Pat. He playfully dabbed mousse on Candi's breasts and belly, began to slowly lick it off. It wasn't long before Candi whispered "Oh, Pat, make love to me. *Please* make love to me." Their bodies thrusted in harmony until orgasm overwhelmed them both. They lay quietly entwined, fell asleep. Pat woke a half-hour later, felt a chill, picked up Candi, who wrapped her arms around his neck, her head resting on his shoulder.

He carried her up stairs to the master bedroom, lay her on the king-size bed, slipped in beside her, and covered them both with the top sheet. He pulled her close, her head on his chest, her right leg draped over over his. Minutes passed, then she spoke in a whisper.

"Pat. Do you think about having sex with anyone special?"

"Well, you're special."

"That's my Aussie cowboy!"

"But you didn't tell me I'm special. You said I'm 'interesting!'"

"Then I said 'that's special'!"

"Okay, thank you. Now go to sleep."

It wasn't long before Candi's breathing was shallow, rhythmic, sound asleep, her head still on Pat's chest.

Pat lay and thought about Colette. *("Now she's special!")*

8

SATURDAY, EARLY AUGUST

It had been a hell of a week, but Pat had planned a relaxing and fun Saturday. The afternoon, he knew, was going to be amazing, and the evening's event should be interesting, fun, a resounding business success.

Colette had agreed to join him for lunch and an afternoon swim. He couldn't believe his luck, vowed to behave, not pressure her, wait to make his move until all his guests had left after dinner this evening. Then he'd see how well his charm worked on Colette, a tough sell, but he was convinced the Ole Clauson Suave would melt her resistance.

Also, the company's penny stock had had a successful launch at $2.00 per share, the price had already tripled to six bucks and was still climbing. If the momentum continued, and he was determined to make it climb, he'd walk out of Fabricated with almost $1,000,000, a nice haul.

And he had the entire management team of Fabricated arriving for dinner this evening, a show of splurge in this mansion, an indication of his implied desire to be considered a member of the Fabricated team. *("Gotta keep up that appearance to allay any impression I might be even a little shady; can't allow that to happen.")*

He met Colette at the front door when she arrived just before noon, her long blonde hair flying in the breeze as she entered the circular drive in her BMW 650 convertible, top down. Fashion sunglasses hid those fantastic eyes. She was gorgeous, the car a 'piece de resistance', a very hot gal in a spectacularly hot car.

She wore a ruffled sleeveless blouse, short shorts emphasizing the length of her gorgeous legs, heeled sandals lifted her height over five-ten. She carried her famous shoulder bag, a warm smile, gave

Pat a friendly wave as she mounted the steps, kissed his cheek when they met. *("Keereist, this is gonna be a bit of alright!")*

"Hi, Big Guy! How's your day?"

"A lot better now that you're here."

"Charmer!" She brushed past him, intoxicating perfume, entered the house as Pat held the door. "Wow! This is some place you have here."

"Thank you, Colette. I'm just renting, was lucky enough to find this home available because the owners are traveling overseas for several months."

"You'll have to give me a tour later on, but right now I'm eager to shed these clothes *("God, can I help!")* and get into my bathing suit so I can hit that pool and lay in the sun. Gonna join me?"

"I can't let you do that alone. My guardian angel would kill me!"

Both laughed. Colette followed his directions upstairs to the master bedroom. No way he was going to stick her in a first floor guest bedroom, wanted her to see the king-size bed, views of the

Bay, upper patio and jacuzzi, hopefully wetting her appetite for possibilities later!

They reached the pool at about the same time and dove in. Pat surfaced first, Colette seconds later. She began swimming the width of the circular pool, back and forth several times in a smooth, almost effortless overhand crawl. She looked professional, wasn't even breathless when she ultimately surfaced near Pat, who was standing in the shallow end admiring her stroke, the torpedo-like move of her sensual body through the water.

"Man, you really know how to swim!"

"I was on my high school and college swim teams, Pat. Grabbed a few trophies and headlines, but that was some time ago."

"Well, you certainly haven't lost your touch, or stroke, or whatever you fish describe it as!"

They both were laughing as they exited the water, dried off, sprawled on side-by-side chaise lounges separated by a small table which held two ice cold glasses of lime squash and a house telephone/ intercom extension. The phone rang, Pat lifted the receiver, heard Nora announce that lunch would be served poolside.

The sun was warm, almost too warm. They both lay absorbing the UV rays, relaxing, little conversation for about five minutes, Pat stealing furtive glances at her luscious, bikini-clad body. Then Colette spoke up without even turning to look at Pat.

"What's the deal this evening, Pat. Why the special dinner, who's coming, what's the occasion?"

Pat swung his legs over, sat upright.

"I thought it would be a good idea to get your company's management team together for a relaxing social evening. I haven't even met some of those folks yet, and I'd like to be considered a member of the team.

"Also, we had a successful launch of the company's stock, as you know. The price has been climbing, a very good performance in such a short time. I'm sure that has been helped by the company's positive second quarter financial results, which Steve announced on July 15th.

"You folks in management are moving into a terrific new office building, and Steve successfully negotiated a multi-million dollar loan with your bankers. So, given all of that happy news, I thought this would be a great way to celebrate our accomplishments."

"Well, it's very nice, Pat, and I'm sure Tom and Steve and the others will be very pleased."

"I hope so, Colette. I'm actually having the dinner catered by a terrific French restaurant here in Newport. I felt like giving Nora the night off, and these folks turn out a terrific feast."

"Good for you."

"I've invited six folks from the company -- Tom, Steve, you, the VP of Manufacturing, VP of Sales, and VP of Government Relations -- I can't even remember all their names. Wives, too, of course, and you're welcome to bring a guest."

"No, that won't be necessary, Pat. The day we went sailing you said I was your date, so you can be my date tonight." She was looking at him above her lowered sunglasses, a bright twinkle in those penetrating eyes, her luscious lips parted in a big smile.

Pat smiled back. "Sounds great to me!" *("Oh my god, this is gonna be a spectacular evening!")*

His revery was interrupted by the telephone, which he again picked up after a single ring, annoyed at the interruption.

"Hello."

"Pat, this is Candi."

"Oh, Hi! How are you?"

"I'm pissed, Pat. You are more than three weeks late with your rent payment on that house, my boss is threatening to fire me if I don't collect it, and despite my earlier calls to you I still don't have your check."

"I'm sorry, Candi. I've been really busy with my client and it slipped my mind."

"Well, you're at the house now, so I'm coming over to pick up a check for the July rent and you better pay us for August, as well. That's eighteen-thousand, Pat, and I want it all. I'm sick and tired of your delays."

"Candi, you can't come over here now. *("Jesus, I don't want her here today while I'm laying next to a gorgeous female in a bikini!")*. I'm with a guest, and I have to get ready for a large dinner party here this evening. I promise to bring you a check Monday morning at nine."

"DAMMIT, Pat!" Her voice was so loud Pat held the phone away from his ear, forgot that Colette was now party to the conversation. "YOU FUCKING BETTER BE HERE BY NINE WITH EIGHTEEN THOUSAND DOLLARS OR I'M GOING TO ROAST YOUR ASS AND MOUNT IT ON MY WALL!"

"I was thinking of mounting a little ass myself, Candi."

The phone went dead.

Colette was sitting up on her chaise. "Wow! Who was that?"

"She's the real estate lady who got me this house. She's also the one who found us the Washington Square building."

"Oh, right. I met her, Candi, right? I was with Tom when she showed us the building. She's a cute little number."

("Shit! I didn't know Colette and Candi had met. I'm damn glad I told Candi not to come over here today.")

"Whose ass are you thinking of mounting?"

"What?"

"You told her you are 'thinking of mounting a little ass.' Whose ass might that be?"

"Ahhh, it's just a figure of speech, Colette!"

"Thank, goodness. I was beginning to get nervous!" She smiled broadly.

They moved over to a patio table where Nora had just spread lunch. Conversation continued, mostly about the company, the key managers coming to dinner this evening, lots of questions about Pat's business, his "associates" in Los Angeles, his "relationships" with the bankers in the UK and law firm in Hong Kong.

Pat was surprised to learn that Colette had worked in Hong Kong before returning to the States to join Fabricated; had been an airline cabin attendant for United, was recruited by a Hong Kong bank as a customer service rep handling mostly U.S. and European clients, knew of the law firm Pat mentioned but did not personally know any one there.

"Thank god!"

Pat's answers to most of Colette's questions were carefully evasive, not enough to arouse suspicion (he hoped), just enough to divert her from prolonging her inquiries beyond surface information. He'd already told her more than he intended the day they went sailing.

Nora interrupted their conversations once to advise Pat that the catering truck had pulled into the garage, the catering staff had taken over the kitchen, was setting the table in the dining room, things were well underway for this evening's dinner party.

Colette stood to leave.

"Pat, you have a lot going on here, so I'm going to change back into my street clothes and get out of your hair."

"You're not in my hair. Please stay awhile longer."

"No, I'm going to take my leave. I'll see you this evening. I'm really looking forward to it, and remember, you're my date."

They shook hands, she brushed his cheek with her lips, ducked into the house. Pat sat down again, buoyed by the fact that she was coming back this evening, and he was to be her date. She said so herself!

+ + +

Colette was on the phone to Tom Mulholland from her car, anxious to fill him in on her lunch conversation with Pat, and Candi's call about Pat owing her firm $18,000!

"How'd it go, Colette?"

"God, you wouldn't believe it, Tom. Tonight's shindig is strictly for show. He wants to be perceived as a member of your team, and he also wants to flaunt his apparent status as a successful financial consultant, but I don't believe he has a pot to piss in!"

"Really!"

"Really! He owes that real estate gal eighteen grand, which is past due. He carefully dodges any detailed discussion of his California partners -- who they are, or what they do -- and he's equally obscure when you try to engage him in a conversation about his London bankers or Hong Kong lawyers. The law firm exists, I know that fact, but I'm not sure they've ever heard of Pat Clauson!"

"This doesn't sound good, Colette."

"Remember, I said it was all a charade."

"I haven' forgotten, and I'm getting more nervous by the day that you might be right."

"I hope not, Tom. I hope I'm wrong. He hasn't done us any damage yet that we know of, but I sure as hell would keep him on a tight rein, Tom. I could be all wet, but I just don't trust the guy, and I'm not saying that just because he's coming on to me with his tongue hanging out. I just don't trust the guy!"

"Well, he's given us thirty grand of his own money so far to renovate the new building, and he's going have to cough up another ten or more to finish the job. That's not costing us anything."

"Yeah, but you're paying the guy five thousand a month, and he's just shuffling his money in and out of the company account because that's where he puts it and he's writing the checks. Steve should make certain the checks are being written properly, and that the contractors are actually being paid."

"What are you suggesting?"

"Come on, Tom. You're not naive! Do I have to draw you a picture? If it were me, I'd write checks to cash, cheat the vendors, and pocket the dough. And I could get away with it until you or Steve figured out what I was doing. Then I'd disappear like dust."

"My god, Colette, you have a sinister mind!"

"I worked for a Hong Kong bank, Tom, and I learned some tricks of the trade."

"Okay, you've given me a lot to think about. Thanks for all you've done today, and I'll see you tonight at the unveiling."

"Your welcome, Tom. I hope I'm wrong about this guy, but I have an itchy feeling."

They hung up and Colette continued home to change for Pat's dinner party.

+ + +

Guests began arriving shortly after six. Tom and Alice Mulholland were the first to show. Alice was about Tom's age, very personable, mid-thirties attractive, carried herself like the wife of a young CEO. Tom disappeared through the living room in the direction of the pool and bar. Alice stuck by Pat's side to introduce him to the arriving guests he did not already know.

Sean O'Brien, VP/Manufacturing, was next to walk up the front steps with his wife Margo. Pat had met Sean, but had little interface with him. He was tall, ruddy, slight brogue, very out-going. Margo was even more so, an easy-going "glad ta meet ya" kind of gal, refreshing. Alice directed them both to the patio and bar as Rick and Alma Harris approached the steps.

Rick was VP/Sales, looked and sounded it. He was medium height, balding, quite plump from too many meals on the road, too many bars with clients. Firm handshake, ready laugh from telling or hearing ribald jokes on sales calls or at conventions. Alma was a salesman's wife, very accustomed to playing hostess or being entertained, pleasant smile, quick with compliments about the house, Pat's "gracious" hospitality, Alice's outfit (she wore what all the women were wearing, a lightweight, colorful summer dress or slacks and blouse, with flats).

Steve and Robin Johnson were right behind the Harris's. Steve was his reserved, rather quiet self, did not show much emotion or friendliness, exhibited a level of frost as he shook Pat's hand. Robin also was somewhat stiff, formal, mirrored her husband's personality, polite enough but no party girl. Might have just been reflecting her husband's attitude.

Alice next introduced Pat to Toby and Jane Colby. Toby as Vice President/Government Affairs, based in Washington, DC, so Pat had not met him previously. He was short, stocky, an extrovert, extremely likable, and Jane was more of the same. Like Rick and Alma, they were very accustomed to entertaining and being entertained.

Only Colette was missing!

They all had ooh'd and ah'd as they entered and caught their first look at the huge living room, the mahogany-paneled ceiling, the open glass sliders to the patio, pool and ocean.

"When we drove up I thought we were entering a palace, and we were!" exclaimed Alma Harris.

"Is this yours, Pat?" Jane Colby.

"Good Lord, No! I'm just renting, but I'm very comfortable, as you might imagine."

"Comfortable doesn't begin to describe it!" Margo O'Brien.

"Well, ladies. if you'd like to take a tour of the house, please don't hesitate. There's a library, den and three en-suite bedrooms on this floor, plus the dining room, of course, and the kitchen. Upstairs is the master bedroom suite, which I really suggest you take a look at. It's awesome, and the views are spectacular."

"Thank you, Pat. I think I will take a tour, but after I wrap my hands around something cold," said Alma.

"Follow Alice and me. The bar's out by the pool."

They all joined the men, dressed in slacks and open-collared shirts, congregated at or near the bar with its top brand liquors and expensive wines, a bartender prepared to serve their favorite libation. In addition to greeting each other and ordering drinks, they expressed admiration for the view, visions of sailboats offshore or bikini-clad women in the pool (*"If only they knew!"*).

"Well, Pat, you've certainly got good taste, know how to live well." It was Tom speaking.

"Thank you, Tom. I was very fortunate to find this place. The owners are traveling abroad for several months. Candi, the real estate lady who showed you the office space, also found this home for me. Great place to hang one's hat!"

"Ahhh, Yes. I remember Candi. Good-looker."

Sean O'Brien caught Pat's arm. "Why didn't we just move the offices into this place, Pat. Awesome impression, better views, and a pool instead of lousy coffee!" He was laughing; Pat and Tom laughed with him. Rick, Toby, Steve and the wives joined the circle engaging in harmless social chatter, several clean traveling salesman stories by Rick Harris.

Colette arrived as the women were ordering their cocktails. She was stunning, adorned in a gorgeous ruby-red halter top which highlighted her full breasts, slim waist. Her long slender legs dropped out of navy blue shorts, her neck accented with a gold necklace, matching earrings. And those eyes!

Pat skipped the handshake routine, slipped his arm around her waist and kissed her cheek. Some in the group, no one less than Tom, were surprised at Pat's public familiarity with his administrative assistant. A catering waitress passed among the group with a tray carrying an assortment of scrumptious hors d'oeuvres.

In Pat's eye, the evening had a wonderful start, his guests impressed with his life style, his taste, his apparent wealth, his social skills, his savoir-faire, his carriage as a well-healed, well-connected international businessman. At a point in time, Pat observed Tom and Colette off to the side engaged in serious conversation. *("What's that all about, I wonder!")*

The social conversation, laughter, cocktails carried on for well over an hour, until a tuxedoed waiter approached Pat to advise that dinner was ready. Pat led the group into the large dining room.

The women, in particular, stopped short to admire the setting, the high mahogany-paneled ceiling and paneled walls, magnificent artwork by assorted masters, the long table set for twelve, lit candles lining the center, wall sconces on dim. Soft background music emanated from recessed ceiling speakers.

Bone china place settings, cut crystal water and wine glasses, polished sterling flatware and candle sticks, white linen tablecloth and napkins, an abundance of bright colored flowers: the room was breathtakingly beautiful.

Pat had also provided place cards, told the caterer to make sure no husband and wife sat together, he wanted the group split up to facilitate more conversation. The only exception: he and Colette were to be seated side-by-each, another signal not missed by any one, especially after Pat's earlier greeting of Colette on the pool deck.

Once wine was served, Tom stood, rapped his glass to silence conversation.

"I'd like to propose a toast to the continued success of our company. I believe we are on the threshold of some exciting developments which will result in significant growth and prosperity. And I'd like to single out Pat Clauson for encouraging us to proceed with a stock issue, which appears to be doing extremely well."

"Hear, hear!" The group response.

"Thank you, Tom." Pat rose. "I'd also like to toast you and, I believe, Sean, for your foresight in founding your company . . . to all of you for making it a substantial success in its first years of operation. And I especially want to congratulate Steve for his control of the finances, and for successfully securing a multi-million dollar loan so you can expand and modernize your manufacturing plant. And, let's toast the early performance of the stock offering . . . hope it continues to grow."

"We'll all drink to that, Pat." This was Rick Harris. Steve was noticeably quiet despite Pat's verbal bouquet.

Pat was seated between Colette on his right, Alice Mulholland on his left. Steve sat on her left, his wife, Robin, at the far end of the table next to Tom. Alice turned to Pat.

"Pat, I understand you are originally from Australia."

"Yes, that's correct, Alice. I was born and raised on a sheep ranch, and left several years ago on a freighter bound for L.A. Haven't looked back once."

"Australia not agree with you?"

"It was the sheep ranch: millions of fleas, and sheep stink!"

"How do you like living in the U.S.?"

"Love it. I was telling Colette earlier that this country really is the land of opportunity. It has been very kind to me."

"How did you get started here?"

"I kind of fell into it, Alice. I had some background in finance and corporate financing, and things just bloomed from there. I've been lucky, and I suppose, very fortunate." He sipped his wine, confident his stretch of the truth remained concealed.

"I've heard you have helped several other firms before Tom's. Would it be possible for you to give us the names so, if the spirit moves us, we could call one or two and ask how they're making out. I'm especially interested in how they progressed with their stock offering, how quickly it grew, what they did after you left to secure a Big Board listing, if in fact they did." Alice was smiling, her eyes sparkling as she lifted her wine glass.

("Oh my god! I can't have her, or anyone from Fabricated, nosing around my past business connections! Dammit, this is a problem.")

"Sure Alice, I can understand your interest. But as I explained to Tom and Steve, my business is quite confidential, and I don't believe any of my clients would appreciate it if I began telling third parties about their business problems."

"Oh, I see." She looked disappointed.

"But, let me make a few calls and I'll see if I can soften one or two of them up. But, please remember, some of that business goes back a number of years, market performance was different than today. There are a lot of factors to consider when attempting to make a comparison with the success of Fabricated's stock."

"Oh, I understand that, Pat. I'm just curious, nothing will most likely come from my curiosity. Although it would be fun to speak with one or two of them to hear how they made out . . . you know, moving from the penny market to a real stock exchange, impact on the company, attitude of shareholders, that kind of thing."

"Well, I'll gladly provide you or Tom or Steve with whatever I'm allowed," Pat lied. He was extremely uncomfortable, suddenly stood and addressed both Alice and Colette.

"Please excuse me for a moment, ladies. I want to check on the caterer in the kitchen."

As he disappeared from the dining room, Alice and Colette smiled at each other, turned to face Steve, who gave them a thumbs up. They all looked toward Tom, who merely nodded his head. Robin was smiling. Alice's conversation had obviously been planned.

Small groups of dinner guests engaged in conversations, exchanged tidbits of information, stories of times past and future hopes, kids, vacations, college expenses, some but not much office gossip. The atmosphere was extremely friendly, upbeat, most of the wives knew each other and their husbands, one great fraternity/sorority gathering, just what Pat had hoped to achieve.

Then he had been blind-sided by Alice's inquiry.

The food was lip-smacking good, the wine extraordinary and readily consumed in quantity by all. Led by Rick and Alma Harris, the couples carried their after-dinner brandies out to the pool deck to admire the stars and the brilliant three-quarter moon shining on the ocean surface. The music also was fed outdoors, a few couples dancing to a romantic waltz, others joined in.

Pat and Colette exchanged glances, moved onto the "dance floor" where Pat leaned forward as if to kiss Colette. She pulled back her head, placed a finger across his lips, moved her hand back to his shoulder. He still held her tighter than required for a simple dance.

The party broke up about one o'clock, lots of handshakes, hugs and thank-you's as couples exited the front door, found their cars and drove off. Colette had not yet made a move to leave.

"May I interest you a nightcap, Colette?"

"Oh, no thanks, Pat. I really should be going. It's way past my bedtime."

"No way I can implore you to stay here?"

"I'm sorry, Pat, No! I had a marvelous time, both this evening and this afternoon, and you have been a very entertaining and gracious host, or should I say date. But I really must be going."

She stood on her toes, brushed her lips against his cheek, turned and found that awesome BMW 650, top still down. She waved brightly as she drove past him and out the driveway.

Pat turned to enter the house. "Godammit! This isn't how I wanted tonight to end. And Alice . . . damn Alice!"

He poured himself a drink at the dining room bar, then moved slowly up the stairs to the mammoth second floor master bedroom and slumped into an over-stuffed chair.

The evening had gone exactly as he had planned, except for that business about speaking to some of his former "clients." He was very bothered by the thought that Alice didn't come up with that on her own; that Tom had probably asked her to raise that possibility.

("Shit! I already told he and Steve why that couldn't be done, but I'll bet they didn't like my answer. So Alice gave it another try. That's not good, not good at all. That means they are beginning to question what the hell I'm doing! They'll start nosing around, and if they do they are bound to discover the game I'm playing with their checking account. I've gotta begin thinking of packing my bags.")

Pat sipped his drink for well over a half hour, his thoughts vibrating around the reality that he was running out of time at Fabricated. How best to extricate himself quickly, latch onto as much company cash as possible, then disappear without leaving a trail Tom or Steve could follow easily?

9

SUNDAY

Alice rose early, left Tom asleep, he needed rest. She went downstairs to the kitchen, made coffee, dialed a local number.

"Hello!" The voice was sleepy.

"Colette, this is Alice Mulholland. I'm sorry to wake you."

"Oh! Hi! That's okay, Alice. What's up?"

"What was your impression of the dinner last night at Pat's place?"

"Oh, lord! It was a staged event just to show off. He wants us all to think he is wealthy and a very clever international financier."

"So what do you really think?"

"Well, he's very clever, but I think he's a con artist. If you don't mind my saying so, he sure as hell has conned your husband. At least in my opinion he has, and I'm not the only one in the office who thinks so. Steve Johnson, our CFO, is positively rip-shit."

"I'm also very concerned, Colette, but I can't get through to Tom on this issue. Are you free for lunch tomorrow . . . I'd like . . . could we have a private chat?"

"You bet! When and where do you want to meet?"

Their lunch arrangements made, Alice hung up and waited for her husband to rise and shine.

They were still in pajamas and bathrobes, seated at their patio table where they had finished breakfast. Tom was engaged with the Sunday *New York Times,* Alice was reading the Book Review section when she lay it down, spoke to her husband.

"Tom, we need to talk."

"Oh, boy!" He was smiling. "What have I done? Should I apologize now?"

"It's not you, Tom. It's that guy Pat Clauson."

"What about him?"

"That entire evening last night . . . that was nothing more than an ego trip for him. He was showing off . . . big expensive house, fancy catered dinner, swimming pool and first class bar. He was trying to impress us all with his savvy, his money -- or maybe it's *our* money! The entire evening was staged!"

"You may be right. Colette spent the afternoon with him, tried really hard to press him on his backers, London and Hong Kong associates, nothing. We're beginning to get the feeling he ain't what he claims to be . . . actually, Steve and Colette have felt that way for some time."

"My god, Tom." She fiend ignorance.

"Yeah. Stupid. I can't figure out where he's coming from."

Alice took a long swallow of her coffee, set down the cup, and stared momentarily into space, then at Tom.

"Well, *you* hired him. What the hell were you thinking?"

"Alice, I've been all over that ground with Steve several times. I've talked with Steve, as you requested, and he has relaxed . . . knows exactly what I'm planning.

"On the plus side, Pat got us into the stock market at minimal cost, and our shares are increasing in value quite nicely. When you and I sell, we'll make a handsome profit. He's also committed to investing $100,000 in the company as a bridge loan until we get our new bank loan. Steve has successfully negotiated that, and the check is due momentarily. We need that money to lease more modern equipment."

"Yeah, I know all that. But you haven't seen the $100,000, have you?"

"He's paid us thirty thousand so far, and he has been using his money renovate our new office space which, by the way, *he* found for us. And he's committed to investing another ten or twenty grand over the next two months . . . new office space at no cost to us!"

"I think that's just a come on, Tom."

"Well, it's been a real bonus for us.

Alice again lifted her coffee cup. She felt she had to find a way to wake Tom up to the risk Clauson posed to the company and to their personal financial stability.

"Steve is real upset because you agreed to give Pat signature rights to the company's bank accounts. How's that going?"

"I told you, Steve and I have talked and he has relaxed."

"Well, I'm damned concerned that Pat has found a way to rip us off. I don't know how, but I'm convinced I'm right. He made no attempt to identify his previous 'clients' when I asked for that information, and his eyes grew wide with fear! I wasn't the only one who noticed that. Steve and Colette also noticed. You may recall, Pat jumped up from the table and disappeared into the kitchen before I could press him any further.

"And you, Tom, you gave us a nod from your end of the table, signifying that I was on the right track. I can't understand why none of you fellas asked that question!"

"I did, weeks ago, and he gave me the same answer he gave you. OK, Alice, I'll take the rap for not pressing the issue. But still . ."

He never got to finish his sentence. Alice exploded!

"YOUR problem, Tom, is you're too damned nice. I'm not. I'm a bitch on steroids when I have a bone in my teeth, as you know, and I'm chewing on a whopper. I intend to check this guy out."

Tom, also, was getting annoyed.

"Really! And just how do you intend to do that?"

"I'm going to call my Uncle Diego and ask him to have a few of his people do the homework you didn't do!"

"Not Diego, Alice. He's in the waste management business, for chrissake. If you're serious, hire a lawyer or private eye, and the company will pay the bills."

"No! My uncle has more contacts and more resources than any damned lawyer, more than you or I can imagine. And he's family. He'll do what I ask for no charge."

"And what do you intend to ask?"

"I'm going to spell out my concerns, why I'm upset. I'm going to ask him to find out what companies Pat has worked with in the past, and what they think of him on a scale of one-to-ten, one being 'crook' and ten being 'saint'. And I'll bet all we own that 'saint' never gets mentioned."

"Maybe you're right."

"Maybe!? You're not one-hundred-percent comfortable yourself, are you. But you've allowed things to percolate for almost four months. If I'm wrong, I apologize. I'll even apologize to Pat. But if I'm right . . . ."

"Yeah! Then what?"

"Then we blow the whistle. Sue the guy, or whatever."

"It's the 'whatever' that worries me, Alice!"

\+ + +

Early Monday, Diego Valenti sat at his favorite corner table in the busy north-end Providence pastry shop he claimed as his "other" office. Heavyset, balding, late fifties, always smoking, he had a deep rasping voice and enormous pride in his Italian heritage, his "position" as a prominent figure in the rough-and-tumble arena of Rhode Island business.

Valenti Hauling had been founded by his grandfather about seventy years earlier. The old man arrived in the U.S. as a child, spoke little English. He held any number of lousy paying jobs until he could scrape together enough dough to buy a beat-up truck and begin hauling yard waste, broken furniture, old mattresses, any other crap his north-end neighbors were sick of tripping over.

He eventually upgraded his truck and landed a contract hauling rubbish for the City of Providence, a deal which involved bribing a state rep and assorted city council members. The bribes were quickly recovered because rubbish hauling became a profitable occupation, especially when he convinced a few other truckers to get out of the business or be taken over by Valenti Hauling. Either way, he expanded his collection routes, multiplied his income.

His only son, Diego's father, Tony, took over the business when the old man's health began to fade. Tony built upon the success of his Dad, vastly enlarging Valenti Hauling into one of the biggest waste management companies in the state. He had a fleet of modern trucks and a large base of employees whose loyalty he secured with cash and assorted off-the-clock assignments.

The business continued to bloom, if that's the right adjective to describe a rubbish business, and Tony became a very influential member of the city's Italian community, far more powerful than his father. His notoriety did not escape the attention law enforcement agencies, which were increasingly suspect of how rubbish contracts were awarded, competition stifled, employees harnessed.

Diego inherited the business from Tony, the third generation to run Valenti Hauling. He re-named the company Valenti Waste Collection, painted his new fleet of trucks environmental green, uniformed his drivers and truck grunts, and even constructed a recycling plant to show the world (especially the Rhode Island legislature and nosey law enforcement) that the name Valenti represented an upstanding community success story.

He also assumed his father's mantle as the leader-among-leaders within the Italian community of Providence. He became known as Diego "The Man" Valenti, an honorarium bestowed upon him because of his ability to accomplish almost anything asked of him by his extended family, friends and troops (i.e., his close acquaintances).

On this Monday morning, Diego was basking in his power and fame, entertaining a few associates with stories of decades past, politicians bought and sold, when the private line mounted on the wall next to him interrupted his monologue. He set down his coffee, picked up the receiver, barked into the mouthpiece.

"Yes!"

"Hi, Uncle Diego. This is Alice."

"Alice! My word, child! Long time, no speak. How are you and Tom?" His personality had shifted in a flash from gruff to honey.

"We're very well, thank you."

"To what do I owe the pleasure?"

"Uncle Diego, I think Tom has gotten himself, his company, and ourselves, into a potential mess, and I was wondering if you could do a little homework for us."

"I'd be glad to, Alice. What's the problem, and what kind of homework do you need?"

Alice spent the fifteen minutes detailing her concerns about Pat Clauson: his "British bankers" and "Hong Kong lawyers"; his demand to have signature rights to Tom's company checking account; his show-off life style; his failure to pay rent on the micro-mansion he was renting; his allusions to having helped companies in Chicago, St. Louis, Atlanta, Kansas City and Oakland; his reluctance to identify any of those firms; his over-bearing personality and "slippery, slimy" behavior in general; his so-called "promise" to invest $100,000 in Tom's company; his mysterious and unidentified west coast "associates".

"Good Lord, Alice. This guy sounds like a ringer! How come Tom agreed to retain him?"

"Well, Tom feels I'm over-critical. Pat has taken the company public at minimal expense, and the stock is doing very well. It trades on the penny market, but is already over ten dollars a share. And, he used his own money to renovate new office space for Tom's firm, space Pat himself found."

"That sounds pretty good to me. What's your hangup?"

"It's too good, Uncle Diego. I think it's a come-on, you know 'Look what I've done for you; trust me with your bank account.' That sort of stuff. And Tom has no references for the guy. If I'm wrong about him, I'll pay to advertise in the *Journal* to tell the world he's fantastic, but I know deep down I'll never have to do that . . . apologize, I mean."

"I see."

"I'm not the only one who feels this way. Tom's treasurer, Steve Johnson, and his administrative assistant, Colette Dubois, also share my concerns, and they're exposed to this guy every day."

The name Colette Dubois caught Diego by surprise. There could be only one woman with that name, and she dated Diego's son Enrique. He decided to keep his mouth shut.

"Okay, Alice. Give me the specifics of what you want to know, and I'll have some of my people check this guy out."

Alice spent another twenty minutes feeding her uncle as much specific information as she could: the company bank account numbers so one of Diego's contacts could pull strings and obtain a printed statement; the cities in which Pat said he had worked with other firms so Diego's contacts in those markets could discreetly query Chambers of Commerce, regional business journals, a few politicians, and other business associations to see who remembered Pat's name and what, specifically, they remembered!

Also, Diego would query the UK bankers and Hong Kong law firms to learn if anyone had ever heard of Pat Clauson; the Newport real estate agent and any other local vendors to see if Pat had paid them for their services; the car rental agency to see if it had been paid; her list went on, and on.

"Okay, Alice. You and Tom relax. Tell Tom to keep his eyes and ears open to anything that might not seem hunky-dory, and I'll get back to you in a couple of days with some preliminary information."

"Thanks, Uncle Diego. I feel better already."

"Take care, Alice. If anything else comes up, be sure to call me."

+ + +

Alice and Colette entered the Italian restaurant together, having met moments before on the outdoor deck. They preferred to eat indoors, less visible from the street and passing crowds. They sat at a small round table, ordered wine and pasta salads, their conversation light, friendly. Once the wine arrived, Alice opened the dialogue she was anxious to pursue.

"Colette, I deliberately did not tell Tom we were meeting today. Have you said anything to him?"

"No! I haven't said a word to him."

"Good, let's keep this between us girls." They both laughed.

"Sounds good to me!"

"Colette, I was very interested to hear Tom say yesterday at breakfast that both you and Steve Johnson are uncomfortable with this fella, Pat Clauson. I am, too, as you know."

"Uncomfortable isn't a strong enough word, Alice. Steve and I don't trust him at all. We both think he's a crook, but have no proof."

"I see." Alice paused, let Colette's words sink in.

"I mean, that dinner Saturday night was a ring job if I've ever seen one, Alice. Pat was in full throttle, doing everything he could to make an impression. I damned near fainted when he put his arm around me when I first arrived, and then he tried to kiss me while we were dancing after dinner. I almost threw up! And after you all left, he tried to talk me into staying for the night, but I got out of there as fast as I could."

"Yeah, that kiss move was sure out of place."

"God, what a jerk! He makes my skin crawl, but Tom asked me to play 007 and pump Pat for as much information as I could pry out of him. I got a lot, I think, but it wasn't fun. I had to do most of it while wearing a bikini on a sailboat or in his pool. He spent most of the time drooling!" Alice laughed, Collette smiled.

"Well, I feel the same way you an Steve do, and I hope you and I can work together to find a way to make Tom listen. He can be stubborn, as I'm sure you know."

"Oh, Yes! I know!" Colette laughed. "He doesn't respond well to theory, Alice, as I'm sure *you know.* But if we can present him with facts, I believe Tom will be very quick to take action."

"Yes! Well, I've taken steps which I hope will secure the proof we need. I really hope, in a way, that I'm wrong, but I don't think I am and I need to prove I'm right to Tom."

"We're on the same page, Alice. But I believe in my heart that you and I and Steve are on the right track. We just need to prove it to your stubborn husband!" She smiled.

"Tell me about it!" Alice also smiled, sipped her wine.

"How are you going about getting proof, Alice?"

"I have a relative who is well connected, and he has agreed to do some snooping around for me."

"That's great! Is he some kind of detective, or something?"

"No! You'll laugh at this, but he's actually in the rubbish business."

"Rubbish business! You're kidding!"

"No! I'm dead serious, Colette."

"Pardon me for asking, but how the hell . . . ."

"Have you heard of Valenti Waste Hauling?" Alice interrupted.

"Yes! I have."

"Well, Mr. Valenti is my uncle."

"My, god! You're kidding me, Alice! You have *got* to be kidding me!"

"No! I'm *not* kidding! What's the big deal?"

"I'm dating Mr. Valenti's son, Enrique!"

"WHAT! That's unbelievable, Colette! Are you serious?"

"Absolutely! We've been dating for two years, and we're *very* serious! We're beginning to plan our future together!"

"What a surprise! I can't believe it! But I'm very happy for both of you. I'm amazed Diego hasn't say anything to me, or didn't when I spoke with him this morning!"

"Well, you know Mr. Valenti. He keeps his mouth shut and only ventures to share information he feels is pertinent to whomever he's speaking."

"Yeah, I know only too well. Tom is somewhat like that, too."

"Two of a kind, Alice." Their salads had arrived and they began to enjoy them.

"But tell me, how is Mr. Valenti going to help you?"

"I'll tell you what I've done, but please, do not let Tom know of your connection to Diego Valenti. I'd rather he didn't know anything about it."

For the next thirty minutes, while they ate lunch and dawdled over coffee, Alice briefed Colette on her conversation with Diego that morning, outlining all she knew about Pat's involvement with Fabricated, and her reasons for asking her uncle to do the sniffing rather than hiring a lawyer or private detective.

She emphasized the extent of Diego's connections to other waste collection firms nationally, and the relative ease with which he could verify claims Pat had made about investors, banking and legal contacts, and former customers he was reluctant to identify.

"This ought to be something, Alice! What a nifty idea!"

"Thank you, Colette. Let's keep this all between the two of us. I won't tell either Tom or Diego that we have met, and I'd appreciate it if you didn't mention anything to them, either."

"Not a chance, Alice. The only thing I've said to Tom is that I know someone who can solve problems, but I didn't mention any names, and I didn't suggest any ideas about how a given problem would be solved. That's really none of my business. I have heard that

Mr. Valenti has scared a few people off when they got in the way of his business, and frankly I don't want to know any more than that."

"That's smart, Colette. Keep it that way."

"I intend to. Our discussion is our secret, Alice, and I think what you've described is a marvelous strategy. I hope it works."

"You and me both, Colette, you and me both!"

+ + +

Pat sat in his office, comfortable in the overstuffed office chair he had rented along with all of the other office furniture for the entire exec-utive staff of Fabricated Structures: attractive oak desks, credenzas and file cabinets, visitor's chairs, secretarial desks, reception room furniture, a large wooden conference table with a dozen upholstered chairs with arms, no expense spared.

He had yet to pay even the first month's rent on the furniture, had the invoice stuffed in his desk drawer along with those from the carpenter, electrician and painter who had renovated the office space, and the carpet company which made the offices and conference room quiet without shoes and high heels marching across hardwood floors.

He had, however, written checks for cash, entering vendor names in the register so it appeared they were being paid. But he didn't pay them, just stuffed the money into opaque and sealed envelopes in a locked drawer of his desk, to be retrieved at the last minute when he chose to flee the scene.

Meanwhile, if Tom or Steve smelled a rat and raised the issue, he could pull some of the cash out of his drawer, dish some of it out to the vendors, hopefully avoid a showdown at the OK Coral. Dicey, but he had done that successfully with other "clients" in the past.

What was making him anxious, however, was Alice Mulholland's questions at his dinner party last Saturday, especially when she asked if Pat would provide her or her husband with the contact names and phone numbers of his earlier "clients".

The hair on the back of his neck began to rise every time he thought about that conversation, fear of discovery beginning to replace his optimism about another successful scam. Even Colette, when they had been sailing Saturday afternoon, had pressed him with questions about his motivation for providing money to Fabricated to renovate the firm's new office space -- space where he was now parking his butt.

Also, both Tom and Steve seemed unusually distant this morning. No verbal greetings, no business talk, not even any socializing before the work day began. Things didn't smell right to Pat, and if he sensed the stink he was reasonably certain Tom, Steve, Tom's wife, and probably Colette, were suspicious that Pat was not the whiz-bang international business executive they had assumed they were retaining.

And if that was true, he really should be plotting to quietly withdraw and head for Rome.

But -- and it was a *big* but -- he had not realized anywhere near the payoff he had been hoping to achieve with this outfit. He had already spent several thousand of his own money in fees, meals and travel expenses on this caper, as well as the new office space. He owed another eighteen thousand to Candi for house rental, had yet to pay a dime to the Here-to-There limo rental company, still hadn't paid Danny his weekly fee.

All he had so far sucked out of this firm was his retainer, about $300,000 of their cash he had hidden in his desk, and a lot of penny stock which he didn't dare ship to Canada for sale while he was still working, so to speak, at Fabricated. His shares were restricted, after all, so he wasn't supposed to be able to sell them. Little did Tom or Steve know!

He had been mulling over this quandary all weekend, knew in his heart he should cut and run, but could not bring himself to do so. For openers, he had not pulled sufficient money from the company to live very well for a long time in Rome, which meant he'd have to find another target pretty quickly, delay Rome, and fatten his wallet.

But that could take several months, perhaps a year, and he felt it would be safer to disappear overseas in the not-too-distant future.

His best bet, Pat realized, was to do everything possible to inflate the price of his 50,000 shares of stock. If it could go to twenty bucks or higher, he'd reap a bundle when he told Kyle to sell through his connection in Canada.

He was on the phone every day, sometimes twice a day, with Danny to learn which brokers he was talking to or meeting with, what he was telling him, and how many shares those guys were moving. Did they have confidence in the stock? Were their customers being supportive? Did any one of them question Danny about Fabricated's outlook financially? Any particular news the brokers needed to hear, or that their customers need to hear?

"Keep feeding me positive, upbeat news about what the company is up to!" was Danny's answer, "and for christssake start paying me!"

Pat's answer to Danny's request for information was to feed him press releases, datelined Newport, RI., in which the company "announced" a new business opportunity of some sort, or a massive sale to a large customer, the promotion of a Fabricated senior executive into a position which implied a substantial broadening of his responsibilities to meet the company's expanding business.

He never alerted either Tom nor Steve to what he was doing. He didn't tell Danny the press releases were unauthorized and didn't reflect accurate developments at the company. In short, Pat was creating proprietary information that didn't exist, passing it off as legitimate, and hoping to god no one discover his ruse. He was breaking a gazillion federal laws.

His press releases were emailed to Danny and selected national trade magazines with very long deadlines, assuring that no one at Fabricated would read the lies in print until Pat was nothing more than an unpleasant memory.

However, he neglected to consider that the brokers might speak with investment analysts; that they, in turn, might call Fabricated itself or a *Wall Street Journal* reporter to discuss the so-called news in order to get a better handle on this growing Newport, RI, firm none of them had ever heard of.

His first few press releases claimed Fabricated had received large orders from, or delivered large orders to, medium-sized companies in the mid-west and West Coast, with a resultant increase in Fabricated's sales and projected earnings.

He also wrote and issued a few announcing the promotion of senior executives into new positions which gave them responsibility for new distribution channels, national sales coverage, international sales, each time implying that the promotions were necessary to keep management in control of Fabricated's expanding business.

His strategy for moving the stock price, while grossly illegal, was having the desired effect of increasing the share price: valued at two dollars per share when offered initially, the stock was now trading over fifteen and continuing to climb.

If he could continue to shield his "campaign" from prying eyes for a few more weeks, the stock price was very likely to break twenty dollars a share while he was hiding in Rome. He could then contact Kyle and tell him to sell and wire the funds to a Swiss bank account.

He glanced up from the national trade magazine he had been perusing in search of a possible new target, suddenly snapped his fingers.

("That's it! Why didn't I think of this earlier?")

He dropped the magazine on his desk, opened to a full-page ad by a company in Cleveland called Aeronautic Supplies, began to make notes on how he intended to approach the firm: What would he suggest? What's his angle of persuasion? Could he pull this off? Why not, he'd strategize the whole thing over the next several days.

("This is gonna work! Tom will be thrilled, and and I'll be able to hang around a little longer. But, I better hedge my bets in case this idea doesn't fly.")

10

WEDNESDAY

Diego's homework was not long in coming. He phoned Alice Wednesday afternoon with a report on the company's bank account, obtained by a friend of a friend.

There had been a number of withdrawals in cash, but when Diego's people called the carpenter, electricians, painter, carpet and office furniture suppliers, no one had been paid. Here-to-There, the local car service, had been waiting for over three months to see a dime, was reluctant to stop providing Pat with car service for fear they would *never* be paid.

Diego's lieutenants also had made calls to British banks and Hong Kong law firms: no one could remember the name Patrick Clauson. He definitely was not an active customer. They could not find any organization in Los Angeles that fit Pat's description, and no "investors" had surfaced in response to their inquiries.

Also, they had called upon "brothers" in the waste disposal unions in each of the markets where Pat said he had worked, but most of that information was not yet available -- except for Kansas City, where the firm which had engaged Pat was prepared to hire a battery of lawyers now that they knew where he was living.

They were advised by one of Diego's people to sit tight for the moment, until information had been collected from the other markets. At that point, several companies might wish to join forces in a larger legal action designed to imprison Pat and bar him from ever again trading in the U.S. securities markets.

"All in all, Alice, it doesn't look good. There's no question your concerns are justified."

"Oh, thank you so much, Uncle Diego. I really appreciate this."

"I expect to have more information for you over the next two or three days, but you have enough to have a serious sit-down with Tom to let him know what kind of character he's dealing with.

"Thank you so much. I'll talk with Tom tonight."

"Okay. Let me know how else I can be of help. Give yourself and Tom a hug for me."

"I sure will. And thanks, again."

They rang off, Alice smiling and pumping a fist. She had nailed that bastard Pat, and was eager to share her information with Tom.

Alice was sitting on the living-room couch browsing through a fashion magazine, her cocktail on the coffee table in front of her, when Tom entered the front door. She rose to greet him as he came into the room, gave him a hug and quick kiss.

"How was your day, Dear? You look bushed."

"The usual . . . prolonged boredom with moments of sheer panic when everything hit the fan. Everything always hits the fan at the same time. And, Yes! I am bushed."

"Well have a seat, and I'll make you a drink. I have some interesting news." Alice turned and headed for the bar in their dining room. Tom set his briefcase on the living room rug, flopped into an easy chair. Alice returned quickly with his drink. He took a long swallow.

"Okay, what's your interesting news?"

"Well, it's both interesting and, potentially, good."

"What does that mean, 'potentially good'?"

"I had a phone call from Uncle Diego."

"Oh, boy!" Tom shifted in his chair. "What has he learned, if anything?"

"Are you aware that Pat has made a number of large cash withdrawals from the company checking account?"

"Yes. He's been paying vendors in cash because that's what they are requesting."

"Really! Well none of them have been paid one red cent. So guess who's holding the cash!"

"Jesus, are you serious?"

"Yes, because Uncle Diego is serious. And he has proof."

"Oh my god!"

"It gets better, Tom. Or worse, depending upon your point of view."

"Like what?"

"Uncle Diego's contacts phoned several banks in London and several law firms in Hong Kong and *no one* has ever heard of Pat Clauson!"

"Oh, come on! How the hell was he going to arranagen a commercial loan from the Commonwealth Bank of London?"

"Obviously, he wasn't. But he most likely would have billed you for hundreds of hours of his time 'arranging' it and 'walking' you guys through make believe due diligence. That's what he did to a firm in Kansas City. The guy's a very sharp con artist, Tom."

"Kansas City?" Tom took another gulp of his drink.

"Yep. He ripped them off for thousands of dollars and they're getting ready to sue now that they know where he's living. But, apparently, Uncle Diego's contacts suggested they wait until Diego hears from the other cities where Pat has been operating. That way all the companies Pat has ripped off may want to join forces and file some kind of class-action suit, or something."

"Holy shit!"

"Uncle Diego says what they will probably want to do is get Pat sent to jail and barred forever from dealing in the U.S. securities markets."

"Wow! Alice, this is unbelievable." He stood, walked over to his wife, and kissed her forehead. "I'm damned glad you went ahead and contacted your uncle. Does Diego have any idea how much of our money Pat has stolen.?"

"He says it appears to be about $300,000!"

"God dammit! How is that possible?"

"Uncle Diego says he just enters the withdrawals in your checkbook as payable to some vendor, but pockets the cash. He also said Pat has most likely hidden the stash in the house he is renting, or in the office somewhere. He says the office is the most likely spot, because if you or Steve caught on, Pat could produce the stash quickly and claim he was getting ready to pay those vendors."

"This is incredible!"

"Well, it's a very hard lesson to learn, Tom. But thank goodness we found out before Pat did some real damage to your company."

"I've got to phone Steve, apologize profusely, and then hammer Pat."

"Frankly, Tom, I think you should wait until Uncle Diego gets a report from some additional markets, so you have a preponderance of evidence with which to confront Pat. And when you do, you might want to have representatives of the FBI and Securities & Exchange Commission in your office with you."

"Is that you talking . . . ."

"Nope. It's Uncle Diego, and I think he's right on. Call Steve to put him on guard, but hold off on confronting Pat. That's Uncle Diego's advice."

"Okay, that sounds reasonable." Tom took another long swig from his drink, draining the glass, then handed it to Alice for a refill. He picked up the phone and dialed Steve's home number.

"Hi, Steve. It's Tom."

"Hi, Tom. What's up?"

"Are you sitting down?"

"Nope! Should I be?"

Yeah! We're going to have a long conversation, and it's likely to wobble your knees!"

There was a few seconds of silence.

"God! Am I being fired?"

"No way, my friend. After what I'm about to tell you, you are going to be promoted! I'm serious."

There was another few seconds of silence, just breathing heard in Tom's earpiece.

"Holy smokes, Tom! Okay, I'm sitting. Let 'er rip!"

Their conversation lasted more than a half hour, and when they finally hung up, Steve turned from his phone and yelled.

"ROBIN!" He hurried toward the kitchen where his wife was preparing dinner. She met him in the doorway and he threw his arms around her, lifting her off the floor.

"Wait until you hear this!"

+ + +

Pat was excited about his Cleveland idea, decided to phone Danny O'Connell at home Wednesday evening to get him thinking. Would not reveal any details of his plan, just drop enough hints to vibrate the guy's thighs and ask for a last-minute check on the closing price of Fabricated's stock.

"Danny, this is Pat." No need for last names, they spoke by phone every day. "How are we doing?"

"The stock closed today at $16.50, Pat. It's on a roll, although I'm sure some of the movement is caused by the fact that the Big Board is pulling everything up as the Dow continues to climb."

"That's really good news, Danny. And I may have a blockbuster announcement for you tomorrow or Friday." *("Can't hurt to whet the guy's appetite; get him thinking about how he'll merchandise the information I send his way next week.")* "I can't share anything with you now, gotta make some calls, but I'm pretty sure I'll have some great news for you."

"Gimme a hint, will you, Pat, so I can mull over my approach to the brokers."

"Sorry, Danny, I can't do that."

"Well, I'll tell you what, Pat." Danny's voice toughening. "Since you guys haven't paid me yet . . . you're into me for several thousand. I'm not going to do a damned thing for you unless, one, I get a check in the mail ASAP, and two, you drop me a hint about the news you think may break."

"Aw, come on, Danny. Don't screw me this late in the game, I'm gonna need your help . . . ."

"I'm not screwing you, Pat, you've been screwing me for several weeks and I'm not going to take it any more. Pay me! Write a me a check as soon as we hang up, and Fed-X it to me for delivery over-night. No checky, no worky . . . you got that? And you also owe me shares of stock. I want that, too, and it want it NOW!"

"Yeah, Danny, I hear you, but I thought we had a better relationship than swapping threats."

"I don't make threats, Pat. I make promises." He was very angry. "And if I don't see some greenbacks from you in the next twenty-four hours, we're done. You've strung me along for several weeks. Our deal was a weekly payment. You're not living up to your end of our agreement, so why the hell should I? Pay me, and give me the shares you owe me, and if your announcement is truly a blockbuster, I'll help make us both richer."

"Okay, Danny. I'll write a check right now and drop it at the local Fed-X office on my way home."

"Don't play games with me, Pat. I'm not in the mood. And don't forget my shares. Fabricated owes me $24,000. Pay me in full or I go to Mulholland on Monday morning. I'm not kidding!"

"I promise you will have your $24,000 by Friday. And I'll work on the shares."

"WORK, on them. You better do better than that!"

"Okay! Okay!."

"Have a good weekend, Pat. Don't call me again if I don't see green by Friday." Danny hung up.

("God dammit! I hafta pay that SOB, which will put a major dent in the company's checking account. I was hoping to squirrel some of that away with what I've already pocketed, but I can't afford to have Danny calling Tom. This entire epic is falling apart on me.)

("I've got to make my idea with Cleveland float; otherwise I'm spinning my wheels and I'm going to come outta this with lint in my pockets until, or if, the stock pays off. I need money for Rome! Lot's of it.")

He was first in the office Thursday morning, much earlier than the traditional 8:30 opening. He took the stairs to the second floor two-at-a-time, snapped on the overhead lights in the reception room and general office area, settled behind his desk.

He was hoping this would be an exciting day.

He planned to phone that company in Cleveland and make his pitch, probably arrange to meet their CEO or a designate in New York, also tip off Danny to begin contacting brokers if everything went as Pat had planned. He was confident it would.

The Cleveland company was Aeronautics Supplies, Inc. The firm's website said it was eighteen months old, specialized in the supply of parts, components and accessories -- radios, GPS, direction finders, altimeters, flight attitude gauges, fuel gauges, cabin seats, tables, a host of other aircraft-related items -- for privately owned aircraft. ASI shipped nationally, although most of their customers seemed to be based at regional airports throughout the midwest, some west coast.

Pat had sketched the pros and cons of several proposals he might make to the CEO or CFO, whomever he could get on the horn. In his mind, ASI seemed to be perfect fit with the larger, more profitable and experienced Fabricated Structures, which sold to larger regional airlines, hoping to break into the national carriers.

Without knowing much about the aircraft business, Pat was certain he could structure a deal between the two firms that would benefit both. The trick would be to convince ASI to form a partnership with Fabricated, or even merge with the company, but the terms of the agreement, however it was structured, could not involve any large cash payout by Fabricated. Pat wanted that firm's bank account to be flush because he had signature rights; if

Fabricated had to shell out a lot of money, he might find himself with signature rights to a bank account with next to nothing in it.

If he could structure the deal "properly", Tom and Steve would look very favorably on the idea, and on Pat for thinking of it and making a successful approach to ASI. The deal would open new markets for both companies, increase their sales, and with Danny's help it would give a serious kick to Fabricated's stock price, a win-win for everybody.

("The stock! That's the answer. Fabricated buys ASI with stock only, no cash; in fact, ASI buys *the stock at a steeply discounted price. Why would they do that? To latch onto Fabricated's more sophisticated sales force, which has contacts with the regionals and nationals. This can work if I can convince the ASI people that {A} their sales will increase, and {B} so will the stock price, so they will quickly recap their investment! Fantastic!")*

Pat was very pleased with himself, rewrote his notes in a logical phone presentation format, a simple synopsis of the deal. He would present the broad outline of his plan, suggest he and the ASI officials meet in New York next week to discuss details, dot the i's and cross the t's, before lawyers got involved in drafting the actual agreement.

He also decided not to tell Tom nor Steve what he was up to, would let the success be a pleasant surprise; or his failure, should it come to that, as an undiscovered secret. He was convinced he had nothing to lose, a lot to gain.

Pat felt his first priority was to conceal more thoroughly the $300,000 he had so far squirreled from Fabricated's bank account under the pretext of paying vendors in cash. The money was wrapped in bundles of five grand each and locked in his desk drawer.

Pat re-wrapped the bundles in another layer of brown supermarket bags, stuffed them into a gym bag under a spare shirt and change of underwear. He placed a folder full of vendor invoices he supposedly had paid with cash in the bottom of the drawer, crammed the gym bag and clothes on top, closed and locked the drawer.

He'd retrieve the bag just hours before his flight to Rome, which he anticipated taking in perhaps a week if this Cleveland idea fell through. If that happened, he'd have only one more week before he put Newport and Fabricated in his rearview mirror.

The office bustle commenced at 9:00, professional staff and secretaries settling into their offices or behind desks, someone making a pot of coffee, people greeting each other, how was your weekend, what's on your docket, that kind of stuff. Steve waved to Pat as he walked into his own office, Tom did the same. Pat felt comfortable; no one questioning anything, moving onto whatever required their attention.

He sipped a cup of office coffee, lifted his phone and dialed Cleveland, asked the Aeronautics Supplies switchboard for the office of the company president. His secretary said he was out of town, could the chief financial officer be of help. He was second in command at the firm.

"Good morning. This Brad Lewis. How may I help you?"

"Brad, my name is Pat Clauson. Please call me Pat."

"Fine, Pat. What's on your mind?"

"Brad, I'm affiliated with a publicly traded company in Newport, Rhode Island. Name of the firm is Fabricated Structures, and our primary business is selling a proprietary product we have developed which we provide in quantity to the private aircraft industry. And, we're also beginning to nurse the regional and major airlines, with some very positive feedback."

"Interesting, Pat. What's your product?"

"We've developed a process for laminating micro-thin layers of carbon fibre in such a way that the molecular structure of each layer is at right angles to the layer above and below. This results in an extremely strong, but lightweight panel -- stronger and lighter than aluminum -- which aircraft manufacturers use for wing, rudder and stabilizer construction."

"Wow! That sounds terrific. How long have you folks been in business?"

"Just about three years, Brad. Our annual sales volume is pushing three million. We went public a couple of months ago and our stock is up more than five-hundred percent since our IPO."

"Congratulations, Pat. We are still privately held; don't feel we are ready to go public, but that day will come, I'm sure."

"That's why I'm calling, Brad." Pat could taste success!

"What do you mean?"

"Well, it occurred to me that it might benefit us both if you folks were to merge with us. We have a solid account base dealing with national aircraft manufacturers who need the kind of equipment you fellas sell, at least I have that impression from your advertising in the trades, and your website. We have a skilled national sales force, and a terrific reputation in the field. The marriage of our two companies seems like a win-win."

"Gosh, Pat, I dunno. We've had no discussions at all about merging with anyone. Bill Enright, our president, is out of the office today, so I can't even run this by him. But even if he were interested, it would take some considerable dialog between your people and us to explore all the in's and out's of the deal."

"I agree, Brad. I'm going to be in New York next week and thought, if you're interested, we could meet over lunch or dinner, and hash through the idea."

"Offhand, Pat, what kind of structure are you thinking of?"

"My thought is that we offer you folks a substantial holding in our company at a dramatically discounted stock price. This would give you access to our customer base, even the use of our field sales organization if that would help you grow.

"Your management, your company name, all of that would remain in place. This would simply be the first step to make certain we both feel the marriage is working as we hope it will.

"Then, when the time is right, Aeronautics Supplies would become a division of Fabricated Structures, or a wholly-owned subsidiary. Your stock would have increased considerably over the discounted price we offer you, so you and Bill and your other management people would pocket a sizable profit personally, and all of us would gain from what I believe could be a dramatic increase in revenues and profits."

Pat was on a roll, smiling to himself, darned near pumping a fist at the "quality" of his pitch. What he didn't say is the stock sale to Aeronautics, even at a discounted price, would fatten Fabricated's financial resources, especially its bank account! Ahh, Yes! That bank account!

"Well, I'll tell you, Pat, I am not in a position to make a decision, or even a recommendation, at this point. Let me talk with Bill when he is back in the office later this week. A meeting here, or in New York, or even Newport will be a must; perhaps New York, at first, and if things pan out we should see your operation in Rhode Island and you folks should see ours here."

"I agree completely, Brad. I'm glad I have piqued your interest, and look forward to hearing from you and Bill next week."

"Thanks for thinking of us, Pat. We'll get back to you."

Pat hung up, leaped out of his chair, excitedly paced his office. This was going real easy, tough work ahead, but if he could pull it off, he'd delay Rome until the deal was done and executed. He'd demand a very large cash fee from Tom for thinking of the idea and getting it launched, then hit the road for several months of R & R in Italy, keeping his 50,000 shares of stock and the $300,000 hidden in his desk, perhaps more by the time he skipped town.

11

FRIDAY

It was the next day when the phone in the Mulholland home rang, and again it was Uncle Diego.

"Good morning, Alice."

"Oh, hi! I was thinking of you. How are you?" She was not about to admit that she knew Diego's son was dating Tom's administrative assistant.

"I think I'm a lot better than you and Tom."

"Oh brother! What does that mean?"

"Well, we've heard from Pat's former 'clients' in Atlanta, St. Louis and Chicago. I think the only one we're missing is Oakland, California, and that firm seems to have gone bankrupt and disappeared. None of the news is good, Alice."

"I guess I'm not surprised."

"The guy seems to pull the same caper each time he gets retained by a company. He says he'll negotiate a sweet commercial loan from some UK bankers, but he has no connections we can find in the UK.

His goal is to run up huge consulting fees without ever delivering on the loan."

"Yes, he tried that with Tom's company, but Tom's treasurer, Steve, put the brakes on that idea."

"Smart move." Diego paused for breath. "At the same time, he offers to handle some projects for the company, and even provides them with some funding which he says he'll use to pay bills. But he never pays them. Instead, as I told you a few days ago, he drains as much cash as possible from the company's bank account, which is relatively easy to do because he demands signature rights on their accounts."

"Yes, I'm aware of that. Tom is very concerned about how much Pat has stolen from Fabricated's bank account, and has his treasurer, Steve, checking that out. It's several thousand dollars, I mean many thousands of dollars. For the life of me, I cannot understand why Tom agreed to give him signature rights to the company's bank accounts."

"Apparently, Clauson makes a very compelling case for doing that, Alice. He's promises the target company a lot of money from his so-called investors, and claims he needs signature rights to protect their investments. But there are no investors, as far as we can tell."

"This is getting really ugly, Uncle Diego."

"I'm not through, Alice."

"Oh, god!"

"He also helps the target company go public on the penny stock market, and grabs a very sizable chunk of the stock as part of his consulting fee. There would be nothing wrong with that, except he illegally hypes the stock to increase sales and run the price up."

"How does he do that?"

"Apparently, he issues a bunch of unauthorized press releases in the name of the company, making all sorts of untrue claims about the success of their business. He does it in such a way that the principals aren't aware of what's happening until he disappears with his stock, leaving management to negotiate their innocence with the SEC.

"In Tom's case, the guy also hired an institutional investor-type to call on brokers who handle penny stocks, compounding the problem by feeding that fella bull-shit which he unwittingly has passed on to the brokers, further hyping the stock price."

"Oh! My god!!"

"That, my dear niece, has the potential to result in legal fees, depositions, court appearances . . . a nightmare Tom, you and others at Fabricated should never have to endure. Besides, Alice, the penny market has a reputation for being a haven for con artists, like this guy Clauson. And, I'm not sure he's actually paid the guy calling on brokers. My colleagues have talked to the guy and he's pissed, claims, Fabricated owes him $24,000 and a boatload of unrestricted stock."

"You're just full of good news!"

"I'm sorry, Alice, I truly am. But you and Tom need to know the hand you've been dealt so you can begin to take remedial action. This guy Clauson is a real slick bible salesman, if you catch my drift. Apparently, he's been walking away from each company he's hit with several hundred thousand dollars: thousands in cash, plus his consulting fee, plus his profits from the immediate sale of stock.

"How does he sell it if it's restricted?"

"He probably sends it to a contact in Canada, because stock restrictions don't apply there. They can sell whenever they want."

"Dammit, Diego!"

"And I'm willing to bet he doesn't declare all of that income on his taxes! If nothing else, the Feds could nail him on tax fraud, but my guess is their case will be a lot broader than that, and most certainly would involve you people in depositions and the need to produce proof that you didn't know what this smooth talking bastard was up to."

"That S.O.B."

"If you folks ever feel you'd like me to step in and shake the tree, just give me a call."

"Well, I'll tell Tom all that you've told me, and I'm sure he'll begin to take some action right away. I don't know what that means, really, but I'm sure Tom is not going to put up with this any longer."

"Okay, dear. Just let me know if I can help."

They both rang off. Alice burst into tears. She was very upset, very angry, and scared to death of the potential legal and financial ramifications she and Tom might face because of "that bastard, Pat."

She picked up the phone and dialed Colette at the office.

"Colette, this is Alice. Can you talk?"

"Yes, sure, Alice. But you sound upset! Is everything okay?"

"No! it's not okay." Alice worked to control herself, then unloaded on Colette, telling her everything Diego had said to Alice, with great emphasis on possible legal action against them by the FBI, SEC or other government agencies.

"Ohmygod, Alice. What do we do?"

"We're going to gang up on Tom, me at home, and you in the office. *WE*, you and I, have got to get him to move on that bastard Pat Clauson. I mean *pronto!*"

"Did you ask Tom to turn Mr. Valenti loose?"

"No! Tom isn't home yet. And when he gets home, I'll be reluctant to tell him to turn Diego loose because I don't know what the hell that means. Do you?"

"No! Not really. I assume it means he'll try to recover the cash Pat has stolen, and then frighten the shit out of him to make him leave town."

"Well, why don't you speak to Diego, and tell him to send Pat back to the fleas in that goddam Australian sheep ranch he's always talking about!"

"I want to talk to Tom first, Alice. I don't dare make a move like that without Tom's okay."

"Okay, Colette. And I'll speak to Tom when he gets home, you can count on it!"

After a few more encouraging minutes, they rung off.

+ + +

Tom was humming as he walked through his front door, caught short by a woman bent on destruction. Alice was so upset she was difficult to understand, yelled, ranted, cried, waved her arms, pointed fingers. Tom tried to calm her down, was hoping to understand the specifics of what she was saying, grasped only that her tirade involved Pat, himself, lawyers, financial security, and "what the fuck were you thinking!"

He finally slid past her, dropped his briefcase in the vestibule and moved through the living room to the bar in their dining room. He poured two stiff drinks, returned to the living room and handed one to Alice, who was scrunched in a chair, crying, holding her head with one hand.

"Okay, Honey. Slow down and tell me what's been happening here today." Alice looked up, her face red and contorted in anger, tears still running down her cheeks.

"I'll tell you what's been happening! Uncle Diego called with a much more detailed report on the activities of that bastard Pat Clauson." She paused to catch her breath. "He's going to ruin us, Tom! Do you understand that? He's going to ruin us!"

"Slow down, please, Alice. Never mind the editorializing, just tell me what Diego had to say, okay."

Alice took a few moments to compose herself, then launched into a detailed discussion of everything she had learned from her uncle. She didn't leave out anything, placed great emphasis on how Pat had ripped off a lot of other companies doing exactly what he was doing to Fabricated Structures. Each time he walked away with hundreds of thousands of dollars, leaving behind a minefield of unpaid vendor bills and depleted corporate bank accounts.

"That's just the easy part, Tom."

"Easy!! Christ!"

"It's the legal ramifications that will curdle your pee." Alice used a cocktail napkin to wipe the tears from her face and blow her nose.

"What legal ramifications?"

"Do you know why the price of that damned penny stock is increasing so rapidly? No, you don't, so I'll tell you." She was warming to the subject, getting angrier by the second.

"Pat has most likely been issuing a series of press releases under your company's name. Releases which claim all kinds of stuff about how fast the company is growing, new business, big sales, and so on. And he feeds those lies to the guy in New York who calls on the brokers. Diego doesn't think that fella knows the releases are lies; he's just an innocent fall guy who is illegally hyping your firm's stock!

"Are you beginning to get the picture?"

"Yes! I am."

"Well, let me complete the image for you. Diego says every-thing Pat is doing is fifty shades of illegal, which will most likely lead to an SEC investigation, shareholder and government lawsuits against you, and me, and Steve, and lord knows who else. Lawsuits, Tom! Expensive and devastating lawsuits!"

"I had no idea . . . ."

"And the kicker: Diego doesn't think the New York fella has been paid yet. He's claiming you guys owe him almost $24,000 plus a ton of stock shares."

Tom slapped his forehead, settled into a chair across from Alice.

"No wonder you're upset, Alice. I am, too, and Steve will shit a brick."

"What in God's name were you guys thinking when you retained that bastard before checking out his line of palaver?"

"You've met him, Alice. He comes across as a very talented, well-connected, savvy international businessman. Sophisticated, charming, well spoken, you know what I mean."

"It's *all* make believe, Tom. The guy's a zero, a con artist, a crook, a fraud. And you guys bought into his crap, hook, line and sinker. And now, we're in a hell of a mess, and so is your company!"

"Okay, we'll take some action right away to cut our losses and get rid of that bastard once and for all."

"Well, you better act quickly, Tom. Lord knows what that guy will be up to come Monday."

"I agree." He set down his drink, stood and gave Alice a hug.

"I'm very sorry, Alice. I obviously didn't deliberately permit any of this to happen, and I'll find a way out, I promise. I'll begin by calling our corporate and personal attorneys."

"Before you do, Tom, call Uncle Diego and hear him out. He may have some ideas about what to do to salvage your business, your reputation and that of Steve, and our financial security."

"He's a rubbish collector, Alice!"

"He has more and better contacts than you do! Look what he's learned in a matter of days that you didn't know over a period of months! Just talk to the guy, Tom! What have you got to lose?"

Tom turned, headed for the bar and made them both another round.

"And, I have more news that will rock your socks!"

"Now what?"

"Colette and I have been talking . . . Talking a lot!"

"Dammit, Alice! Talking about what?"

"About how to convince you that Pat is a scumbag, so we can get you to wake up and take some action against him."

"Jesus, Alice, will you stop meddling in my company affairs. I have enough trouble managing that place without you interfering, and confiding with Colette!"

"Then do something about that crook. And be warned, on Monday you'll probably get an earful from Colette, and Steve, as well."

"That's just what I need, a terrific way to begin my week. Thank you so much!"

"You're welcome. Now go make us another drink, we both need it!"

He did, and they sat calmly, at last, talking about their future, their hopes and dreams, their children. They moved to the couch, hugged, kissed, held onto each other tightly, vowed they would get out of this mess with as little impact as possible.

+ + +

Earlier that same Friday afternoon, about 4:30, Pat had decided to call it a week, began making plans for his weekend. It hadn't been a good week. He remained concerned about Alice Mullholland's inquiries at last Saturday's dinner party. Colette's comments also bothered him, Tom and Steve had been "cold" all week. In total: not a comfortable omen.

But, the weekend loomed. He relished company to help him relax, break the monotony of developing the potential wealth strategy he had put into motion with his call to Cleveland. It was a risky plan for a host of reasons, but if it worked he could most likely rekindle Tom's comfort level (maybe Steve's, too), probably shelve concerns about the outlook for his own financial take!

Candi was clearly off limits. She was still upset that he had not delivered a rent check as promised. He had sent her roses with a warm note, hoping they would placate her feelings and forestall any move to make noise and get him in hot water. She had returned the thorny rose stems, stripped of the beautiful flowers, with a note suggesting he "stick these where the sun don't shine."

Colette also was out of reach. She had rebuffed his advances at least three, maybe four, times. He got the message loud and clear that she had no interest in wrapping her gorgeous legs around his hips. Very disappointing, but there are other fish in the ocean.

Ione was a terrific fish, so he placed a call to the number she had given him.

"Hello!"

"Good afternoon, Ione. This is Pat Clauson, the player from Australia."

"Patrick! So nice to hear from you. How are you?"

"I'm doing well, but I miss you. What are you up to tonight, or even the weekend? Can we have dinner? Go sailing? Dip in my pool?"

"Ahhhh, Patrick, you are an operator and an opportunist, as Colette has told me!"

('Uh-oh! What does that mean?")

"Really! What did she say, exactly?"

"Patrick, we ladies must retain some secrets. She was very complimentary, said you are very nice, handsome, courteous, with a sly streak I should be aware of."

"No kidding! Have I been 'sly' with you?"

"No, not really. But a Friday afternoon phone call to see if I can join you this evening . . . a girl has to assume food is not foremost on your mind."

"Well, that's only partially true, Ione. I would very much like to have dinner with you, because I enjoy your company, your conversation. And, should you agree to find my home comfortable enough to spend the night, or even part or all of the weekend, well I certainly would not object. If that's being sly, then Yes! I'm sly!"

"Patrick, I hope I have not hurt you with my frankness. That is not my intention."

"No, I'm not hurt at all. Let me start over; can you join me for dinner this evening, despite my late invitation?"

"I regret, Patrick, that I cannot join you this evening. I have another social commitment. I have just returned from a week in New York. I'm very tired, intend to have a quick bite with a friend, and retire for the evening. However, I will gladly join you for part of the weekend, if that invitation is still extended."

"By all means, Ione. I am sorry about tonight, but hope to see you tomorrow for as long as you wish to stay."

"Thank you, Patrick. Why don't I plan to see you at your home about two o'clock. Perhaps we can go for a swim, and have dinner."

"That sounds wonderful, Ione. Do you like lobster, or steamers, corn?"

"Yes! That sounds marvelous. New England lobster is my favorite, and the beauty of steamed clams is they do not taste like like sperm!" She burst out laughing, as did Pat.

"Okay, Ione. I'm sure Nora will prepare a fabulous meal for us that will excite your palette even more than oysters. The rest will be up to me, I guess!"

Pat rolled out of bed about 8:30 Saturday morning, shaved, showered, slipped into his bathing suit, grabbed a pencil and notepad, asked Nora to prepare a full breakfast and serve it on the patio. He settled into a seat at one of the round tables ready to work all morning, scoping notes for a possible mind-blowing week when he would reveal his acquisition or merger proposal to Tom and Steve, assuming Cleveland bit.

After breakfast, he gave Nora cash and instructions to buy lobsters, steamers, corn, two bottles of Far Niente Chardonnay and a bottle of Sir Winston Churchill champagne. He collapsed on one of the chaise lounges with the morning newspaper, read for awhile, his eyes began to close, the newspaper slipped out of his hands, Pat dozed.

He awoke with a start in response to a light tap on his shoulder: Nora holding a glass of ice water. He thanked Nora profusely, set the drink on the small table next to his chaise and jumped into the pool. The water was refreshing, washed the sleep from his eyes, and he swam and splashed around for half an hour, then returned to his chaise to await Ione's arrival.

A horn blew in the driveway, Mini Cooper, he could tell by the sound. He rose from the chaise. Nora had already opened the front door, Ione stepped out of the living-room in dark blue Bermuda shorts and yellow blouse, sunglass, large rimmed straw hat, flip-flops.

"Good afternoon, Patrick. How are you?"

"Hi, Ione." He gave her a hug, pecked her on both cheeks. "It's really good to see you. I'm glad you can spare me the time."

"Don't be silly, Patrick. The pleasure is mine."

She dropped the beach bag she was carrying beside one of the chaise lounges, sat herself facing Pat who was again stretched out on the other chaise.

"The pool is wonderful, Ione. Are you going to swim?"

"No, not yet. If it is alright with you I would like to lie in the sun for a while, and swim a little later to cool off."

"Sounds good. You can change in the bathroom downstairs or go up to the master bath. You know the way."

"Yes, but there is no need, Patrick."

She stood and began to undress: blouse, bra, shorts, panties, stark naked she sprawled face down on the chaise lounge next to Pat, who was goggle-eyed! Ione was clearly not the least concerned or embarrassed.

"Patrick, there is some suntan lotion in my bag. Would you mind putting some on my back and legs?"

"Lord, No! How about your butt?" He began laughing.

"Yes, that would be nice, also." She looked at him and smiled. "Just behave."

"Behave? If I behave like the horn-toad I am, you won't get much tan. So I'll try to control myself, but even that won't be easy!"

"Now, now! You must behave, or control, or whatever else calms a horn-toad!" She laughed. "Will you join me in tanning?"

"Ione, if I take this bathing suit off, I can guarantee you my blood will rush out of my head and I'll pass out." They both laughed heartily. "You can imagine where my blood will be going."

"Yes, I believe so."

"Let me find that suntan lotion and if I can stop thinking when I rub it on you, you'll be safe!" He laughed, she giggled!

Pat applied the suntan lotion to her body liberally, slowly. He managed to complete the application without embarrassing himself, although when finished he jumped into the pool to calm himself and cool down. He was hoping that, at some point, she would roll over and ask him to do her front; *that* would present an extreme challenge, one he almost certainly would fail. (*"Man, what a tease! I'm going crazy! And she knows it!"*)

Pat lay back on his chaise lounge, sunglasses on so he could gaze at Ione's body without being too obvious. She lay very quiet, rhythmic breathing, almost asleep. He was concerned she might fry, although her dark complexion could obviously handle the sun, and this clearly was not her first exposure of the season.

Pat was in and out of the pool several times during the afternoon to maintain his control. Ione remained inert on the chaise lounge. She finally rose after baking for almost two hours, never did ask Pat to apply suntan lotion to her front -- not that she couldn't have done that herself, but he was hoping -- slipped into the pool, swam and splashed around for several minutes.

She retrieved a towel from her beach bag, stood naked on the patio to dry off. Pat watched her enticing body, struggled to avoid standing next to her or grabbing her for a long kiss.

"Patrick, I wish to take a shower upstairs. What is our dress for dinner this evening? Anything special?"

"Not at all, Ione. Just the blouse and shorts you were wearing earlier. I'll be dressed the same way, plan to change also. I've been in this bathing suit almost all day."

"Well, I will put on something more appropriate." Ione slipped on her shorts, sans panties, to walk through the house and up the stairs to the master bedroom and baths.

Pat watched her all the way, strolled over to the dining room bar, poured himself a stiff Chivas on the rocks, and made his way upstairs to the master bedroom. The door to one of the two bathrooms was closed, Ione inside humming.

+ + +

She was standing beside the pool, gazing at the ocean, a cold drink in her right hand, when Pat came out the living room sliding door.

She turned to face him, a smile on her face. He stopped short, caught his breath. She was positively beautiful, sheathed in a flowered green sundress, a matching ribbon across her forehead and tied behind her head in a bow, the long ribbon ends trailing down her glistening black hair. As she walked toward him, Pat could tell she was not wearing a bra. They hugged, kissed quickly.

"Man alive, Ione, you look marvelous!"

"Why, thank you, Patrick. I wanted to look special for you this evening to celebrate our lobsters and clams, no oysters!"

"Hopefully, that's not all we'll celebrate." They both laughed.

"Now, now! Control and good behavior. Those are the key words for you to remember!"

"I've already forgotten them, and I'm going to slide over there and make myself a drink so I continue to forget them."

They each enjoyed a cocktail, then switched to the Sir Winston Churchill champagne. Nora served their dinner on the patio while it was still daylight: steamed clams, broiled lobsters, corn on the cob, salad, washed down with a bottle of the Far Niente Chardonnay, a delayed dessert of fresh fruit and chocolate macaroons.

They lingered at the table conversing for quite some time. Pat opened the second bottle of Chardonnay and they toasted "the spectacular sunset", sat admiring the stars.

"Tell me something, Patrick. How did you graduate from a sheep farm in the Australian outback to a career in international finance?"

"Well, first of all, it was a sheep *ranch* and it was not in the outback. It was fairly close to Sydney. And second, I am not an international financier, just a financial consultant with experience taking companies public, issuing stock, trading on the stock exchanges, that sort of thing."

"Oh, I see. But you do not work alone, correct? Colette says you have a staff in California."

("Oh my God! Tread easy! This conversation is heading in the wrong direction.")

"Yes, Ione," he lied. "I have people there who provide support; some are not my employees, just interested investors who help me provide funding to my client firms." Another lie.

"Really? What do they get out of it?"

"I give them a percentage return based on what I earn from working with a company." *("Lie!")*

"Like Fabricated, Colette's company?"

"Yes, that's right." *("Jesus, I'm digging myself a hole. Gotta stop this.")*

"She said you convinced her bosses to issue a lot of stock for public trading, and also that they shelled out some to key employees as well as you."

"That's correct, Ione. My shares, and those of the Fabricated management people, are restricted so they cannot be sold for several months. That prevents people, including me, from immediately selling their shares. It's a benefit, really, because the hope is the share price increases, so several months from now the shares will be worth a lot more than the day they were issued to us."

"And the price has been climbing," she said.

"Yes, quite nicely. It's an interesting company."

"But it may be months before you can pay your investors?"

"Yes, but they understand that." *("Lie.")*

"One thing really baffles me, Patrick." She sipped her wine; no thumb and finger slide on the stem of the wine glass.

"What's that?" *("Be on guard! This could be really tough.")*

"She said that, before you agreed to help the company, you insisted on being given signature rights to their bank accounts. That strikes me as really ballsy, and I'm amazed they agreed to it. I would not have."

"Well, you're in a different situation than Colette's company. I need that security to protect my investors and the money we sink into Fabricated. They need new manufacturing equipment, a larger plant to put it in, and an upgraded office complex, which I have already arranged for them."

Ione sipped her wine, sat back smiling.

"Yeah, but in my book that still doesn't warrant putting your name on their bank accounts. Do you actually write checks?"

"Yes, I do. I pay vendors for work I have been authorized by management to commission." *("Lie.")* "I was forced by my investors to demand signature rights." *("Lie.")*

She still held a frozen smile, head tilted, a question in her eyes.

"But how does Colette's superiors control the checks you write? I'm not suggesting you are dishonest, Patrick, but my God, you are in an amazing position to drain cash, if you were so inclined."

She continued smiling, not really a comfortable smile, almost sarcastic, as if she didn't believe him. Pat was getting nervous, didn't like the direction of her comments or questions.

"Well, obviously, I have to walk a very delicate line, Ione. They trust me, and I like them and their company. If I were to rip them off, my reputation would collapse. I'd never get any other business. I just cannot afford to be negligent in the execution of my responsibilities. *(Lie.)*

"I guess I understand, Patrick. And I wish you success." She glanced at her watch: 9:15. Looked at Patrick, raised her wine glass. "A toast to a lovely and interesting evening, Patrick. I regret I must make it end."

"You're leaving?" He was visibly upset.

"Yes, my dear, I am afraid I must go home and pack. I have an early flight tomorrow morning to Antigua to visit my mother and some friends."

"Oh, hell! I was very much looking forward to spending the night with you."

"Control, Patrick. Remember control!" She laughed.

"I really don't want control. I want you." He was not laughing.

"Next time, Patrick. I will be in Antigua for two weeks, but we should plan to get together upon my return. I will phone you, I promise." She looped her arms around his neck and they kissed, quick but moist.

"Do not walk me out, Patrick. I know the way, and you should stay here and admire the stars." She turned, picked up her beach bag, entered the living-room and was gone.

Patrick slumped back into his chair, disappointed, angry, concerned that Ione had asked so many questions about his business activities at Fabricated. *("What was her take-away? Did she buy all that I told her? Probably not. I better be damned careful.")*

+ + +

Ione slid behind the wheel of her Mini Cooper, drove slowly out the circular driveway, in less than ten minutes was parked in front of her waterfront condo. Once inside, she dropped her beach bag, picked up her phone, dialed a number from memory.

"Colette, this is Ione."

"Hi, how'd you make out?"

"We didn't 'make out' in the usual sense, but we did have a long conversation about his business and what he is doing for your firm."

"And . . . ."

"I wouldn't trust him as far as I can throw him. He's a real smooth talker, as you know, but there is nothing between his ears accept greed. I frankly don't believe he has any 'colleagues' in California because no intelligent investor is going to wait months for Patrick to sell stock before the guy gets a return on his money. That's just bullshit!"

"Yeah, I agree."

"We never talked about British bankers or Hong Kong lawyers, but if he's lying about a California staff and so-called investors, you can bet the rest of his song is also nonsense."

"Gotcha!"

Ione was on a roll.

"Also, this whole thing about getting signature rights to your firm's bank accounts. What was your boss thinking? That's just asking for trouble, Darling, and I'll bet you're going to get it. I don't have any proof, mind you, but it doesn't take a genius to figure out that Patrick knows what he's doing even if your bosses don't!"

"Well Steve, our treasurer, keeps an eye on the check register."

"Big deal, Sweetheart. If it was me, I'd write checks to cash, tell you people that's how the vendors wish to be paid, and pocket the money. Sweet, clean, and very doable."

"Yes, I understand that, Ione. Did he admit to that?"

"Of course not! But that's what I would do if I was so inclined. And I think Patrick is inclined. Tell your treasurer to check and see if vendors are really being paid. I'll lay you two-to-one they aren't!"

"I won't be surprised, but my CEO will be!" Colette was not shocked at Ione's assessment of Pat, but surprised at the audacity of the guy if he was really plundering the firm's bank account. Tom and Steve will have a fit!

"And, to your point, Colette. I got whatever information I did because I stripped and sunbathed naked in front of him." They both laughed. "He thought I was a sure bet to join him between the sheets so, when I began hitting him with questions, he answered, hoping I was going to stay the night. Poor little Aussie!" They laughed again.

"Ione, I want to let you in on a little secret."

"Oh! Gossip! I can't wait!"

"Not really gossip, but facts. My boss's wife and I have been conspiring to secure information which confirms that Pat is a crook, and we've pretty much got it. Now, all we have to do, I think, is reveal what we know to my boss, and hopefully he will blow the whistle."

"My god, Colette, you gals are brilliant."

"You wanna know what's amazing -- the father of the wonderful guy I'm dating is the nephew of my boss and his wife. She's his niece, and it's her uncle, my boyfriend's dad, who's getting all this information for us. And none of us were aware of the connection."

"Small world, Colette, small world."

"I'll say, and my boyfriend's dad has some amazing contacts."

"Well, I hope for your sake everything works out okay."

"Thank you, Ione, thank you so much for making yourself available this evening. I'm sure it was not a lot of fun, and I'll find a way to make it up to you."

"Don't be silly, Colette. What are friends for?

"Well, you went a lot further with Pat than I ever did."

"You're talking about sex! I am partly French, Colette. We thrive on sex and escargot! Besides, all I let him do was rub suntan lotion on my back and butt, and it drove him crazy!" She was laughing heartily.

"Well, thanks again, Ione." They rang off.

Colette clapped her hands, laughed to herself, couldn't wait to tell Tom and Steve on Monday what she'd heard from Ione. She was fascinated by Ione's take on the corporate bank accounts. Is it even remotely possible Pat was stealing cash from the company? If so, that would be a hell of an eye-opener for Tom, especially.

12

MONDAY

Pat's first move upon reaching the office was to phone Danny-Boy in New York. He wanted to brief him on the Cleveland opportunity, play it cool and calm regarding the reality: just give Danny enough sizzle to get him started talking to brokers, encouraging them to call their accounts about a significant development in Fabricated's business outlook.

Danny appeared to be jumping out of his seat when Pat told him a Cleveland company was considering a sizable investment in Fabricated Structures, a development that was bound to trigger a considerable uptick in Fabricated's stock price.

Danny had received the $24,000 from Pat and was eager to run, but Pat held the reins tight, suggesting that Danny not make any calls until Pat could email him a press release with the specifics. With that document in hand (Pat did not advise him that he would put the release on Fabricated's website, also), Pat would release the reins and Danny was free "to go nuts!"

That is exactly what happened. Pat drafted the release Monday afternoon, issued it only to Danny, who began a barrage of telephone calls about the time the stock markets were closing. Pat then put the release on Fabricated's website, simultaneously issued it to a variety of monthly aircraft industry trade publications so the statement would receive maximum industry exposure. But because of long lead times, those magazines would not be public with the "announcement" for at least another four or five weeks.

He deliberately avoided the national financial publications and wire services, all of whom had short deadlines. He knew they would ultimately hear the news, but it would most likely be a week or longer before Tom, Steve or Aeronautics Supplies got wind of Pat's public disclosure. By then he'd be in New York, hopefully meeting with an executive or two from the Cleveland firm to close the deal and everything would hunky-dory.

The news would hit at the earliest next week, exactly as Pat had intended, thanks to his "ingenuity" and Danny's efficiency and enthusiasm.

But Pat's activity did not remain hidden from Tom, Steve or Aeronautics Supplies anywhere near as long as Pat had expected. And the explosion was catastrophic.

+ + +

Tom had hardly shed his suit jacket and settled behind his desk when he called for Steve and Colette to come into his office, urgently.

Once they were settled in chairs -- Tom had asked Steve to close his office door -- he began a long discourse on everything he had learned through Alice from her uncle. He was not interrupted, Steve and Colette each taking notes.

"How about them apples?" was his closing comment.

"Son of a bitch!" That was Steve.

"Frankly, I'm not surprised." That was Colette. "I assume your wife spoke to you this weekend about my boyfriend's father."

"Yes, Colette, it's fair to say we talked, endlessly!"

"What the hell are you two talking about? What does Colette's boyfriend and his father have to do with any of this?"

"It's a long story, Steve, and I'll let Colette fill you in. In brief, my wife's uncle owns Valenti Waste Hauling, and he has connections all over the country through other waste collection firms, their union, and so on.

"At Alice's request, her uncle made a lot of inquiries and turned up amazing information about the other firms Pat claims to have helped. He actually ripped them off, just like he's trying to do to us. And, it turns out Alice's uncle is the father of Colette's boyfriend. We were unaware of the connection until the two gals, Alice and Colette, decided to have lunch on the QT to share mutual concerns about Pat, and the rest is history, as they say."

"Well, I'm damned interested to hear what they have to say."

"Connect with Colette after this meeting and she'll blow your mind!"

"Okay, and thanks for letting me in on the secret!" Steve was angry and it showed, shifted in his seat before continuing. "Tom, we are definitely short about $300,000 in our bank accounts, but what concerns me the most is our exposure to potential law suits.

"None of us knew what the hell this guy was up to behind our backs, but that's going to be damned hard to prove. It's going to look like were were complicit in a scheme to hype our stock."

"That's the issue we have to focus on first, Steve. We'll worry about the missing cash later. Is Pat here this morning?"

"He was earlier, Tom, behind a closed door. But I saw him leave just as I was coming here to see you."

"Okay, Colette. Thanks. Let me know if he returns."

"You got it. Is today showdown day?" Colette was smiling, so was Steve.

"If there's going to be a shoot-out, Tom, I'd love to be a fly on the wall!"

"I can't say for sure that there will be a shoot-out, but when there is, Steve, you will be an active participant, not just a fly on the wall." Tom was smiling.

"How about me, Tom? Can I watch and cheer from the sidelines?"

"Please, you two. Let's drop that for now. I'll move when our lawyers say I can move, not before." Tom turned serious. "Now, Steve, call that fella in New York and turn him off. You should be speaking on behalf of the company, not some guy we don't even know, and who doesn't really know us.

"Tell him to get us the name and email address of every broker he's talked to, even those others that brokers have spoken to, and draft for me an email which explains what the hell has happened to us. Deny any claims Pat may have made in his releases, and for Christ sake, find us copies so we know what he's been lying about."

"Okay, Tom, I'm on it." He stood to leave.

"Colette, you should be clear of any legal concerns, although you have spent time alone with Pat and that has the possibility of implicating you, as well."

"Oh, that's just dandy!"

"We'll protect you, we'll cover your legal expenses, and any other costs."

"I'm worried about my reputation, Tom." She was boiling. "If word gets out that I'm somehow involved in a stock swindle I may as well kiss my career good-bye."

"You and me both! And Steve. You're not alone in this."

"I'm not even 'in this', to quote you. All I did was go swimming and sailing with the prick, had a couple of dinners -- at your request, I might add -- and now I may be meat for a pool of legal sharks! I'm thrilled, Tom, fucking thrilled!"

"Let's not get hysterical, Colette." Tom rose, moved into the chair next to her, put a hand on her shoulder. "We all need to stay calm and think carefully about how we proceed."

She was near tears.

"Yeah, okay. What do you want me to do?"

"Write down everything that has occurred when you and Pat were together. Where were you? Anyone else there? What did you talk about? When was this? What time of day? Absolutely everything. Don't leave out any facts.

"Also re-construct your conversations with Steve and me after you met with Pat. Same kind of detail. And do *not* give either Steve nor me copies of what you prepare. That way no one can suggest the three of us have rehearsed our answers to questions."

"So you've already been talking with a lawyer."

"Two, actually. My personal attorney and the company's legal counsel. They're telling me the same thing I'm telling you and Steve: remain cool and calm. Our corporate counsel is calling the SEC this morning to alert them to our problem. She is confident we will come out of this okay.

"So, I want you to relax, and behave in the office as if nothing has happened. Apparently, it is in our best interests not to start pulling our hair out until our legal counsel has had a meeting with the SEC folks in New York. That's most likely going to happen tomorrow or Wednesday."

"Okay, Tom. It's just that I have never been involved in anything like this, and I'm as nervous as a pregnant nun!"

"I understand, Colette. So am I . . . well, not as a nun, but nervous. I'm sure Steve is as well, but I remain optimistic that we all will survive this with unblemished reputations."

"What about jail?"

"Stop, Colette! Don't start thinking like that, because it ain't gonna happen. Take my word for it.

"And one last item. Do not sell your Fabricated stock, even after it becomes unrestricted. Just let it sit, let it sit for another year. If you sell, that will be another quill in some lawyer's quiver, claiming you were part of the problem. And you're not!"

"Thank you, Tom. I'll try my best."

"I know you will, Colette. We all will."

+ + +

It was shortly after lunch when Tom's secretary announced that he had two unexpected visitors who insisted on meeting with him. They were shown into his office, two tall, slim, well-dressed executive types in dark navy suits, white shirts and colorful ties. They both flashed gold badges as they approached his desk. Tom stood to greet them.

"How can I help you, gentlemen?"

The taller of the two men spoke.

"Mr. Mulholland, I am agent Russ Thomas of the FBI. And this is my partner, Agent Howard Bowling."

"FBI!" Tom's heart skipped a beat, his stomach knotted.

"Yessir." They sat in chairs facing his desk. "We have reason to believe you have some sort of arrangement with a gentlemen named Patrick Clauson, who apparently is doing some work for your company relative to its listing on the penny stock market."

"Oh, that son-of-a-bitch!" The relief on Tom's face was visible.

"What is your relationship with Mr. Clauson?"

Tom took the better part of fifteen minutes to describe how and where he met Pat, the consulting arrangement he has with Pat's firm, the recent discovery that Clauson was not who he claimed to be, was falsifying information about the company to enhance investor interest in the stock.

"All of this information has come to me in the past few days, gentlemen. I have already spoken with our legal counsel, who is telephoning the SEC today and planning to meet with their people on Wednesday in New York.

"I'm moving as fast as I can to shut this prick down and get him out of our hair. This is the last thing we need. We are a very reputable company, and I do not want our reputation tarnished by a fucking scumbag." Agent Bowling seemed to be writing all of Tom's comments in shorthand.

"I understand your concern, Sir. But things have gone beyond just the reputation of your company. Mr. Clauson is apparently engaged in a massive stock fraud."

"I've just been made aware of that this weekend, and I had a meeting with my Chief Financial Officer this morning to plan our steps to get out from under this jerk's behavior. We are notifying all of the brokers handling our stock today that there is a major problem we were unaware of."

"Well, that's good to hear, Sir." This was Agent Thomas. "Please give us the name and phone number of your legal counsel."

"Sure, no problem. I've also spoken with my personal attorney. Would you like her contact information also?"

"Yes, please, that would be fine. We'll need a copy of your legal agreement with Mr. Clauson?"

"Sure. It's actually just a letter of agreement which I drafted myself. There were no lawyers involved, unfortunately, now that I understand what he's been up to."

Several more minutes of "interrogation" passed, somewhat uncomfortably for Tom. The FBI agents were not about to settle for Tom's plea of complete innocence unless he could produce a paper trail to prove it. But Tom had no copies of the false press releases Pat had been sending to New York.

"Have you seen this one, which landed on your company's web site this morning?" Agent Thomas handed Tom a single sheet of paper. It was a press release, printed on Fabricated's letterhead, which said the company "was in discussion" with a firm in Cleveland, named Aeronautic Supplies, "to merge for the mutual benefit of both firms as they aggressively pursue regional and national airlines with their unique product portfolios." The release went on to describe a meeting of senior executives to be held in New York City "this week to further explore the merger opportunity."

Tom was flabbergasted. Read the release twice, lay it on his desk, and muttered "that fucking bastard."

"I take it you were not aware of this."

"God, No! Give me a minute."

He punched a button on his phone, spoke to Steve.

"Pat has put an announcement on our web site claiming that we're talking with a Cleveland outfit about merging. Please delete it immediately, and then come into my office. Two FBI agents are with me."

Steve entered his office less than two minutes later, shook hands with the two agents, settled in a third chair facing Tom's desk.

"Steve, these fellas are investigating Pat's relationship with us, and the goddamned shit he has been feeding that guy in New York to hype our stock price. I have no idea what he's been telling or send-ing that fella, and I assume you also were not aware that he was sending Danny anything."

"No, I'm not. In fact, Pat doesn't have authority to send Danny anything he doesn't run past me first."

"Well, apparently, he has been fast and loose with the truth to bump the stock price, a tactic he has used with other firms in the past. Call Danny and tell him not to pay any attention to anything Pat says or sends him. And make it clear Danny works for you, not Pat.

"Also, as we discussed this morning, ask Danny for a list of the brokers he has been contacting with Pat's bullshit, and prepare a written denial of whatever the fuck Danny was told to feed them."

"I've already talked to Danny this morning, Tom, following our meeting. He's really upset, as you might imagine, because Pat has tarnished his reputation as an honest institutional financial consultant. I think he's ready to shoot Pat, and I don't think he's alone!"

That last comment raised eyebrows of the two FBI agents, who did not find any humor in a discussion of gun violence.

"Steve's comment was a figure of speech, gentlemen! Not to worry!"

The four exchanged several more minutes of questions and answers, Tom's secretary delivered a stack of papers to the two agents, as they had requested, and they stood, shook hands with Tom and Steve, advising them that this was not the last they would see of hear of the FBI as their investigation proceeded.

Tom slumped into his chair after the agents departed, elbows on his desk, hands cradling his head. Steve sat stunned.

Tom's secretary stuck her head into his office.

"Are you okay, Tom?"

"I hope so! Ask Colette to join us for a minute."

She stood before his desk and Tom briefed her on the FBI's visit, the depth of their questioning, the "announcement" on the firm's website about a "merger" with a Cleveland company none of them had ever heard of.

Colette listened in silence, remained standing, turned without saying anything, and walked out of the office. Steve swore, and he, too, stood and left.

\+ + +

"Well, I can tell you've had a sparkling day." Alice was smiling as she greeted Tom when he stepped through the front door looking a little like he'd been hit by a two-by-four.

"You won't believe it, Alice."

"Yes, I will. I had a phone call from Colette after the FBI left your office."

"Colette called and told you that!"

"Yep. We talk frequently since our lunch together. I consider her a friend."

"God help me!" Tom looked apprehensive. "I hope she'll be smart enough to keep her mouth shut and not blab all over the office that she's your confidante, or your hers."

"Don't worry,Tom. She is nothing if not discreet."

"I sure hope so!" He dropped his briefcase, poured them both a stiff drink.

"So what's the latest news."

"Well, I know Pat was in the office this morning, but I didn't get a chance to speak with him. I suspect he doesn't know the FBI was in to talk to us, but it won't be long before he hears about it, probably from that guy in New York that Pat has been screwing with false information about our company. Steve spoke with that fella this morning, before our visit from the Feds, and the guy is furious because Pat has compromised his reputation as an honest and reliable institutional finance advisor.

"Pat, it turns out, has been screwing a lot of people, not just us. And as your uncle has discovered, this isn't the first time he's pulled this crap."

"It's a tough lesson for everybody."

"I had a long meeting with Steve and Colette this morning, before the FBI showed, so they both are up to speed on what Diego has found out for us. Steve has called the fella in New York to tell him to sit tight until we bring him to Newport to sit down with us and brief us on everything he's been doing. I also told Steve to get his hands on all of the press releases Pat has been issuing so we know what kind of bullshit he has been peddling."

"What a mess, Tom."

"Tell me about it. I'm trying to run a business and instead I'm playing cops and robbers with a scumbag, lawyers and the FBI. I don't have time for this. As soon as the lawyers tell me to pounce, I am damned well going to throttle that bastard."

"Just be careful, Tom. You don't know what that guy might be capable of."

"Yeah, I will." He slumped into a living room chair, leaned his head back, starred at the ceiling, closed his eyes.

13

TUESDAY

Tom hardly had time to shed his jacket and sit behind his desk when he was buzzed by Colette.

"Tom, there's a fella named Brad Lewis on the line from a Cleveland company called Aeronautics Supplies. He's really ripped about something to do with Pat, wants to speak with you."

"Dammit! What now? Okay, I'll pick him up." Tom pressed a button on his phone. "Good morning. This is Tom Mulholland."

"Good morning, Sir. My name is Brad Lewis. I'm the CFO of a company here in Cleveland, Aeronautics Supplies, and we have a real problem with one of your employees."

"Yes, I'm sorry to hear that, Brad. I understand your headache is with a fella named Pat Clauson. He's not an employee, thank god, he's just a consultant we retained a few months ago and, frankly, wish we'd never heard of the bastard."

"That's the guy, Sir. Sounds like you have your hands full."

"That's one way to phrase it. We had the FBI in here yesterday afternoon asking a lot of questions about Pat. He's supposedly a financial consultant, but we've since learned he's a goddamned con artist. So what's he done to you folks?"

"I assume you are aware that he has told Wall Street your firm and ours are discussing a merger. I don't mean to insult you Tom, but frankly we have never heard of you people."

"That goes both ways, Brad. I was shocked beyond belief when the FBI handed me a press release which they had printed off my company's web site yesterday. Christ, I was furious, had it removed immediately, and my CFO has already talked to the fella in New York who was unwittingly forwarding the bastard's lies to the investment community."

"Is that New York fella guy part of the scam, do you think?"

"No, Brad. We don't believe so. He was as shocked as we were, and is contacting all of his accounts immediately. But, as you might imagine, he is in a very awkward position. He got duped, just like we did, and he's struggling to save his reputation."

"Well, he sure as hell wasn't the only one shocked, Tom. My phone's been ringing off the hook, and we're issuing a statement this morning to deny the merger talk."

"We will do the same, Brad. My CFO, Steve Johnson, is drafting that we speak. And our statement will include an apology to you folks for the disruption this mis-information has caused you."

"Thank you, Tom. That would be very helpful."

"Brad, I'm extremely sorry about this. I have already had a discussion with our corporate counsel and she is meeting with the SEC tomorrow. As far as this guy Pat Clauson is concerned, we're looking for him now -- we think he also may be in New York -- and I'm going to fire him. And we are most likely going to join with the other firms he has ripped off and file a class action suit to bar him from having any connection with the stock exchanges in this country."

"Thanks, Tom. I appreciate anything you can do to put a stop to this. We also have our sales people calling all of our customers."

"Brad, thank you for your call. I promise you we are on top of this. Let's stay in touch as we all try to wind this down, just to keep each other in the loop so we're all on top of it."

"That's a very good idea, Tom. I'll touch base with you every morning for the next week or so, and will call immediately if there's an development that catches us short."

"Good move, Brad. Again, my apologies that this even happened."

"Thanks, Tom, Sorry to screw up your day!"

"I'm glad you have."

They both hung up, Tom's neck and face were red with anger. He hit another button on his phone.

"Steve Johnson."

"Steve, Tom. Get in here now, please!" Anger in his voice.

Steve was in Tom's office in less than a minute, a bunch of papers in his hand, slumped into one of the visitor's chairs facing Tom's desk.

"Is Pat back here yet?"

"No! He's not, Tom. I'm looking for him myself, called his house and his cell phone, but he's not answering. Colette says he was going to New York for a meeting with that Danny guy who's calling on stock brokers for us. But I've already told Danny not to listen to him, and Danny's been calling brokers to make them aware of our problem.

"Danny's also sending me a complete broker list so we can issue an email of our own. He sounds like a nice guy, Tom. Really upset that

Pat pulled this shit on him; wants to assure us he had no knowledge of what Pat was doing."

"Thank God. Give him all the assurances he needs that we do not hold him responsible, nor liable, for the lies Pat has been feeding him as our corporate news. Also tell him the FBI was here yesterday asking about Pat, and I have talked with our corporate counsel and my personal attorney. I want Danny to understand we mean business."

"All of that has been done, Tom. Danny and I have had about a dozen phone calls in the past twenty-four hours. He's as ripped as we are because Pat's antics have clobbered his business."

"This is the last straw, Steve. We cannot wait any longer before thumping that bastard Pat's forehead!"

"Well, I've got more bad news for you. See these," holding up his small stack of papers, "I just printed these out. They're recent press releases I found on line about stuff we're supposed to be doing, thinking of doing, or not doing. They're also the work of Pat. He's obviously going overboard to hype our stock to get the price up, but he's walking a damn fine line -- in fact, he's crossed the line!

"Danny's going to call me as soon as Pat arrives in his office or calls him."

"Shit, we've got to shut this guy off! Where the hell does he get off issuing press releases without our knowledge, especially when they aren't true, not even remotely accurate!"

"Tom, as you know, I've been skeptical about Pat from the get-go . . ."

"I know, I know. I accept full responsibility for agreeing to work with him, not listening to you. Even Alice reamed my ass when we got home from that Saturday shindig at Pat's house. And then she had her uncle do all of that homework which confirmed her, and your, suspicion that Pat is a fucking fraud. Even Colette was smarter about that bastard than I've been, but for different reasons."

"He IS a fraud, Tom. There's nothing behind Pat's eyes except his wallet. But don't beat yourself over the head for failing to recognize that. We now know he's pulled his shit on several other companies in the past. I think we'd do the world a favor if we shut the guy down."

"Yeah, I agree."

"There's more, unfortunately. I went through Pat's desk, and this stack is all of the unpaid invoices from vendors he was supposedly paying in cash. One drawer in his desk is locked. Frankly, I think these bills are just the tip of the iceberg. Some of them are over 90 days old, and my secretary, Beth, has been getting nasty calls in recent days."

"Who are they from?"

"Everybody Alice's uncle identified: the carpenter, electrician and painter who renovated this office space for us. The carpet company, the firm we're renting our office furniture from, even the temp agency that's supplying us with two secretaries and a billing clerk. And his GD limo service!"

"Mother of god!" Tom stood, was pacing.

"And that $300,000 missing from our bank account! Just as we've come to suspect, Tom, Pat has been making cash withdrawals, entering notations in our check register to indicate he was paying these people in cash at their request. But he hasn't paid them, so you can guess where the $300,000 has ended up. That's fraud, Tom. Embezzlement, and that's a felony."

"The guy has to be bat-shit crazy!" Tom slapped his forehead with a closed fist.

"Okay, Steve. I've heard all I need to hear. Give me a few minutes. Call Danny again, make sure he understands he reports to you, and

I think you had better go to New York and meet him personally. Or, invite him up to see us. I like that better. Get him up here. And tell him to shut up!"

"Okay, Tom."

"Second, draft a release of our own denying any intended relationship with the company in Cleveland. Walk your draft past me, please, before it hits the internet. I want to read it to our corporate counsel before you put it on line. And on your way back to your office, ask Colette to join me."

"You got it, Tom. Sorry this has become such a mess."

"It's my mess, Steve. And I have every intention of cleaning it up."

Steve rose and left Tom's office, carrying the papers with him. Within a minute or two, Colette entered the office and occupied the seat just vacated by Steve. Tom asked her to close his office door.

"I have had it, Colette. Actually, *we* have had it. I want Pat stopped. We've got the FBI, the SEC, what a fiasco!"

"Oh, god, Tom, what's going to happen to us?"

"Nothing, Colette, nothing. None of us, including you, have done anything wrong, except that I was not as vigilant as I should have been . You are in the clear. Don't worry."

"Well, I have more interesting news. I happened to overhear a telephone conversation between Pat and that real estate lady, Candi. Apparently, he has not been paying the rent on that house, and she's ready to kill him."

"She'll have to stand in line!" He gave a short laugh. "I want this bastard silenced, Colette. He's a curse on the human gene pool."

"Should I speak with Mr. Valenti?"

"Oh, lord! Diego! Alice's uncle!"

"Yes, and Enrique's father!"

"Right, of course, Enrique's father . . . My nephew's father!" Tom paused, ran his hand through his hair. "You say Diego is a Mr. Fixit kind of guy? I just know him, slightly, as my wife's uncle. But you say he can fix problems!"

"Yes, and I think your wife agrees with me."

Another pause, Tom shuffled some papers on his desk.

"Yes. I don't know how he intends to solve our problem, and I don't care. I want our $300,000 returned, and I want Pat Clauson out of our company, my life, our lives, forever.

"I can't think of a good way to retrieve our 50,000 shares of stock unless we go to the expense of a lawsuit and prove Pat is guilty of fraud. That will cost us thousands in legal fees and months of anguish, Colette, for which I do not have the patience nor the resources."

Tom was pacing behind his desk.

"Our lawyers may change my mind, but right now I don't give a damn about the stock. It's frozen. But I want that Pat guy out of our lives!"

"Okay, Tom."

"Fuck it -- just tell Diego to help us however he can. And I don't care how he spooks the guy . . . gets him to flee the state . . .flee the country . . . flee the planet. Just get the fucker out of our hair!"

"Okay, I'll make that call momentarily."

"Pat apparently is in New York, Colette, trying to meet with Danny. Steve's already cautioning Danny and is taking steps to publicly deny any discussion between the Cleveland firm and us regarding investments or a potential merger of any kind.

"And Steve is making it crystal clear that Danny reports to him, and is not to open his mouth unless Steve says it's okay. In fact, he's ordering Danny to fly up here so we can have a powwow."

"That's a very good idea." Colette stood. "I know Pat is in New York. He is due back here sometime Friday afternoon."

"Okay, sic 'im, Colette. And many thanks for whatever you can do, or Diego, can do."

Colette shook hands with Tom, returned to her office and picked up the phone. She was smiling as she made a local call.

+ + +

"This is Diego."

"Good morning, Mr. Valenti. This is Colette."

"Well, good morning, Colette. It's great to hear your voice, although I'm sure you're not calling me. But Enrique isn't here, Dear, he's on the road. Can I give him a message?"

"Sure! Tell him I love him. But I really want to speak with you."

"Well, I'm flattered, but what can an old duffer like me do for a gorgeous mademoiselle like yourself?"

Colette spent no time unloading on Diego; described in detail all of Mulholland's concerns, plus her own fear of being involved in lawsuits, ruined reputation, and so on. She also broke the news that she and Diego's niece, Alice Mulholland, had become friends and shared their concerns about Clauson.

"I hate to admit it, Mr. Valenti, but Alice and I kind of ganged up on Tom to convince him it was time to deal with Pat Clauson as the crook he really is, and this morning Tom said okay.

"He told me to call you as Mr. Fixit, said he doesn't care how you solve our problem, he just wants the $300,000 Pat has stolen from the firm's bank accounts, and he wants Pat out of our lives forever. Tom's hoping you can scare the be-jesus out of Pat so he flees the state, or even the country. Those were Tom's exact words, especially the part about not giving a damn how you address his concerns."

"Sounds like Tom has had it up to here." Colette envisioned him drawing a hand across his neck.

"I think it's fair to say we're all in that camp, Mr. Valenti: Tom, Alice, Steve and myself. All in all, Pat Clauson has been a nightmare for us, just as he apparently was for the companies he screwed earlier. Frankly, I'm just scared stiff I'm going to be sued or go to jail, and I don't deserve either."

"Calm down, Colette. You will not be sued or jailed, you have my word on that." Diego's voice was very soothing, calming. "Leave it to me, and everything will turn out okay. I promise."

"Thank you, Mr. Valenti. Thank you so much."

"You calm down now, Colette, and I'll have Enrique call you as soon as he's back in the office. I'm sure he'll rush over to your place to give you a hug, and lord knows what else."

Colette laughed, thanked him again, hung up.

Diego never put down his phone, simply depressed the hang-up button, immediately dialed the number of a guy he knew well; a guy with a reputation for getting things done without necessarily divulging, even to Diego, how he accomplished his "assignments."

Vince was in his late 20's, dark hair and eyebrows, a face that rarely smiled. He was a native of North Providence, a neighborhood of three-story tenements where he and most of his close friends had bailed out of high school as sophomores to pursue life on the streets.

Vince made his living pushing a little pot, breaking and entering, stealing cars which he sold to a local chop shop that salvaged parts for re-sale and ground up the rest as scrap metal.

He had been in and out of the slammer several times, most recently for violating his parole by threatening a gas station owner with a handgun. He didn't give a shit, and as soon as he was released, he looked up a "friend" who made arrangements for him to purchase a hot Glock. Vince didn't feel comfortable unless he was carrying, didn't hesitate to wave his weapon in anyone's face as a threat he was more than eager to fulfill.

Word on the street was "don't fuck with Vince, he's nuts!"

Diego wasted no time in explaining why he was calling.

"What shape are you in, Vince?"

"I'm ready to roll, whatever. I've got what I need."

Diego had an idea what that meant, preferred not to know for sure. Ignorance was bliss.

"Okay. I've got two or three people who are really ticked off with a guy named Pat Clauson. He claims to be some sort of financial genius from California . . . he's really Australian . . . but he spends his time ripping people off and ripping off their companies for really big dough. I mean, *really* big dough, stocks, and so on."

"Okay. Gotcha."

"I have no idea what this guy looks like, but he's flying into T. F. Green on Friday afternoon and is always picked up by a black Town Car from Here-to-There."

"Okay."

"If you can lay your hands on a similar car and put his name on a handheld sign, pick him up at the airport and help him understand he better return the $300,000 he's stolen from my friends, and that he better get the hell out of Rhode Island and forget he ever heard of the place."

"Yeah, I can do that. No problem."

"Okay, Vince. I don't care what you say to this guy to bring him around, my contacts just want him gone. Can you handle that?"

"Yes, Sir. Not a problem."

"Okay. And you and I never had this conversation. Do I make myself clear?"

"Absolutely, sir. Leave everything to me."

"Okay. But I don't want any screw-ups. This guy Clauson is a bonafide con artist and my friends want him out of their lives forever. Got that? They'd just as soon he moved to another planet!"

"Yes, sir. I'll make certain of that."

"Good show, Vince. Gimme a call when you're done."

"You bet. I'll call you Friday evening."

"Remember, no screw-ups!"

They hung up.

+ + +

Pat checked into a Fifth Avenue hotel following his afternoon landing at LaGuardia, stayed in his hotel room, flopped fully dressed onto the bed. He had been extremely troubled since his dinner party, when Tom's wife, Alice, began making noises about contacting companies Pat had previously worked with. That was not a good sign.

He also was becoming more and more concerned about Ione's questions last Saturday evening. Add the two together, and it didn't smell like roses. And even Colette had become somewhat stand-offish, which may not mean anything, but on the other hand . . . .

He wasn't clear what he should do. Logic argued for bailing out of Fabricated ASAP and hiding out in Rome, but he wasn't yet happy with his financial haul. He'd finessed the firm's checking account to hide $300,000, but that didn't give him the kind of bucks he was after. If the Cleveland deal went through, there'd be hope, but it was a long long shot. He hadn't heard anything; it looked dead.

He still held 50,000 shares of Fabricated's stock -- actually the stock certificate was being held for him by Kyle Mullen, with Pat's Power of Attorney -- but it might be several more months before the stock reached or broke twenty bucks. Then Kyle was at liberty to forward it to Pat's contact in Canada and deposit the money in an overseas bank account Pat had yet to establish. He'd open an account tomorrow with a big New York international bank.

This entire caper just hadn't gone right from the outset, and now it seemed to be roaring over a cliff.

Pat was beside himself with anxiety, uncertainty, and fear. He spent the entire afternoon and evening wrestling with his problem, his potential exposure, and if that occurred, what Tom and Steve's response might be. He ordered room service, never even turned on the TV, just paced and sat and paced, mulling over his options.

He thought of going downstairs to the bar in hopes that Cecily might be there, decided against it. He could phone her, her number still in his briefcase, but decided against that, too. He just wasn't in the mood, felt so distracted he might not be able to perform. Cecily would be a waste of money; maybe tomorrow night.

Sometime around ten o'clock, he decided to phone Kyle and ask if they could meet in the morning. Kyle wasn't happy to get the call.

"What's wrong with you, Pat? It's after ten o'clock!"

"I know, Kyle, but I have to see you. Something's come up and I need your counsel. Can we meet in the morning?"

"That's a hell of a lot better than ten o'clock tonight. What's your problem?"

"It's complicated, Kyle. I can't describe it on the phone. Can we meet or not?"

"Yes, we can meet. Where are you?"

He gave Kyle the hotel name and his room number.

"Wanna do breakfast?"

"No, Kyle, I don't want to talk in a restaurant. Let's meet in my room about 9:30. I'll order up some coffee and danish, if you like. Plan to stick around for a couple of hours."

Pat rose Wednesday morning after a fitful night of almost no sleep. The bathroom mirror reflected a mess. He shaved, showered and dressed, hoping that would improve his looks and temperament. It didn't.

He retrieved the *Times* and *Journal* from outside his hotel room door, hung the 'Do Not Disturb' tag on the knob, retreated to an easy chair to scan the newspapers. Couldn't concentrate. Ordered coffee and danish for two, awaited Kyle's arrival.

Kyle was very prompt, rapped on Pat's door at precisely 9:30, recoiled slightly when he saw Pat's appearance.

"Man, what the hell hit you? You look like your pigeon died!"

"Thanks, Kyle. I appreciate the compliment." He wasn't smiling.

They moved into the living room, Kyle settled on the couch, Pat back in his chair.

"So what mess have you created for yourself this time?"

Pat jumped into a long monologue, described most of what he'd been doing since he first met Tom Mulholland in London. Talked about his idea of a one-point-five million dollar commercial loan from his banking contacts in London, with a hundred-thousand dollar fee for him, an idea which got shot down by Fabricated's treasurer, Steve Johnson.

"Whoa, hold on a minute. Do you even have banking contacts in London?" Kyle was leaning forward, couldn't believe what he was hearing.

"Well, I know a guy . . ."

"You 'know a guy'! Dammit, Pat, what were you thinking?"

"I could have made that work, I think. But it's a moot point; the Newport guys didn't bite, and so I was screwed out of a hundred grand!"

"You were screwed! Are you nuts! You were tucking it to those guys big time, and the CFO said 'Hold up, Cowboy. I own the silver bullets!'".

"Yeah, that part of my plan didn't work."

Pat next described his offer to invest $100,000 of his own money into their company over a twelve-month period, had already given them over thirty thousand with another ten grand promised every month for the next six months. And they promptly had him use his own money to renovate the new office space Pat had found for them.

"Pat, you are nuts. You were trying to con them, and instead they conned you into renovating their new offices with your own money. What on god's green earth were you smoking?"

"I am not planning to invest the other sixty-thousand of my offer, Kyle. I was, and still am, planning to bolt before any more of my money is due. And I agreed to hire and supervise the contractors, and pay them, in order to get my hands on the company's checking account. That's the only way I could do it."

"So you wrote company checks against your own money in their bank account?"

"No! I drew out money in cash, filled out check stubs as if I was paying the vendors, but I kept the cash."

"Dammit, Pat, you are nuts! How long did you think that ruse would work?"

"Well, it's worked for several months and I got my thirty back, plus almost three-hundred thousand of their company money! I'm actually holding two-seventy of theirs, plus my thirty!"

"Pat, I don't wanna hear any more. I don't wanna know. I don't like the smell of this whole thing. You want my advice, I'd return the money, beg forgiveness so these guys don't come after you legally, or otherwise."

"What do you mean 'otherwise'?"

"What do you know about Providence?"

"Not much."

"Well, for your information, at one time Providence was a mafia stronghold. A lot of that has changed in recent years, but you can't tell me there isn't a lingering fringe of heirs eager to re-establish their namesake's reputation on the street, so to speak. A whacko like you is a perfect way to do that."

"Oh, come on! We're talking a few hundred grand, not a bloody fortune!"

"It is to some people. And they won't like the way you got it! They do not enjoy being ripped off!"

"Well, I've made up my mind. I haven't had any feedback from the Cleveland outfit -- did I tell you about them? Well, screw it, that deal's dead. I have tickets from New York to Rome out of Kennedy tomorrow night. I'm going to hang out there until things blow over."

"Italy! You think that's clever! People have relatives in Italy, lots of relatives."

"Will you stop it, Kyle! I'm not concerned, I made these plans months ago and I'm sticking to them. In fact, I'm going to fly to Providence tomorrow afternoon, pick up my stuff in Newport, and fly back to New York to catch my flight overseas."

"Why the hell are you risking another visit to Newport?"

"My money is still there."

"*Your* money! Oh, for Christ's sake, Pat. Leave it there and get the hell out!"

"Naw, I'm okay."

"Horse shit! You're trying to be a hero instead of a zero, but you'll probably end up under a rubber sheet in some morgue."

"Come on, Kyle. You're not frightening me!"

"Look, I brought your stock certificate and Power of Attorney. I want you to hold onto this stuff; think about hanging it in your jail cell!" Neither guy laughed.

"No! I'd rather you kept it safe for me. I won't be able to follow the penny market very carefully from Rome, and the POA permits you to sell whenever you think the time is right. If that occurs before the stock restriction is lifted, transfer the stock to your guy in Ontario who can sell it on the Canadian market and wire the funds to my special account in New York."

"So what's the number and where is it?"

"I'll open an account this afternoon and email you the bank name and account number."

"If your stock sells in Canada, you'll take a beating on the exchange rate."

"I'll lose some, but nothing compared to what I'll net."

"God, this whole thing stinks! Why don't you send the stock certificate to Canada now? Get me outta the loop. Why do you need me involved?"

"I'd rather sell in the U.S. and avoid the exchange rate problem, but that means I couldn't sell until the restriction is lifted. I want better flexibility."

"Well, it still stinks, and I'm not comfortable being your shill!"

"Come on. I'll make it worth your while."

"Damn, I hate you! Don't send me any emails. I don't want a paper trail. Just phone me. And you better take care of yourself. But understand, if I'm ever asked, I'm going to deny I ever knew you!" He was not joking.

Kyle stood, they hugged, Pat pledged to stay safe, Kyle patted him on the back as they moved toward the door. Final handshake, and Kyle disappeared.

14

THURSDAY

Danny Boy was settled behind his desk as usual, telephone receiver stuck in his left ear as his smooth voice romanced some penny stock broker about the benefit of buying heavily into a new listing. His secretary suddenly rushed into his office, wildly gesturing about something or someone in the reception room.

Danny disengaged from the phone conversation and the somewhat distraught gal mentioned something about FBI agents. Danny stood, brushed past her, entered the reception area to find two well dressed men in blue suits, white button-down collared shirts, colorful ties. He knew instantly they were feds.

"Good morning, gentlemen. How can I help you?"

"You're Daniel Grady?" It was really a statement, not a question.

"Yes, Sir."

"Well, I'm FBI Agent Harold Windsor and this is my colleague, Agent Charles Dempsey. We need to ask you a few questions."

"Sure." Danny was beginning to sweat. "Come into my office."

The three sat around a small conference table. Agent Demp-sey produced a pad and a pen.

"Mr. Grady, we understand you have a contract with a Rhode Island company called Fabricated Structures, and you have been distributing press releases provided by that company to brokers who handle their stock in an effort to escalate the price. Is that true?"

("Oh my god, what the hell has Pat been doing?")

Danny began to fidget in his chair, gripped the edge of the table with both hands.

"Yes, I have a letter of agreement with the company to keep brokers informed of the firm's growth. I thought it was growing very rapidly. However, I've had several conversations with the chief financial officer who tells me I've been getting a lot of false information from a consultant they hired to keep me informed of the company's growth. I don't mind telling you I'm pissed."

"We can understand that, Sir."

"That damned bastard has almost ruined my business, my reputation. I've been calling every broker I do business with to alert them to this problem, and while they understand I'm not the guilty party they are still upset because they've put their own reputations on the line. It's a damned mess."

"Yes, Sir! It is. I assume you're telling us you had no idea the claims Mr. Clauson has been making about Fabricated's business are, in fact, false."

"Lord, No!" Danny began pacing. "I had no idea. I sure as hell have no desire to ruin my business, nor my reputation as an honest financial resource for the brokers. And, I'm ticked off at Fabricated's management for not checking out this guy Clauson so none of us would be in this mess."

"I understand."

"Just how bad is it?"

"It's real bad, Sir." The Agent let that sink in for several seconds.

"Son-of-a-bitch! Wait until I get my hands on that prick, I'll kill him."

"We don't recommend that, Sir!" Agent Windsor cracked a small smile. "We are building a case against Mr. Clauson. Apparently, he has pulled similar schemes against firms in other markets, and he appears to be very clever at his game."

"Goddammit, I just don't need this. What the hell do I do?" He sat down again.

"We will need copies of as many of the press releases as you have. Also copies of all correspondence between you and Fabricated management or this fella Clauson, any correspondence between you and brokers, and a detailed statement from you describing the manner in which information was received by you and transmitted by you to stock brokers.

"Jesus, you might as well take my file cabinets."

"Okay, that can be done. I'll phone my office now and there will be a battery of FBI personnel here within the hour. They will be carrying a search warrant . . . standard procedure, Sir. And we will need you to come to our office this afternoon to give us a statement detailing everything you can tell us about your working relationship with Mr. Clauson."

"Okay! Do I need a lawyer?"

"That's up to you, Sir. You are not under arrest, and are not being charged with a crime. At least not yet."

"Not *yet!*" Danny ran his hand through his hair, his forehead dripping perspiration. "Goddammit, that fucking bastard."

"I'm sure this is very stressful, Sir, but if you're telling us the truth, and your files back that up, you have nothing to be concerned about other than trying to pacify your brokerage clients. We know from experience they will pitch a tantrum because fellow agents will be visiting them, as well."

"Oh god! I've already been in touch with most of them, and I know the management of Fabricated Structures is also going to contact them. Can I at least contact them to let them know the FBI will be calling?"

"No, Sir, we cannot allow that because they might begin to destroy some of their files before our Agents visit them, and that wouldn't go over very well with us."

"Aww, I see, hadn't thought about that." Danny buried his head in his hands, remained still for several seconds, then looked at Agent Windsor, tears streaking his cheeks. "What the hell do I do now, Sir? I'm terrified the brokers will never trust me again. They'll be furious because I fed them fraudulent information, even unintentionally, and they'll really be rip-shit when the FBI comes calling. They need that like a hole in the head! Me, too, for that matter!"

"I regret this is necessary, Sir. We're simply doing our job. I'm sure you understand that."

"Yeah, I do. I'm just very upset."

"Understandable, Mr. Grady. Our colleagues will be here shortly to pack up your files and move them out. And we'll expect you in our offices this afternoon, okay."

"Yes, I'll be there."

The two agents stood, shook hands with Danny, and prepared to leave. Danny's secretary wrapped on his office door, opened it a crack.

"Danny, Pat Clauson is on the phone!"

Danny leaped for the phone on his desk, was grabbed by FBI agent Windsor, who whispered instructions.

"Sir, take it easy, please. Ask him where he is. Don't tell him we're here. We're trying to find him."

Danny pulled his arm free, grabbed his desk phone.

"You god-damn mother-fucker! What the hell are you doing to me!"

"What are you talking about?"

"I'm talking about your press release on that firm in Cleveland and merger plans with Fabricated. It's all fiction, Pat, a damned lie. And I have been spreading your lie to all of my clients, the brokers, all of whom will be very pissed at me, and it's your fault!

"You've been feeding me lies about that company for weeks! What the hell's wrong with you?"

"Jeez, I'm sorry, Danny. All I'm trying to do is get the stock price to climb. And it's been working, right!"

"'Working!' You idiot, you're lucky we're not being sued, or worse. I'm getting calls from Steve, the treasurer, who is mighty upset. And I now work for Steve, not you. Are you in the city, at your usual digs? If I had time, which I don't, I'd show up an strangle you or cut your balls off!"

"Come on, Danny."

"Come on my ass, Pat! Don't ever, *ever,* call me again. I'm going to pretend I never heard of you . . . unless I get sued. Then my attorney will be all over you like a swarm of hornets."

"I'm really sorry, Danny. Really, I am."

"Goodbye, Pat. And fuck off!" He hung up.

Danny turned to the FBI agent, he face bright red, bulging veins on his neck.

"Is he at the hotel?"

"He didn't say, but I'll bet you dollars-to-donuts he's there. That's where he always stays when he's in New York."

The Agent Windsor turned to Agent Dempsey.

"Charlie, call the office, get backup and see if you can find this guy Clauson at his hotel. Mr. Grady and I will go to the office as soon as our investigation team gets here."

Danny asked if he could let his secretary go for the day.

"No, Sir. The investigation team will want her to show them through your files, and they will also most likely want to ask her a few questions, too."

"Jesus, what a mess!"

It wasn't long before a team of FBI personnel entered the office to begin searching, and Danny and Agent Windsor left for the FBI's New York office. Danny's secretary was frightened, crying when they walked out.

+ + +

Pat replaced the receiver, stood shocked at Danny's anger, surprised Pat already knew the Cleveland release was a phony, must have been the FBI who were at Fabricated earlier this week.

His plan had been to hibernate in his room, take a short nap, then call Cecily to see if he could connect with her. But Danny's FBI comment rattled his mind. *("Christ, maybe they're closing in on me! Danny's statement that I'm probably at my favorite hotel. . . FBI may have been in his office!")*

He quickly packed his suitcase, checked out of the hotel, told the desk he had to catch a train to Washington, took a cab to a steak house on 44th Street. He used a pay phone to dial Cecily's phone number, and by a small miracle she answered.

"Cecily, this is Pat Clauson, the Australian guy you helped relax several weeks ago. We met in a hotel bar."

"Oh, Yes! Pat. It's good to hear your voice. How are you?"

"That's a debatable issue, Cecily. Any chance I can see you?"

"Do you need to relax?"

"You better believe it!"

"Let me make a phone call to cancel something. Where are you and what time is good for you?

He gave her the name and address of the restaurant.

"What's a good time to meet, Pat?"

"I'm ripe for your company, and I'm already at the restaurant. Let's meet now, if you can, for an early drink and dinner. I need to get back to Newport."

"Okay, I'll be there shortly." Pat slipped onto a tall chair at the bar, ordered a double Chivas Regal on the rocks.

Cecily sat back in her living-room chair with nothing to cancel, asked herself why she had agreed to meet with Pat. She had dropped out of the "entertainment" business several weeks ago, didn't like it any more, never really did like it; only sold herself (she hated that thought) on rare occasions when she was short of cash.

But even the money had become distasteful.

So why Pat? She struggled to answer her own question, thought of phoning him at the restaurant, tell him "no go, something has come up." But she didn't. Just a drink maybe, for old time's sake, but no roll in the hay. That may be what he's expecting, but he did say he has to get back to Newport.

Pat was halfway through his Chivas when Cecily slipped onto the stool next to him. She looked ravishing.

"Hi, Cowboy! How are you?"

Pat slipped his arm around her waist, pulled her close, gave her a quick kiss on the lips.

"You're the second or third person to call me 'Cowboy'!"

"What's her name?" Cecily was laughing.

"Ahhh, I don't remember," Pat lied, also laughing.

"It must have something to do with that sheep ranch you grew up on."

"Yeah, well I wasn't really a cowboy. I was more like a good shepherd!" Both were laughing.

"It's good to see you, Pat. How have you been?" She was looking at him intently, her tongue swung across her painted red lips. Pat stirred, ordered her a flute of Sir Winston Churchill.

"It's good to see you, too, Cecily. And I'm glad you were not previously engaged this evening."

"What's up? You sound like you've lost your best friend."

"That, my dear girl, is an understatement." Pat sipped his scotch, proceeded to tell Cecily a very shortened version of his headaches of the past several days, the failure of his deal in Newport, his plan to hang out in Rome for a couple of months. Didn't say anything about the FBI hunting for his tail.

"I'm sorry to hear things in Newport didn't work out for you. But Rome sounds exciting."

"Yeah, I'm really looking forward to it. I haven't gotten away for quite awhile, need to veg out, see the sights. It's supposed to be a beautiful city, and very historic."

"That's what I hear."

"Have you been to Rome, Cecily? I haven't."

"No! Neither have I, but everything I've read or heard has made it seem like a fairy tale . . . lots of ancient history, marvelous old architecture, and fantastic art, much of it from the Renaissance era."

"You like art, Cecily?"

"Yes, it's sort of a passion. I don't own any, certainly nothing like a masterpiece, but I have several coffee-table books about the works of Raphael, Caravaggio, Leonardo da Vinci, Michelangelo and other famous Italian Masters." She sipped her champagne.

"No kidding! I never would have suspected that."

"Why? Think someone formerly in the entertainment business doesn't have a brain?" She looked at him quizzically, teasing.

"No! That's not it, by any means. I just never thought . . . What do you mean by 'formerly'?"

"I've given up the so-called relaxation business. It was demeaning at best, and I just cannot bring myself to hit the sheets with strange guys who only want a quick screw. That's really not who I am, or who I want to be, or how I want to think of myself."

"Well, I'm disappointed, although I can understand where you're coming from." He sipped his scotch. "But you said 'strange guys'. Am I a strange guy or friend."

Cecily didn't respond, sipped her champagne, stared down at the bar, finally raised her head, flipped her long blond hair, and looked directly into Pat's eyes.

"Obviously, you are not a strange guy, but I'd call you more of an acquaintance than a friend because we really don't know each other very well."

"So, you're saying we're not going to make love this evening."

"Let me rephrase your question, Pat. We're not going to have sex this evening; that's different than making love, don't you agree?"

"Shit!" It was Pat's turn to sip his drink and stare at the bar.

"Okay, Cecily, so we need to be friends. So, how about this . . . It's a wild idea, but let me try it out on you."

"It better not involve animals!" She smiled, Pat roared!

(*"Here comes his goddamn pitch!"*)

"How about coming to Rome with me?"

"You *are* crazy!"

"Why? Has something in jerkwater New Jersey got you bottled up?"

"No! But my gosh! When are you leaving?"

"Tomorrow night, nine o'clock at Kennedy. Alitalia."

"Ah, come on, Pat. It's nice of you to offer, but I'd really need time to think about it."

"Do you have a passport?"

"Yes! Of course."

"I'll have your ticket waiting at the Alitalia counter. First class. I'm flying back to Newport tomorrow to pick up some stuff, and I'll return to JFK mid-day tomorrow, well in advance of the flight to Rome."

"Wow! You really are a take-charge kind of guy! Let me think on it." (*"Rome! A free ticket to Rome! Now there's an offer!"*)

"Can you think while we have dinner?"

"Pat, I'll have dinner with you here, but that's as far as I'm willing to go, ticket or no ticket. Believe me when I say I do not turn tricks. And I will *not* be your concubine in Europe or anyplace else." She looked and sounded dead serious, and Pat sensed it.

"Yeah, I understand, Cecily. So let's just say Rome will give us a chance to become real friends, and we'll throw ourselves on the mercy of Mother Nature." He was smiling, assumed his Australian charm and accent would win her over eventually -- not for a serious relationship, but for a month or two of wild sex.

"I really need to think this through, Pat. It's a very nice offer, but it's not easy for me to just pick up and leave town. And I am *not* interested in screwing myself across Italy with you or anybody else. So don't press me, okay? I can do dinner, if you'd like, but then I intend to go home."

"Well, dinner is better than nothing, so let's find a table." Pat wasn't smiling, reluctantly resigned to a night alone.

Their dinner conversation was directed largely by Pat, who waxed enthusiastically about Rome, it's museums and art-laden churches, it's ancient ruins, it's extraordinary restaurants. Every day, he assured her, would be one excitement after another. He never mentioned their nights and what he really relished.

Cecily wasn't stupid, knew exactly what was foremost in Pat's mind. But a free first-class ticket to Rome! How could she pass that up? And once in Rome, she could shut down Pat's sexual advances like a defensive lineman. *("Let him chase Italian whores!")*

Cecily finally agreed to meet him at the Alitalia departure gate about 8:00 o'clock Friday night. He was smiling when they parted, she wasn't. She anticipated a struggle when she wouldn't allow him near her bed, or even in her hotel room. But she was determined to stick to her guns, free ticket or no.

Pat retrieved his suitcase from the hat check girl, camped out in a crumby by-the-hour flophouse in mid-town. Didn't really sleep.

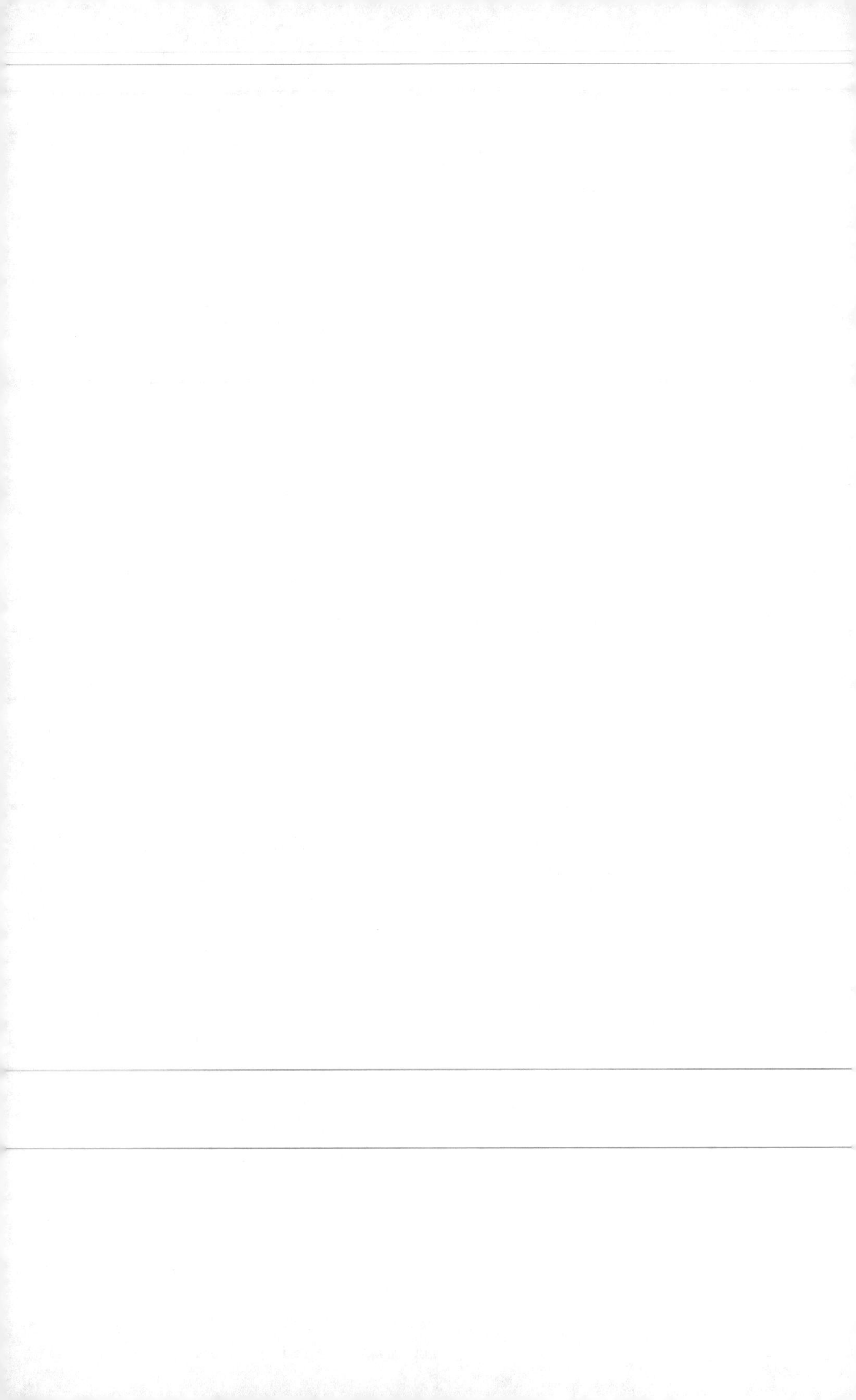

15

TODAY

Vince had been told by The Man that two of his friends had a problem with a fella named Pat Clauson. The Man wanted it fixed quickly, no screw-ups, didn't care how the fix was accomplished, left that for Vince to decide. Vince would collect $5,000 if all went well.

Given the background information he had, Vince knew this guy was always picked up at T.F. Green Airport by a chauffeur-driven Town Car from Here-to-There, easy for someone with Vince's ingenuity to secure. The guy had no trouble spotting Vince standing next to the car as he exited the terminal.

They had driven to the guy's office in Newport, where the fella picked up something at his office, and here they were in the middle of a noisy car wash, water splashing, soap covering the windows, loud piped-in music, Vince thinking *"neat bit of planning, if I say so myself!"*

Clauson sat terrified in the back seat, Vince's pistol aimed at his forehead.

After a few moments of sheer panic, Pat found his voice, picked up his briefcase, pulled out a wad of $100 bills, and held them up for Vince to see.

"There's three-hundred thousand in here. It's all yours if you want it." He thrust his briefcase toward Vince. "Go ahead, take it!" He thrust the briefcase toward Vince. "Please, don't hurt me. Please! I haven't done anything to you. *PLEASE!!*"

Vince used his left hand to take the briefcase from Pat, kept the pistol in his right hand aimed at Pat's forehead. He had to act quickly, the car was still moving through the car wash, approaching the end.

Clauson never heard the shot that killed him.

Vince exited the car wash, turned right, parked beside the building, got out and opened the back door. Moving quickly, he pulled Clauson's body off the back seat onto the floor, grabbed a handful of drying towels from a wooden bin, covered the body, wiped the rear seat and window clean of splattered blood, shut the door, and drove off.

He went only a few blocks before turning into an automobile junkyard, stopped right beside a large concrete burn pit. He retrieved Clauson's briefcase, opened it and saw the several bundles of $100 bills, tucked it under his arm for The Man.

He threw his Glock onto the floor, dropped the car keys next to it, exited the Town Car and waved to the operator of a large forklift. Vince entered a beat-up Ford 150 pickup nearby and disappeared into rush-hour traffic.

The forklift operator drove the two blades straight through the driver-side windows of the Town Car, shattering the glass and forcing the two blades clean through the car until they shattered the passenger-side windows as well. He raised the car about four feet off the ground, within minutes had all four tires and rims removed for re-sale. He considered pulling the satellite radio as well, thought better of looking inside the car. Didn't want to know!

He remounted the forklift and suspended the car over the burn pit. He dismounted again, picked up a long crowbar and punched several holes in the fuel tank to let the gasoline drain into the pit. Left in the gas tank, the fuel would explode like a bomb; freed to drain into the pit, it would simply ignite and burn the car so thoroughly every thing -- cloth, rubber, plastic, glass, fiberglass and flesh -- would incinerate into ashes or melt into globs of twisted metal.

He lowered the car into the pit, cleverly withdrew the forklift and backed it a safe distance away. Then he lit a torch, threw it into the pit, and hurried back behind the forklift as the pit erupted into a hot, viciously hungry fire. It burned for more than a half-hour. There was very little left of the Town Car, just a charred frame of metal, most of it bent in melted odd shapes from the intensity of the heat.

Once the ravished metal had cooled, the forklift operator raised it out of the burn pit, dropped it into the junkyard's crushing machine, and compressed it into a metal block about the size of a small table. Some people actually bought the crushed metal blocks and used them as such.

Good-bye Town Car, good-bye Pat, good-bye Phil, Pat's regular driver, whose dead body had been locked in the trunk.

+ + +

The wall clock was closing on 8:20 PM. Cecily had waited at the Alitalia check-in counter until the flight to Rome began boarding. Pat never showed. Her baggage was checked, she held her ticket.

("That son-of-a-bitch isn't coming! But I've got this ticket, and I intend to use it. I'm going to Rome to see the art!")

Cecily turned and entered the jetway to the Alitalia flight, settled quickly into her first class seat. She smiled warmly at the good-looking gentlemen seated across the aisle: early thirties, dark hair, dark eyes. A cabin attendant served her a chilled champagne, which she raised in a silent salute to Pat Clauson.

("Go to hell, Cowboy. Thanks for the ticket!")

The good looking guy across the aisle leaned slightly toward Cecily, raised his glass.

"A toast to an interesting flight." He was smiling.

"Yes, sir! I'll drink to that." She smiled back.

+ + +

It was November. Kyle Mullen had not heard from Pat for over four months. He had learned from Danny-Boy that Pat had disappeared shortly after leaving the Rhode Island firm. He had no idea how Pat handled his departure from Fabricated, assumed he was in Rome.

Danny also said the FBI were hot on Pat's tail, but hadn't heard if they'd caught him. He bored Kyle with a long, sad tale of all the FBI had done to him: thorough searches of his office files, his condo, warrants to search his client brokerage files, depositions, interviews, *ad nauseum.* His business had not recovered, many of the brokers reluctant to do business with him or even be friendly with him. Press reports in the New York dailies and local TV news gave him the kind of celebrity he would rather have avoided.

Kyle was not overly concerned about Pat's silence because the guy had a habit of disappearing for weeks or months after he had completed one of his "market tests", as he liked to call them. But he usually contacted Kyle at some point by email, postcard, or phone to brag about the fact that he was romping in London, Vienna, Paris,

Singapore, anywhere, and he was living the good life on someone else's money.

This time was different. Pat's whereabouts remained a mystery; Kyle had not heard a word, nada, damned unusual. He occasionally thought about his last conversation with Pat, and his advice that Pat might be careless to go back to Newport before heading for Italy. That, too, was a lousy choice of destinations. But, what the hell. This is real life, not some scripted television show.

He still held Pat's certificate for 50,000 shares of Fabricated's stock. Pat had said to hang onto it and either sell it when the stock became unrestricted, or whenever he felt it made sense to do so, as long as the per share price had hit twenty dollars or higher. Pat's Power of Attorney gave Kyle that permission. So where *was* Pat?

Kyle didn't have the foggiest idea. What the hell.

The stock was no longer restricted and was trading at $23.50, so Kyle sold all 50,000 shares.

He pocketed $1,175,000.

Screw the bastard!

End

Printed in the United States
By Bookmasters